MR. DARCY, VAMPYRE

MR. DARCY, VAMPYRE

AMANDA GRANGE

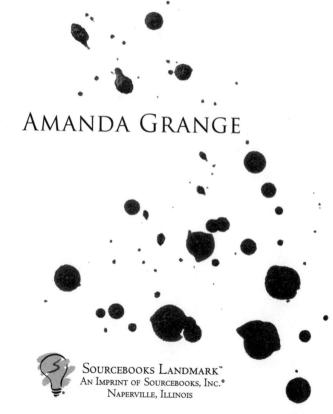

SOURCEBOOKS LANDMARK™
AN IMPRINT OF SOURCEBOOKS, INC.®
NAPERVILLE, ILLINOIS

Published by Sourcebooks Landmark, an imprint of Sourcebooks, Inc.
P.O. Box 4410, Naperville, Illinois 60567-4410
(630) 961-3900
FAX: (630) 961-2168
www.sourcebooks.com

Library of Congress Cataloging-in-Publication Data

Grange, Amanda.
  Mr. Darcy, vampyre / Amanda Grange.
     p. cm.
  1. Darcy, Fitzwilliam (Fictitious character)—Fiction. 2. Bennet, Elizabeth (Fictitious character)—Fiction. I. Austen, Jane, 1775-1817. Pride and prejudice. II. Title.
  PR6107.R35M69 2009
  823'.92—dc22
                              2009024137

Printed and bound in the United States of America
LBM 10 9 8 7 6 5 4 3 2 1

This book is dedicated to Catherine Morland

Prologue

December 1802

My dearest Jane,

My hand is trembling as I write this letter. My nerves are in tatters and I am so altered that I believe you would not recognise me. The past two months have been a nightmarish whirl of strange and disturbing circumstances, and the future…

Jane, I am afraid.

If anything happens to me, remember that I love you and that my spirit will always be with you, though we may never see each other again. The world is a cold and frightening place where nothing is as it seems.

It was all so different a few short months ago. When I awoke on my wedding morning, I thought myself the happiest woman alive…

CHAPTER 1

OCTOBER 1802

E LIZABETH BENNET'S WEDDING MORNING was one of soft mists and mellow sunshine. She drew back her bedroom curtains to see the dreaming English landscape lying serene and beautiful beneath a soft, white quilt. The mist was at its thickest by the river, lying voluptuously over the water, then thinning out as it spread over the fields and pastures before disappearing, wisp-like, into the trees.

The birds were silent, but there was a sense of expectancy in the air. It was as though the world were waiting for the sun to rise and burn away the gauzy veil, revealing the true colours of the countryside, not muted white and grey, but green and blue and gold.

Elizabeth sank onto the window seat and pulled her knees up in front of her. She wrapped her arms around them and her thoughts drifted to the ceremony that was to come. Images floated through her mind: she and her father walking down the aisle, Darcy waiting for her, the ring slipping onto her finger...

She was not the only one to have risen early. Her mother was already awake, complaining to anyone who would listen to her about her nerves, and Mary was playing the piano.

Kitty was calling out, 'Has anyone seen my ribbon?' and Mr Bennet was adding a full stop to his dry reply by closing the library door.

Beside her, Jane was still sleeping.

As she watched the world waking outside the window, Elizabeth thought of the past year and of how lucky she and her sister had been. They had both met men they loved and now, after many trials and difficulties, they were to marry them.

Elizabeth could not remember whose idea it had been to have a joint ceremony, but she was glad to know that her sister was to share the happiest day of her life—no, not the happiest, for she was sure that was yet to come—but the happiest day of her life thus far.

As the sun rose and the mists began to lift, Jane stirred. She blinked and then lifted herself on one elbow, pushing her fair hair out of her eyes and smiling her slow, beautiful smile.

'You're awake early,' she said to Lizzy.

'And so are you.'

'Here.' Jane climbed out of bed and took a wrapper from its peg behind the door, then draped it over her sister's shoulders. 'You don't want to catch cold.'

Lizzy took the wrapper and put it on, then she caught her sister's hand impulsively and said, 'Only think, in a few more hours we will be married. I will be on the way to the Lake District for my wedding tour, and you will be on your way to London to visit Bingley's relations there.'

Jane sat down on the window seat opposite Elizabeth, and Elizabeth made herself smaller to give her sister more room. Jane raised one knee and let her other leg dangle over the edge of the seat, with her foot swinging idly an inch or two from the floor. She looked absently out of the window and twirled one fair curl round her finger, then she turned to face her sister and she said, 'Do you wish we were going on our wedding tours together?'

'Yes,' said Lizzy. 'And no.'

Jane nodded thoughtfully.

'I will miss you, Jane, but we need some time alone with our husbands,' said Lizzy, 'especially to begin with. You will write to me, though, won't you?'

'Of course. And you will write to me?'

'Every day. Well, perhaps not every day,' said Lizzy with a sudden smile, 'and perhaps not at all just at first, but I will write often and tell you what I am doing, and you must do the same.'

They heard the sound of footsteps on the stair and they knew it was their mother, who was coming to hurry them into dressing, even though the ceremony would not begin for another three hours. They greeted her with affection, being too happy to worry about anything this morning, and listened to all her anxieties, both real and imagined. They reassured her that Kitty would not cough during the ceremony and that Mrs Long would not steal Mr Bingley for her niece at the last moment—'for I am sure she would be capable of trying,' said Mrs Bennet.

'Mr Bingley loves Jane,' said Lizzy.

Mrs Bennet smiled complacently.

'I cannot wonder at it. I knew she could not be so beautiful for nothing. Now, girls, you must come downstairs. Breakfast is ready in the dining room.'

Elizabeth and Jane exchanged glances. They could not face the thought of a family breakfast with their mother fussing and Mary moralising.

'I am not hungry,' said Elizabeth.

'Nor I,' said Jane.

Their mother protested, but they would not be persuaded, and at last Mrs Bennet went downstairs, calling, 'Kitty! Kitty, my love! I want to speak to you...'

Elizabeth and Jane breathed a sigh of relief when they were left alone again.

'We should eat something, though, even if we don't really want it,' said Jane.

'I couldn't eat a thing,' said Lizzy. 'I'm too excited.'

'You should try,' said Jane, standing up and looking at her sister with affection. 'It will be a long morning and you don't want to faint in the church.'

'All right,' said Lizzy, 'for you, I'll eat something, but only if we don't have to go downstairs.'

Jane swirled her own wrapper from the peg and let it fall round her shoulders, then she drifted out of the room.

Elizabeth leaned back against the window and her eyes looked towards Netherfield. She imagined Darcy rising, too, and preparing himself for the wedding.

Her thoughts were recalled by Jane, who returned with a tray of delicacies, and together the two of them managed to make a passable breakfast. They broke off small pieces of hot rolls and ate them slowly in between sipping hot chocolate.

'What do you think it will be like?' asked Elizabeth.

'I don't know,' said Jane. 'Different.'

'You will still be here, at Netherfield,' said Elizabeth, 'but I will be living in Derbyshire.'

'With Mr Darcy,' said Jane.

'Yes, with my beloved Darcy,' she said with a long smile.

She thought of herself and Darcy at Pemberley, wandering through the lush grounds and living their lives in the luxurious rooms, and she was lost in happy daydreams until her mother came in again, saying that it was time to dress.

The two young women rose from the window seat and went over to the washstand, where they stepped out of their nightgowns and washed in the scented water before slipping into their chemises. They sat patiently whilst Hill arranged their hair, threading seed pearls through their soft chignons, and then they put on their corsets, tying each other's stays and laughing all the while.

They became quieter when it was time to put on their wedding dresses. They had wanted their dresses to be similar but not the same. Both gowns were made of white silk, but Jane's dress had a round neck decorated with ribbon whilst Lizzy's dress had a square neck trimmed with lace. Elizabeth helped Jane to begin with, lifting the gown over her sister's head. It fell to the floor with a whisper of silk and Elizabeth fastened it, then stood and looked at Jane in the mirror. She kissed her on the cheek and said, 'Bingley is a lucky man.'

Then Elizabeth raised her arms so that her sister could slip her dress over her head. It fell lightly around Elizabeth's form, dropping to the floor with a satisfying rustle.

Elizabeth looked at herself in the mirror and thought that she looked somehow different. Elizabeth Bennet had almost gone, but Elizabeth Darcy had not yet appeared. For the moment she was caught between the two worlds, neither one thing nor another. She would be sorry to let the former depart and yet she was longing for the latter to arrive: a new name and with it a new world and a new life.

The two young women looked at each other and then hugged and laughed. They put on their veiled bonnets, pulled on their long white gloves, and picked up their bouquets, releasing the scent of roses into the air. Then, hand in hand, they went downstairs.

'So here we are, two brides,' said Elizabeth as they reached the bottom of the stairs, and suddenly, she shivered.

'What is it?' asked Jane.

Elizabeth's voice was queer.

'I don't know. I just had a strange feeling, almost a sense of foreboding.'

'Hah! That is nothing but wedding nerves,' said her father's warm voice behind her, and turning round, she saw him looking at her kindly. 'Everyone has them on their wedding day.' He became suddenly serious. 'Unless you have changed your mind, Lizzy? If so, it is better to say so now. You have only to say the word, you know that. It is still not too late.'

Elizabeth thought of her beloved Darcy and the way he looked at her as though she was the only woman in the world, and said, 'No, of course not, Papa. It is as you say, just wedding nerves.'

'Good, because I could not bear to let you go to anyone who did not deserve you or anyone you did not truly love,' he said searchingly.

'I do love him, Papa, with all my heart,' said Elizabeth.

'Well then, the carriage is ready, and your bridesmaids are waiting for you. Your mother has already gone to the church. It's time for us to go.'

He offered them each an arm and then, with Lizzy on his right and Jane on his left, he led them out to the carriage.

∞

The streets of Meryton were full of the townspeople going about their daily business, but they all stopped to look and smile as the Bennet carriage drove past. It was the centre of attention as it drove the mile to the church. When it arrived, Elizabeth and Jane saw that the lich gate had been decorated with flowers.

'That was your sister Kitty's idea,' said Mr Bennet as he handed his daughters out of the carriage.

Kitty, climbing out of the carriage behind them with their other bridesmaid, Georgiana Darcy, flushed with pleasure at their obvious delight.

'Your sister Mary, however, thought it a well intentioned but futile gesture as the state of the lich gate would not have any bearing on your future happiness; indeed, she had already discovered a learned extract on that very subject,' Mr Bennet added drily.

Elizabeth laughed, but as she walked up the path to the church, she felt her humour leave her and nerves began to assail her.

Would Darcy be there? Would he have changed his mind? *Would he be wearing his blue coat?*

The mischievous thought slipped into her mind and made her realise how foolish her worries were, and she laughed quietly to herself.

When they reached the church door, Mr Bennet paused.

'Well, girls, let me look at you for one last time,' he said with something that looked suspiciously like moisture in his eyes. 'Yes, you will do very well,' he said at last with a fond smile. 'In fact, you will do more than very well. You are undoubtedly the two loveliest brides in England.'

Then, giving them an arm each, he led them inside.

As they entered the church, Elizabeth and Jane saw that their family and friends had all gathered to witness their wedding. Mrs Bennet was sitting on one side of the aisle with the Gardiners and the Phillipses, whilst Caroline Bingley was on the other side with her sister and brother-in-law. Friends and neighbours were scattered about, all eager to witness the ceremony.

Mr Collins told everyone, in a loud whisper, that, as a clergyman, he was ready to perform the necessary ceremony if the Meryton vicar should suddenly be taken ill; but as Mr Williams was a young man, and as he was already standing in front of them, this did not seem very likely.

The two prospective bridegrooms stood at the front of the church, smiling nervously at each other and asking their groomsmen repeatedly if the wedding rings were safe. They were both looking very handsome and were dressed immaculately in black tailcoats and white breeches. Their cravats were newly starched and their white shirts were ruffled at the wrist.

As Elizabeth and Jane began to walk down the aisle, Mary, who was seated at the church organ, struck up a sonata and everyone turned to look at the brides. A murmur of appreciation went up, gradually fading away to nothing.

When Elizabeth and Jane reached the front of the church, they gave their bouquets to Kitty and Georgiana and then the bridesmaids stood to one side. There were a few coughs, though mercifully none from Kitty, and the vicar began.

'Dearly, beloved, we are gathered together here...'

Elizabeth stole a look at Darcy. He was looking more nervous than she had ever seen him; more nervous, even, than he had been when he had visited her at the inn at Lambton after their estrangement. But when, feeling her eyes on him, he turned to look at her, she saw his nervousness fade, and smiling, they both turned back to the vicar.

'Who giveth this woman to be married to this man?' asked the Rev Mr Williams.

'I do,' said Mr Bennet, with a look of paternal love and pride.

Mr Darcy took Elizabeth's hand in his own right hand and repeated after Mr Williams, 'I, Fitzwilliam Charles George Darcy, take thee, Elizabeth Eleanor Anne Bennet, to be my wedded wife. To have and to hold, from this day forward, for better or for worse, for richer or for poorer, in sickness and in health, to love, honour, and cherish, till death do us part.'

As he did so, there were sighs from the congregation, most notably from the corner where Caroline Bingley was sitting.

Elizabeth and Darcy loosed hands, and then Elizabeth took Darcy's right hand in her own right hand and made her vows in a clear voice that set Mrs Bennet mopping her eyes with her handkerchief, and when Darcy slipped the ring onto Elizabeth's finger, a murmur of approval ran round the church.

Their vows made, they went through into the vestry to sign the register, accompanied by Jane and Bingley, whose vows had been made in no less loving tones. As Mary played another sonata, Elizabeth and Jane signed their names as Bennet for the last time.

When they came out of the vestry, Elizabeth distinctly heard her mother whispering in exultant tones, 'Oh! Mr Bennet! Just think, of it, our Elizabeth is now Mrs Darcy! Oh my goodness, ten thousand a year!'

They walked back up the aisle to showers of congratulations. As they emerged into the sunshine, they were met by Sir William Lucas making a stately speech, and then confronted by Mr Collins bowing obsequiously before them and peppering his rambling congratulations with '…esteemed patroness, Lady Catherine de Bourgh…' before they were free to walk down the path.

When they reached its end, Mr Gardiner handed Mr Darcy some messages which had arrived from well wishers who could not attend the service. Mr Darcy read them to Elizabeth as they went out to the road, where the Darcy coach was waiting.

Elizabeth climbed into the coach, where she was met with the smell of polish and the feel of leather seats, so different from the Bennet coach with its musty interior and its patched upholstery. Even the blinds in the Darcy coach were made of silk.

To the happy cries of the congregation the coach set off on its way back to Longbourn for the wedding breakfast. As Mr Darcy seated himself opposite her, Elizabeth caught an expression of such pure love on his face that she felt a catch in her throat.

She turned away, momentarily overcome, and he continued to read the goodwill messages whilst Elizabeth waved at the young Lucases who were laughing and cheering as the coach drove past. But she could not keep her eyes away from him for long, and they strayed to his reflection, longing to see his face again… and then her heart missed a beat, for the look of love on his face had been replaced by a look of torment.

She felt suddenly frightened. *What can it mean?* she wondered.

For one horrible moment, she wondered if he regretted their marriage. But no, surely not. He had given her so many proofs of his feelings, loving her constantly through her blind prejudice, her angry rejection of him at Rosings, and her sad and uncomfortable awkwardness when they had met unexpectedly at Pemberley, that she was sure he could not regret it. And yet, there had been a look of torment on his face.

She had to know what it meant. Bracing herself for the worst, she turned towards him, only to find that the look had gone and that he was calmly reading through the messages.

She was startled, but then wondered if the glass had distorted his features. It was not a mirror, only a window. It was not meant to give reflections, and the light could play strange tricks even on the smoothest surface. Certainly there was no trace of any anguish on his face now.

The coach turned into the drive of Longbourn House, and seeing the crowd waiting to welcome her, she dismissed the matter. Neighbours who had hurried ahead were waiting to greet her, full of smiles.

The mood was infectious. Darcy helped her out of the coach and then shook hands with all the guests as both he and Elizabeth were showered with rose petals and good wishes.

Jane's carriage, which had been behind Elizabeth's, now arrived, and to the cries of 'Congratulations, Mr and Mrs Darcy!' were added cries of 'Long life and happiness, Mr and Mrs Bingley!'

Elizabeth, banishing the last of her uncertainties, seized a handful of rose petals and threw them joyfully over her sister.

Mrs Bennet cried and said, 'Three daughters married!' and Mr Bennet cleared his throat more than was necessary for a man without a cough.

The whole party went inside. The hall had been decked out with flowers, and the guests passed through with much talk and laughter. They went into the dining room, where the wedding breakfast was laid out. The tables were spread with snowy white cloths and the crystal sparkled whilst the silverware shone. As the guests took their places down either side of the table, Mrs Bennet fussed in and out of the room, until Mr Bennet told her that Hill had taken care of everything.

'Sit down, my dear, and leave everything to Hill,' he said as Mrs Bennet bobbed up from her chair for the dozenth time.

In the centre of the table, a variety of food was arranged on china plates decorated with crystallised flowers. Cold chicken, snipe, woodcocks, pheasant, ham, oysters, and beef vied with colourful salads, the last of the year, and by their side were fruit tarts, syllabubs, and cheeses. In the very centre of the table were two wedding cakes iced with the initials E and F, and J and C.

The voices faded away as people began to eat, with only the clink of glasses and the chink of knives on plates to break the silence.

When at last the guests had eaten their fill, Sir William Lucas rose to his feet.

'And now,' he said, 'I would like to propose a toast: To the fairest jewels of the country, Miss Bennet and Miss Elizabeth Bennet—'

'Hear, hear!' came the cries.

'—who are now to be carried away by their fortunate husbands as Mrs Bingley and Mrs Darcy.'

There were more cries and cheers, and Mrs Bennet could be heard to say, 'I am sure it will not be long before my other girls are married. Kitty is very obliging and quite as pretty as Lizzy, and Mary is the most accomplished girl in the neighbourhood.'

The wedding breakfast eaten and the speeches made, it was time to cut the cake. Elizabeth and Jane rose to their feet, standing side by side with their husbands behind them. The cakes were the pride of the Longbourn kitchen. The rich fruit cake had been steeped in brandy before being topped with marzipan and covered with smooth, white icing. Elizabeth and Darcy, and Jane and Bingley, each put one hand on their respective knives and cut into their cakes. As they did so, Kitty called out, 'Make a wish!'

And suddenly, a cold draught whipped its way around Elizabeth as, with a sudden frisson of some nameless dread, she knew she must have an answer to her forebodings. She turned to Darcy and said in an undertone, 'I wish you would tell me truly, do you regret our marriage?'

His smile was gone in an instant and she saw some great emotion pass over his face. His hand closed convulsively over her own, squeezing it tight. And then she saw a look of resolution on his face and he said fervently, 'No. Never.' He applied pressure to her hand, forcing it downwards with disturbing speed and strength, and together they cut down to the bottom of the cake.

But despite his words, he was ill at ease, and as soon as the last cheer had faded away, he said to Elizabeth, 'It is time for us to go.'

He took her hand and held it firmly in his own. He thanked the assembled company for their attendance and their good wishes, then said that he and his wife must be leaving as they had a long way to travel.

There were more good wishes as he led Elizabeth to the coach and handed her in. Just as Elizabeth was taking her seat, she heard him call up to the coachman, 'There has been a change of plan. I want you to take us to Dover.'

'Dover?' asked Elizabeth in surprise as Darcy climbed into the coach and sat down opposite her. 'But I thought we were going north, to the Lake District. Dover is in the opposite direction.'

'We can go to the Lake District at any time. You cannot

have a very strong attachment to the idea; the plan has been of short duration, and I would like to take you to the Continent instead. I want to show you Paris.'

'But isn't it dangerous?' she asked.

He looked at her in some perturbation and leant forward in his seat.

'What have you heard?' he asked her.

'Nothing,' she said, startled by his change of mood. 'Only that the war with France could break out again at any time, and that when that happens, the English will no longer be safe there.'

'Ah, so that is all,' he said, sinking back into his seat. 'You have nothing to worry about. It is perfectly safe. The Peace will last awhile yet. I have friends and family in Paris, though, people I would like to see again and people I would like you to meet.'

'You have never spoken of them before,' she said curiously.

'There was never any need. But you will like them, I am sure, and they will like you.'

'I have never been to Paris,' she said musingly. 'I have never been out of England.'

'Paris is changing, but it is still a city of great elegance and the Parisians are charming. Sometimes too charming,' he said, and a shadow crossed his face. Then his mood lightened and he said, 'I will have to guard you well.'

CHAPTER 2

THE DARCY ENTOURAGE WAS a large one. Behind Darcy and Elizabeth's coach was a second carriage which contained Darcy's valet, Elizabeth's maid, and trunks of clothes. There were footmen to guard the party from attack and outriders to go ahead of them and pay the tolls, so that when the Darcys arrived, the turnpike was open and the coach could pass straight through.

It was all very different from the journeys Elizabeth had taken with her family in the past. Then, she had been subjected to all the delays and discomforts which accompanied a less luxurious style of travel. She had been packed in with six other people who had laughed and squabbled, exclaimed or complained all the way.

The coach soon left Hertfordshire behind and they began to travel in a south-easterly direction. To begin with the road was familiar to Elizabeth. She had taken the same road the previous Easter when she had visited Charlotte at Rosings Parsonage. This time, however, she did not break her journey in London but continued straight on to Kent. The coach passed through towns and villages, but for the most part, it rolled through the countryside, which was rich with autumn fruitfulness. Blackberries glistened in the hedgerows, and apple trees, laden down with fruit, grew in the fields.

Darcy said little on the journey. He appeared to be thinking about something and Elizabeth did not like to disturb him. His look, at least, was not tormented, merely abstracted, and she found herself wondering if he were prey to strange moods.

She asked herself how much she knew of him, really. She had seen him at Netherfield and Rosings, and at his home in Derbyshire, but there had always been other people present and she knew that, in company, men were not always what they were alone. She had been alone with him as they had walked through the country lanes around Longbourn after their engagement, and yet even then they had not been truly alone: there had always been a neighbour going shopping, a farmer going to market, or a servant on an errand. But now it was just the two of them and Elizabeth found herself both excited and disturbed at the prospect of learning more about him. She wondered what other new facets of his character would be revealed over the coming weeks; she also wondered what further changes of plan there might be before the end of her wedding tour.

This thought led to another and she smiled.

Darcy looked at her enquiringly.

'I was just thinking that I seem destined never to visit the Lake District,' she said. 'I was meant to be going there last year with my aunt and uncle, until my uncle's business concerns made us change our plans. And now, the plans have been changed again. I wonder if I will ever see the lakes?'

'I promise you we will go there, but if we don't take the chance to visit the Continent now, then it might be years before we have the chance again. Napoleon might talk of peace but I have seen men like him before, and whatever they say, they think only of war. There is a small break in the hostilities. We must make the most of it.'

The light soon began to fade. Although the day had been warm, it was October and the days ended early. Darcy pulled down the blinds in the carriage but Elizabeth, eager to see the sunset, moved to stay his hand. He continued with his work, saying that they would be warmer when the blinds were drawn. There was something in the way he said it, some unusual quality in his voice, that made her unwilling to go against him.

They travelled on in silence and Elizabeth thought, with a vague sense of unease, that this was not what she had expected. She had been looking forward to the journey, thinking it would be full of conversation and laughter, and perhaps the kind of love that marriage brought with it, but her husband seemed preoccupied. He sat with his face turned away from her and she watched him, examining his profile. It was strong, with handsome features, yet there was an air of something she could not quite place. He was the man she had married and yet different, more reserved, and she wondered if it was just because of the tiring nature of the journey or whether he were reverting to his former aloof ways.

Although she could see nothing outside the coach, Elizabeth caught the changing sounds and scents of the world beyond them as they neared the coast. The soft song of blackbirds, robins, and thrushes was replaced by the raucous cry of the gulls, and the smell of grass and flowers was replaced by the sharp tang of salt. It permeated the carriage, finding its way into Elizabeth's nostrils and onto her lips and tongue.

The carriage, which had been rolling smoothly over muddy roads, began to jerk and jolt as it travelled over cobbles, and the clattering of the wheels added itself to the harsh sound of the seabirds. Impatient to see where they were, Elizabeth released one of the blinds, and her husband made no move to stop her.

The first thing she saw was the black bulk of Dover castle rising over the landscape. She gave a shudder because, in the darkness, it seemed like something huge and malignant, a massive guardian standing watch, but whether it was protecting or imprisoning the town she could not tell. And then she saw the cliffs. They were as white as the bone of a cuttlefish and, in the pale moonlight, they had a pulsating glow. Outlined against them were the skeletons of tall-masted ships which rose and fell with the tide. Their mooring ropes groaned and sighed as they moved, like the whisper of unquiet souls.

Then the carriage turned a corner and everything took on a more cheerful aspect. Ahead of her, Elizabeth could see an inn. There were lights blazing out from the windows and a brightly-painted sign was hanging outside. The coach rolled into the yard, where the lighted torches made it almost as bright as day. There was noise and bustle, and warmth and colour, and Elizabeth laughed at herself for the nameless fear that had gripped her as they drove into the port.

The coachman pulled the horses up and the coach rolled to a smooth halt. There were no delays or frustrations, as there were when she travelled with her family, no time wasted in trying to attract someone's attention. Instead, as soon as the coach stopped, the horses were attended to, the door was opened, the step was let down, and the Darcys were welcomed obsequiously by the innkeeper. He escorted them into the inn, bowing repeatedly whilst enquiring after their journey and assuring them that they had stopped at the best inn in Dover.

'There is a fire in the parlour when you are ready to dine,' he said, 'and I will have fires lit directly in your rooms. You may rest assured that your every comfort will be attended to.'

Darcy stopped just inside the inn.

'You go ahead,' he said to Elizabeth. 'I have to go down to the harbour and arrange for our passage to France.'

'Cannot one of the outriders make the arrangements?' she asked.

'I would rather do it myself,' he said.

He made her a bow and went outside, and Elizabeth, wondering again at her husband's unexpected actions, was shown upstairs by the innkeeper's wife. The woman threw open the door of a well-appointed apartment and then stood aside deferentially as Elizabeth went inside. The room was bright, with sprigged curtains at the windows and a matching counterpane on the four-poster bed. There was a fireplace in the corner where one of the chambermaids was already lighting the fire, coaxing the wood into life.

The innkeeper's wife then threw open an interconnecting door to another bedroom. The room was slightly larger and the colours were darker than in the previous room. It had obviously been fitted out for a gentleman, with solid oak furniture and paintings of ships on the walls.

'Thank you, these will do very well,' said Elizabeth.

'Thank you, Ma'am.' The innkeeper's wife dropped a curtsey. 'When would you like to dine?'

'As soon as my husband returns,' said Elizabeth.

'Very good,' said the woman, and with another curtsey, she withdrew.

Elizabeth lingered in what was to be Darcy's room. The counterpane had been turned down and she imagined his head on the pillow, with his dark hair showing up against the white bed linen. She was filled with a sudden longing to touch his hair, to feel its texture beneath her fingers, and to inhale the scent of it.

She returned to her own room to find that the chamber maid had already placed a jug of hot water on the wash-stand. She stripped off her clothes, feeling suddenly travel-stained, and standing in a pretty porcelain bowl, she washed all over, squeezing her sponge so that the water trickled down her soapy body, leaving clear channels in its wake. As the water began to cool, she rinsed herself more efficiently and then she went over to the bed where her maid had laid out her new blue dress, which had been bought especially for her trousseau.

Annie, her lady's maid, emerged from the dressing room and helped her to dress, dropping her lace-trimmed chemise over her head and then lacing her stays. As Annie pulled the strings tighter, Elizabeth thought how strange it was to be dressed by someone she didn't know. At Longbourn there had always been her sister Jane to help her, and they had laughed and talked whilst they had dressed for balls; and there had always been Hill to give them more help if needed, to scold and worry them into getting ready more quickly, and to stand back and admire them when they had finished. There had been her mother, too, and Kitty and Mary and Lydia, but here there was no one except Annie, who was new to her, because at home she had had no need of a lady's maid.

As she finished dressing, pulling on her long white eve-ning gloves, Annie opened her mouth and then closed it again. Then she opened it and wiped her clean hands on her apron in a nervous fashion.

'Yes, Annie?' asked Elizabeth.

'Well, Miss—Ma'am—I was just wondering, Ma'am, if it's true, that's all, like the others are saying, are we going out of England, Ma'am? Are we really going to France?'

'Yes, we are,' said Elizabeth, stopping in the middle of fastening the button on her glove and looking at Annie. 'Does that worry you?' she asked.

'No,' said Annie uncertainly. 'But some of them aren't so sure. There's bad things happen in France, so they say, very bad things.'

'Some terrible things have happened in France over the last few years, but they're are over now,' said Elizabeth, wishing she could feel as certain as she sounded. 'If there is any danger, we will not stay.'

Annie nodded, looking as though she only half believed her, then Elizabeth gave her one last reassuring smile and went down to the private parlour where a fire was blazing. The window gave a view of the front of the inn as well as the road beyond and she looked out, hoping to see Mr Darcy when he returned. At last, she grew tired of watching for him and she turned away from the window, only to see that he was already in the room. She felt a frisson of surprise as she wondered how he could have opened the door without her hearing him.

And then all else was forgotten as she saw his appreciative glance and he said, 'You look beautiful.'

'Thank you.'

He stepped forward and took her hand and kissed it.

'Elizabeth, if I seem—preoccupied—it is only because I have a lot to think about at the moment. I will make you happy, I swear.'

'I know you will,' she said.

He stroked her cheek, then his hand stilled as the innkeeper entered the room. A look of frustration crossed his face but he dropped her hand and took his place at the table, as she took hers.

'Did you manage to arrange a passage for us?' she asked politely as the meal was served.

With the servants coming and going she could not say anything more intimate.

'Yes, we sail on the morning tide. Are you a good sailor?' he asked.

Her eyebrows raised.

'I don't know. I've never been on a ship before.'

'Then this will be your chance to find out. You will enjoy it, I think. The captain says the sea will be calm tomorrow. He's a man of some ability and he's used to my ways. I often sail with him when I cross to the Continent.'

They continued to talk of the journey and their plans for the morrow until at last their meal was done and Elizabeth retired for the night. Her husband said that he must speak to the innkeeper so she went upstairs, anticipating the moment when he would join her.

She undressed with Annie's help and put on her new nightgown, trimmed with expensive Bruges lace, and then she dismissed her maid.

She was nervous as she thought about all Lydia's bawdy, soulless tales of married life. *Would it be like that for Darcy and her?* she wondered.

She thought not.

To help pass the time, she went over to the travelling writing desk she had brought with her and started a letter to Jane.

My dearest Jane,
    You will be surprised when I tell you that we are not going to the Lake District after all, we are going to France...

She found it difficult to keep her mind on her letter and she lifted her head, listening for Darcy's foot on the stair or the click of the interconnecting door, but the inn was silent, save for the murmur of voices coming from below.

She turned back to her letter. She wrote about the journey, about the inn, and about her hopes for the morrow, but still her husband did not come.

…Tell me, Jane, is marriage what you thought it would be?

she wrote.

Does Bingley have strange moods? Does he change his mind rapidly? Does he have caprices? I never thought that Darcy would be like this, with strange quirks and fancies, and such rapid changes of mind, and I never thought he would abandon me on our wedding night, either, but I have been in my room for an hour now, Jane, and I am still alone. Perhaps he is tired after the journey, or perhaps he thinks that I must be tired—unless I have done something to offend him. But no, what could I have done?

She wrote on until the clock struck midnight, and then beyond, until at last she fell asleep in the chair.

❦

Elizabeth was awoken by her maid. She was stiff and sore from spending the night on the chair and she was ashamed that her maid had seen her abandoned, but the woman gave no sign that she had noticed anything unusual. Instead, she busied herself with preparing Elizabeth's things. An hour later, Elizabeth, somewhat refreshed by highly scented soap and water, and dressed in clean clothes, went downstairs.

Darcy was in the dining room. He looked up when she entered the room and his eyes widened when he saw her, telling her more clearly than words that he found her lovely. He took her hand and kissed it, then led her to the table, but he made no mention of the night before and she could not say anything in front of the servants.

They made a good meal and then set out for the docks. Elizabeth, missing her daily walks, rejected the coach and they went on foot. The day was uncommonly fair. It was October, but it felt more like September in its mild air, brisk soft wind, and bright sun. Everything looked so tranquil, with the shadows pursuing each other over the landscape, that Elizabeth wondered how she could ever have found the castle, the sea, and the cliffs menacing. They were now picturesque, adding charm to the scene before her.

Darcy was affable and their thoughts were in tune when they made a comment on the port or the people or the bustle all around them. There had been rain in the night, and Darcy teased Elizabeth when her skirts dragged through the dirt.

'Mrs Darcy, are you aware that your petticoat is six inches deep in mud?' he asked her.

She laughed, recalling the time, almost a year ago to the day, when she had walked to Netherfield because Jane was ill and had arrived looking very bedraggled.

'Caroline would be horrified!' she said as she looked down at her muddy hem.

'She was certainly horrified last year.'

'What a sight I must have looked! You must have thought me a strange creature, to turn up at the house in all my dirt.'

'Not at all. It is true that I thought it unnecessary for you to have walked all that way to see your sister when she had nothing but a trifling cold—yes, I really was so pompous, I must admit it—but your eyes, I distinctly remember, had been brightened by the exercise. In fact, your whole face was glowing. I don't think I had ever seen anyone looking more lovely. I believe it was from that date I started to feel myself in some danger from you, although of course I did not admit it to myself at the time.'

'You are determined, I see, to concentrate on my bright eyes instead of my wild appearance!'

'Naturally! Your good qualities are under my protection, if you remember, and I have your permission to exaggerate them as much as possible.'

She laughed, remembering their exchange in the summer.

'But if you would like to avoid the dirt in the future, there is a way to do so, if you are willing. If you would let me buy you a horse, we could ride and spare your gowns,' said Darcy. He looked at her thoughtfully. 'I have always wondered why you don't ride. Jane doesn't have an aversion to horses; I remember her riding to Netherfield, but I have never seen you on horseback.'

'I don't have an aversion to horses, either, but riding takes so long. First of all, I have to ask for the horse and then it has to be made ready—if Papa can spare it, that is—and then it walks so slowly that I am tempted to jump off and carry it instead of letting it carry me.'

'Ah, I see, you don't have any objection to riding, just to inconvenience.'

'Mr Darcy, are you teasing me? I do hope so. Otherwise, I must appear sadly spoilt.'

'Never that,' he said. 'I am glad you do not object to

riding. I will buy you a horse in Paris and you will see what a difference it makes to have a well-chosen mare with good paces instead of a farm horse. You will also see what a difference it makes to have an animal that is ready to go when you are, instead of one for which you have to wait; and one that can actually walk faster on its four legs than you can on your own two!'

'Will there be anywhere to ride?'

'Of course. What do you think the Parisians do?' he asked her teasingly.

'I suppose they must have somewhere to ride, it is true. Very well, you may buy me a mare and I will endeavour to find that I prefer riding to walking.'

'But you will not be afraid to tell me if you do not.'

'No. You know me too well to doubt that I will abuse the exercise if I have a mind to do so.'

He drew her hand through his arm and they walked on, going down the street to the harbour. It was a busy scene. There was noise and bustle everywhere as ships were loaded and unloaded, and carts brought cargo to and from the docks. Sailors lounged about if they had no ship, or shouted to each other as they worked if they were due to sail.

'Which is our ship?' asked Elizabeth.

'That one,' said Darcy, indicating a fine sailing ship. 'The *Mary Rose*.'

The *Mary Rose* bobbed on the water, her sails furled and her rope tied securely to the mooring post. All around her was a scene of activity. Darcy's servants were seeing to the safety of the coach, which was being hoisted on board, and the grooms were leading the horses up the gangplank and onto the ship. The animals were restive but the grooms spoke to them calmly and the animals traversed the narrow plank without mishap. Their possessions followed, the trunks being carried on board by stocky sailors, who carried them as though they were nothing.

Finally, when all was safely stowed, the Darcy entourage walked up the gangplank, all except one of the outriders who, saying that France was a heathen country, refused to go. He was paid off without delay, for the tide was ready to turn.

One of the sailors approached and offered to help Elizabeth board the ship, but she only laughed and walked confidently up the gangplank, laughing as it jostled and jolted beneath her feet. Darcy followed her and they were welcomed on board by the captain.

'It's a good day for sailing,' he said. 'We'll have you across the channel in no time. Have you made the crossing before, Mrs Darcy?'

'No, never,' said Elizabeth.

'There is nothing like being at sea. I am sure you will find it interesting.'

She looked around the deck, seeing coiled ropes and all the appurtenances of sailing, then noticed the cannon.

'Is it usual for a packet ship to be armed?' she asked with some apprehension.

'It is not uncommon in these troubled times,' he said. 'A few modifications to the ship and a few skilled crew can make all the difference to a ship's safety. As often as not, the very sight of them keeps everyone safe.'

'But I thought we were at peace,' said Elizabeth.

'And so we are, but there's never any telling when a foreign captain might get it into his head to forget his orders, and then there are always privateers,' said the captain. 'But don't you worry. We're not likely to meet with any trouble on our voyage. I'll have you in France before you know it.'

'Are there any other passengers?' asked Elizabeth.

'No, just you,' said the captain. 'I've had a cabin made ready for you. It has everything you'll need on the voyage.'

The mate appeared and the Darcys followed him down to the cabin. Elizabeth found it small and cramped, although Darcy told her it was spacious by ships' standards. It had a table and two chairs as well as two bunks, and Elizabeth was surprised to see that the furniture was all nailed down.

'In case of storms,' said Darcy. 'It prevents everything from moving around.'

Elizabeth nodded thoughtfully.

She did not stay below deck for long. Although the cabin was well equipped, the air was stuffy and Elizabeth knew she would be happier out in the open. They went on deck and watched the ship set sail, with the rope being cast off and the sails unfurled. The white canvas billowed out in the wind and drove the ship forward.

It was exhilarating for Elizabeth to feel the wind in her face, and she laughed as it whipped her hair free of its chignon. Darcy smiled and stroked it back, his finger tracing a searing arc across her cheek.

At his touch, the world disappeared and she was held, mesmerised, looking into his eyes. Nothing and no one else mattered. Nothing else seemed to exist.

It was only when one of the sailors bumped into her that she came out of her trance. The sailor apologised, but as she became more aware of her surroundings again, Elizabeth could see that she was in the way. She stood aside and leaned over the rail, feeling the salt spray in her face as it was thrown up by the ship, which cut its way through the waves. Darcy stood next to her, his hand resting lightly in the small of her back.

'Have you been to France many times?' she asked him.

'Yes, I have; many, many times.'

There was something in his voice she did not understand and she glanced at him to find that he was looking unseeingly into the distance.

'Were things very terrible?' she asked, wondering what he was thinking about.

'No, on the contrary. I haven't been to France for some years,' he explained. 'When I last visited the country it was before the revolution.'

'You must have been little more than a child, then,' she said.

'I was certainly younger than I am now,' he agreed. Then, drawing his thoughts back to the present, he said, 'You are a good sailor.'

'Yes, I believe I am,' said Elizabeth, 'at least today, when the weather is fine. Although I am not very steady on my feet!'

'It takes time to get used to the movement,' he said. 'Have you never been on the water at all, not even on a pleasure boat?'

'No, we seldom went to the seaside. Mama always wanted to go. She talked constantly of Lyme and Brighton and Cromer when I was younger, but Papa was always content to stay at home. The furthest she could ever persuade him to go was to London, to visit my Aunt Gardiner and her family, except on one occasion when she told him that her nerves would benefit from some sea air.'

'And did they?'

'No, which is why he never took us again. He said that she had promised him once that her nerves would benefit but that it had ended in nothing and that he would not go on such a fool's errand again!'

'And did you never want to visit a resort?'

'I never thought about it. There was always something new to do or see at home, so much change in the people around me, that I never thought to pine for something else. But now I think I would like to go to the seaside again. Perhaps we could all go to Ramsgate, if it would not remind Georgiana too much of her time with Wickham.'

'I think it would be better not to go to Ramsgate, but there are plenty of other resorts we can visit.'

He told her of the places he had been to and then they turned their attention to the ships they saw around them. Some were naval vessels, some were merchantmen, and some were packet ships; some were going to England and some were going to France; some, indeed, were going further afield, being in the service of the East India Company.

When they were about halfway to France, Darcy went below to make sure that the horses were comfortable and not too distressed by the voyage, and to give instructions for their disembarkation when they should land. Elizabeth remained on deck, watching the other ships and from time to time seeing nothing but the ocean as the seas filled and emptied around her.

It was during one of these lulls that she saw a solitary sail on the horizon. She watched it lazily, but as it drew nearer, she became aware of a change in the atmosphere and she felt a tension amongst the sailors. They began to look up from their work and to shade their eyes with their hands, turning in the direction of the vessel.

'What is it?' asked Elizabeth. 'Is it a French vessel?'

'It's trouble,' said the mate.

'Aye,' said one of the sailors. 'Privateers. Pirates.'

Elizabeth watched the ship with mounting alarm. It was closing fast and she could already see the figures of people on deck. They became more distinct as the ship grew closer, changing from shapeless blobs to well-defined forms.

A flurry of activity broke out all around her as the mate gave orders and the sailors swarmed up the rigging, furling and unfurling sails to try and bring the ship about. But it was no use; they could not turn or run quickly enough, the pirates were almost upon them. Elizabeth was afraid. She backed away from the side of the ship, keeping her eyes on the pirates and hoping for a change in the wind or a sudden calm, anything that would keep their ship from hers. But still it came on. She could see the pirates' faces now, full of savage glee.

She turned to go down to the cabin and found herself walking into her husband. He had come back on deck again with the captain, and he put his arm around her. She felt an unusual strength emanating from him and a sense of raw power.

'Darcy!' she said thankfully, taking refuge in his nearness. 'The pirates…' she said, looking again at the fast approaching ship with its crew of murderous men.

And then suddenly, she saw the pirates go pale and their expressions changed. Their look of triumph gave way to one of fear and their anxious mutterings could be heard as they started to back away from the rail. Then they broke apart and began swarming up the rigging whilst their captain hurled abuse at them. The ship veered away, and then it turned and ran, disappearing into the distance as quickly as it had appeared.

She stood watching the empty water where it had been for a few seconds.

'What happened?' she asked the mate as she felt her pulse begin to return to normal.

'I don't rightly know,' the mate answered her with a frown.

'I do,' muttered one of the sailors darkly. 'There's something on board that frightens them. And there's not a lot will frighten men like that.'

'Aye, our cannon,' said the captain with satisfaction.

Elizabeth looked to the side of the deck where the small cannon had been placed, but the sailors still muttered and one of them said something that sounded like albatross.

'Albatross?' said the mate, and spat.

'You will have to excuse him, Mrs Darcy,' said the captain apologetically. 'My men are a good lot but they don't have drawing-room manners.'

'What did he mean by albatross?' asked Elizabeth.

The captain shook his head.

'Sailors are a superstitious lot, and as soon as the least little thing goes wrong, they must find a reason for it. They say it is bad luck to shoot an albatross, and so, when something strange occurs, of course it must be because someone on board has shot one of the birds. That is, of course, a far more reasonable explanation than that the pirates were afraid of our guns!'

Elizabeth smiled, but the air of unease lingered. As the captain escorted them below, having invited them to take luncheon in his cabin, there were still mutterings amongst the crew. Some of the mutterings were in English and some were in a mixture of other European tongues. One phrase seemed to rise out of the others and one of the sailors asked another, 'What does he say?'

'Old one,' said the sailor sullenly.

The captain looked startled, but then said, 'Old one!' with a laugh. 'Why, there is nothing old about our cannons, or our ship either! Both are new. Well, new in naval terms, Mrs

Darcy, and certainly new enough to scare away any other malcontents who should happen to cross our bows.'

They went below. A simple meal had been laid out on the captain's table and soon the three of them were eating. Darcy was content to listen to the captain instead of saying very much himself and Elizabeth was content to watch him. Her eyes were drawn to his fingers, and she watched them as he carefully peeled an orange. He took advantage of the captain leaving the table for a few seconds and put the orange on her plate. She broke it in two, separating the soft segments, then gave half back to him.

'We'll soon be there now,' said the captain as their meal at last drew to an end. 'It's been a pleasure having you on board, Mrs Darcy. Your husband I've transported on many occasions. But I hope I will have the pleasure of carrying you again. You did not find your first trip too unpleasant, I hope? I assure you that our little bit of trouble was unusual and is not likely to happen again.'

'I am not so easily frightened,' said Elizabeth, earning an admiring look from her husband. 'I think I would be more alarmed by a rough crossing!'

'Aye, that can be unpleasant, but you have the look of a sailor about you, Mrs Darcy. I'll wager you'd find your sea legs whatever the weather.'

Elizabeth glanced at the porthole, which allowed daylight into the cabin, and through it she found that she could see the dim and distant outline of land.

'Is that France?' she asked, going over to the porthole to look.

'Aye, it is,' said the captain, rising to his feet as soon as Elizabeth rose. 'Will you be staying long?'

'For a few weeks, perhaps,' said Darcy, rising also.

'There are many fine sights to be seen. I hope you enjoy them,' said the captain with a bow.

He had a few things he wished to discuss with Darcy, and Elizabeth took the opportunity to return to her cabin where she tidied her hair, which had been blown about by the wind, before going on deck again. Darcy was already there. He put his arm protectively round her as the shoreline drew gradually closer, until the buildings and then the people on shore could be discerned.

'Is it far to Paris?' asked Elizabeth.

'It will take us several days to get there,' said Darcy. 'We will travel in easy stages, seeing the sights on the way. There is a great deal I have to show you.'

The ship eased its way into the harbour and the Darcys disembarked.

As she set foot for the first time on French soil, Elizabeth looked about her with interest and wondered what the next few weeks would bring.

CHAPTER 3

My dearest Jane,

It is almost a week since I wrote to you last, and indeed I have been very negligent for I have forgotten to post my last letter to you. Never mind, I will post them both together and you will have the pleasure of two letters at once; or, more likely, you will receive one after the other. The post from the Continent is not very reliable, I hear.

We are now established in Paris, and it is the most beautiful city. I was apprehensive about coming here at first, but my fears were unfounded. The city is unexpectedly civilised and the French, so far, seem friendly. We have had some trouble with the food, which is laced with garlic, and several of the servants have been ill; indeed one of our footmen has left us, saying that he will be poisoned here if he stays any longer. Fortunately, he has not been difficult to replace. My maid refuses to eat anything except the bread and cheese she buys at the market. I must confess, I have joined her in this simple repast on more than one occasion. Darcy too eats very little here. But that is a small matter. The shops are elegant and numerous, and there are splendours to be seen everywhere. My dear Darcy has a wide circle of friends and relatives, and I pity poor Mama for telling him that we were able to dine with four and twenty families in Hertfordshire, for I must already have met a hundred of his friends. Last night we went to a soirée and tonight we are to go to a salon given by one of Darcy's cousins. Does that not sound grand? Perhaps I will start a fashion for salons when I return home. You and I can hold them, Jane, and be the most fashionable women in England!

How are you finding London? Are you and your dear Mr Bingley happy? I am happy with my Darcy, and yet, Jane, he has still not visited me in my bedchamber and I do not know why. I wish you were here, then I would have someone to talk to. The people here are all very welcoming, but they are strangers, and I cannot say the things to them that I could say to you.

Write to me as soon as you can at the address below.

Your affectionate sister,
Elizabeth

She addressed the letter and gave it to one of the footmen to post, together with the letter she had written in Dover, then went upstairs to dress. As she did so, she was conscious of the gulf between her old and new lives. Her experiences of Paris had, for the first time, shown her how truly different Darcy's life was from her own. Before their marriage, she had seen him at Pemberley with his sister, at Rosings with his aunt, and at Netherfield with Bingley, but she had never seen him in society. Now, however, it was very different.

She thought of Lady Catherine's visit to Longbourn a few short weeks before, when Lady Catherine had tried to dissuade her from marrying Darcy by saying that she would be censured, slighted, and despised by everyone connected with him, and that the alliance would be a disgrace; that Elizabeth herself, if she were wise, would not wish to quit the sphere in which she had been brought up. To which Elizabeth had replied angrily that, in marrying him, she should not consider herself as quitting her sphere, because Darcy was a gentleman and she herself was a gentleman's daughter.

And that had been true. But only in Paris had she realised how wide was the gulf between a gentleman's daughter from a country manor house and a gentleman of Darcy's standing. The people he knew in Paris were quite unlike the country gentry of England. They were beautiful and mesmerising in a way she had never encountered before. The women undulated, instead of walked, across the rooms with the sinuous beauty of snakes, and the men were scarcely any less seductive. They spoke to her in low voices, holding her hand lingeringly and gazing into her eyes with an intensity which at once attracted and repulsed her.

Nevertheless, she liked Paris, and by the time she arrived at the salon, she was ready to enjoy herself.

The house was insignificant from the outside. It was situated on a dirty street and had a narrow, plain frontage, but once inside everything changed. The hall was high ceilinged and carpeted in thick scarlet, and a grand staircase swept upstairs to the first floor. It was crowded with people, all wearing the strange new fashions of the Parisians. Gone were the elaborate styles of the pre-revolutionary years, with wide hooped skirts and towering wigs. Such signs of wealth had been discarded in fear, and simplicity was the order of the day. The men wore their hair long, falling over the high collars of their coats, and at their necks they wore cravats. Beneath their coats they wore tightly fitting knee breeches. The women wore gowns with high waists and slender skirts, made of a material so fine that it was almost sheer.

There was a noise of conversation as the Darcys began to climb the stair. One or two people raised quizzing glasses so they could stare at Elizabeth. She felt conscious that her dress was English and appeared staid by the side of the Parisian finery. The fabric was sturdier and the style less bare.

Darcy introduced her to some of the people and they welcomed her to Paris, but it was not the warm welcome of Hertfordshire; it was an altogether more appraising greeting.

Elizabeth and Darcy made their way to the top of the stairs where they waited to be announced.

The doors leading to the drawing room had been removed and the opening had been shaped into an oriental arch. It framed the hostess so perfectly that Elizabeth suspected it was deliberate. Mme Rousel, reclining on a *chaise longue*, was like a living portrait. Her dark hair was piled high on her head and secured by a long mother-of-pearl pin, from which curls spilled artistically round her sculptured features and fell across her bare shoulders. Her dress was cut low, with the small frills which passed for sleeves falling off her shoulders before merging with a delicate matching frill at her neck. The sheer fabric of her skirt was arranged around her in folds that were reminiscent of Greek statuary, and on her feet she wore golden sandals. A dark red shawl was draped across her knees, flowing over the gold upholstery of the *chaise longue* in an apparently casual arrangement. But every fold was so perfect that its placement could only be the result of artifice and not the negligence it was intended to convey. Elizabeth realised that that was why she felt uncomfortable: because the whole salon, from the people to the clothes to the furniture, was the result of artifice, a carefully arranged surface which shone like the sea on a summer's day but disguised whatever truly lay beneath.

The Darcys were announced. At the name, many of the people already in the drawing room turned round. Even here in Paris, the name of Darcy was well known. They stared openly, in a way the English would not have done, with a boldness that was unsettling.

They went forward and Mme Rousel, Darcy's cousin, welcomed them.

'At last, Darcy, I was wondering when you would pay me a visit. It is many years since I have seen you.'

'It has not been easy to visit France,' he said.

'For one of our kind it is always easy,' she said reprovingly. 'But you are here now, and that is all that counts.'

She held out her hand, with its long white fingers covered in rings, and he kissed it. She then withdrew it and placed it precisely in her lap, exactly as it had been before.

'So you are Elizabeth,' she said. 'You must be very special to have won Darcy's affections. I never thought he would marry. The news has taken many of us by surprise.' She looked at Elizabeth and then at Darcy and then back again. Her expression was thoughtful. Then she bowed slightly to Elizabeth with a small incline of her head before wishing them joy of her salon.

'You will find many old friends here and some new ones, too,' she said to Darcy.

Darcy and Elizabeth moved on into the large drawing room so that Mme Rousel could greet her next guests.

Darcy was at once welcomed by four women who walked up to him with lithe movements and lingering glances. Their dresses were rainbow hued, in the colours of gems, and flimsy, like all the Parisian dresses. Their hair was dark and their skin was pallid.

'You will have to be careful,' came a voice at Elizabeth's shoulder.

She turned to see a man with fine features and tousled hair. He had an air of boredom about him, and although Elizabeth did not usually like those who were easily bored, there was something strangely magnetic about him. His *ennui* gave his mouth a sulky turn which was undeniably attractive.

'They will take him from you if they can,' the man continued, watching them all the while.

Elizabeth turned to look at them, and as she did so, she was reminded of Caroline Bingley and her constant efforts to catch Darcy's attention. He had been impervious to Caroline and he was impervious to the Parisian women as well, for all their efforts to enrapture him. As they talked and smiled and leant against him, flicking imaginary specks of dust from his coat and picking imaginary hairs from his sleeve, they looked at him surreptitiously. When they saw that he was oblivious to their attempts to captivate him, they redoubled their efforts, one of them whispering in his ear, another leaning close to his face, and the other two walking, arm in arm, in front of him, in order to display their figures.

'It is not right, what they do there, he being so newly married,' said a woman, coming up and standing beside the two of them. 'But forgive me, I was forgetting, we have not been introduced. I am Katrine du Bois, and that is my brother, Philippe.'

There was an air of warmth about the woman which was missing from many of the salon guests, and Elizabeth sensed in her a friend. And yet there was something melancholy about her, as though she had suffered a great disappointment from which she had never recovered.

'It is not right, no,' said Philippe. 'But it is nature. What can one do?'

He turned to look at Elizabeth with sympathy but Elizabeth was only amused.

'Poor things!' she said.

Darcy wore the same expression he had worn when she had first seen him at the Meryton assembly; and despite the difference in the two events, the noisy vulgarity of the assembly and the refined elegance of the salon, he was still above his company. His dark hair was set off by his white linen and his well-moulded face, even in such company, was handsome. His dark eyes wandered restlessly over his companions until they came to rest on Elizabeth. And then his face relaxed into softer lines, full of warmth and love.

'I wish a man would look at me the way that Darcy looks at you,' said Katrine.

'I am very lucky,' said Elizabeth, and she knew that she was.

She had not married for wealth or position; she had married for love. She wished that she was not in company, that she and Darcy had stayed at the inn where they could have been alone, but she knew they would not be in Paris forever. The calls and engagements would come to an end and then they would have more time to spend, just the two of them, together.

'You are,' said Katrine. 'I have many things; I have jewels and clothes, carriages and horses, a fine house and finer furnishings, but I would give them all for one such look.'

Darcy's companions claimed his attention and he turned reluctantly away. As he did so, his hand moved to his chest as though he were lifting something beneath his shirt, pulling it away from his chest and then letting it drop again.

'What is it he does there?' asked Katrine. 'Does he wear something round his neck?'

'Yes, I bought him a crucifix yesterday. The shops in Paris are very tempting,' said Elizabeth. 'He refused to take it at first, but he had given me so much and I had given him so little that I insisted, and at last he allowed me to fasten it around his neck.'

Katrine's voice was reverent. 'He must love you very much,' she said.

'Yes, I believe he does,' said Elizabeth.

'And now, we have talked of Mr Darcy for long enough,' said Philippe. 'Any more and I will grow jealous. I will pay you out by talking of our hostess's many perfections. Do you not think she is beautiful?' he asked, casting his own longing look in her direction.

'She seems charming,' said Elizabeth.

'Yes, she is, very charming,' he said with warmth.

'But does she always receive people whilst reclining on a sofa?' asked Elizabeth, unable to suppress her mirth.

'Ah, you find it amusing,' he said, seeing the humour in her eyes. 'And so it is, an amusing affectation. Our great hostesses all like to have them. Do your hostesses at home not like to make an effect?'

'I cannot say; I rarely go into society,' said Elizabeth, 'or at least not this sort of society, and no one in Meryton would dress in such a way or spend the evening lying on a sofa unless they were ill!'

'Your husband does not take you to the London salons then?' asked Philippe. 'I was certain he would do so.'

'I hardly know where he takes me—or perhaps I should say, where he will take me. He has only been my husband for a week.'

'Ah, yes of course. Being so newly married you will have better things to do with your time than to go to salons,' said Philippe, raising his eyebrows.

Elizabeth, much to her surprise, blushed, and Katrine, seeing it, said, 'Take no notice of my brother.' She tapped his arm
reprovingly with her fan. 'He is very French; he does not understand the English idea of good taste. He thinks of nothing
but the pleasures of the flesh, and he has no reticence in him.'

'*Ma soeur!* You wrong me,' he said, pretending to be
wounded. 'What impression of me will you give to *la belle*
Elizabeth?' Then turning to Elizabeth he said, 'I think of
many things, of my horses and carriages, my friends and family, of art and music… see, I will prove it to you. I will take
you to meet our resident genius, and you shall see how I
listen to him with rapture in my eyes!'

He offered her his arm with such an air of gallantry that
she could not refuse, and he led her to the other side of the
room, where a young man was starting to play the piano. He
was surrounded by a devoted coterie of women who leaned
over the instrument or stood adoringly by his side.

He was very handsome in the French fashion, with a high
brow, sleek hair, and pronounced features. He played with
exquisite taste, his fingers running over the keys more quickly than seemed possible, blending the notes in a strange and
rippling liquidity. It flowed out from his fingers and into the
room, filling the space with the hypnotic melody.

'I have brought someone to meet you,' said Philippe.

He introduced Elizabeth to the three women leaning
across the piano and then to the pianist, Monsieur Huilot, 'a
young musical genius.'

Monsieur Huilot took the compliment gracefully, never
once breaking off from his hypnotic melodies, and asked
Elizabeth if she enjoyed music. When she answered that she
did, he said, 'That is good. Music feeds the soul, and the soul,
it needs feeding.'

He continued to play, his tapering fingers caressing the keys, and the music was gorgeous. But Elizabeth could not keep her eyes on him, for they kept wandering to Darcy, who was still watching her whilst the women around him tried to catch his attention.

There was a lull in the music and Darcy stood up, crossing the room to Elizabeth and saying, 'Will you not play?'

'You of all people know that I am an indifferent pianist,' she replied.

She had played before him on a number of occasions, first in Hertfordshire, when they had both been guests of Sir William Lucas, and later at Rosings, the home of Darcy's aunt. She had not wanted to do so, even in such small gatherings, and she was even less disposed to play here, where there was so much musical talent.

'I beg to differ; you play very well. Besides, you cannot mean to refuse me, now that I have come in all my state to hear you,' he said with a wry smile.

Elizabeth laughed, for it was the complaint she had made against him at Rosings. He had been aloof and superior, and she had suspected him of trying to discomfit her; though she had been quite wrong, for he had just wanted to be near her.

'Very well,' she said, adding to the other guests, 'you have been warned.'

She played and sang, and received a polite response, despite the fact that she was in truth an indifferent pianist, for she was not willing to devote several hours a day to practise. But this lukewarm response was more than made up for by Darcy's look, and by his saying to her, not long afterwards, 'We have been here long enough. What do you say to our going to the Lebeune's ball? I would like to dance.'

She needed no urging. The sumptuous atmosphere was starting to oppress her and the strangely sinuous people were unsettling. She was relieved to get outside and breathe the fresh air.

Night hung over the city like a dark mantle, pierced with the light of flambeaux, and up above, there seemed to be a thousand stars.

There was as much activity as there was in the daytime. Paris was a city which did not sleep. Carriages rolled through the streets taking brightly dressed passengers to balls and *soirées*, and light and laughter spilled out of the taverns. English voices could be heard mingling with the French, as Elizabeth's compatriots took advantage of the peace and visited Paris in great numbers.

And yet despite the colour and laughter there was a lurking horror beneath the brightness, a sense that violence could erupt again at any time. For all its elegance, Paris was a city torn apart by destruction. The revolution had left its mark.

'You're very quiet,' said Darcy.

'I was thinking,' said Elizabeth.

'About what?'

'About the revolution. About how it changed everything.'

'Not everything,' he said, touching her hand.

The carriage pulled up outside a long, stone building and they went inside.

The Lebeune's house was shabby, full of faded splendours and battered grandeur. The marble columns in the hall were dull and the carpet covering the stairs was worn into holes. As Elizabeth ascended to the first floor, she looked at the portraits hanging on the walls, but they were so begrimed that she could not discern their features and she could see nothing beyond a dark and gloomy outline. Their frames too were begrimed, and although they were gilded, they had long since lost their sparkle. There was a chandelier hanging from the ceiling, splendid in size and shape, but so denuded of candles that it gave out no more than a dim glow.

The people too were faded. The men's coats were shiny with wear and their shoes were scuffed, whilst the women's dresses were mended and patched. They wore the old style of clothing, heavy gowns with full skirts and damasked fabrics. Elizabeth had met their type before, in England, people who had once been wealthy but who now lived on the charity of their friends—not by taking money, but by accepting invitations to dinner or to stay, which both parties knew they could never return.

But despite the weary air of both people and surroundings, Elizabeth preferred it to the Rousel house. There, the surface had been dazzling and the undercurrents jaded; here, it was the other way about. Beneath their wary smiles, the people were warm and friendly. They had known sorrow and loss, but their spirit survived.

Elizabeth felt herself begin to breathe more freely.

She was introduced to a dozen people. She told them of England and talked to them of their own city, but at last she could resist it no longer, and with a glance at Darcy, she invited him to lead her onto the floor.

'A married couple. How *outré*!' was the whisper as they took their places, for it was not done for married couples to dance together.

But Elizabeth did not care. It was like the days of their courtship. She and Darcy talked freely of everything they had seen and heard that day. They talked of art and music, of the people they had met and the people they still hoped to meet.

'My cousin liked you, as I knew she would,' said Darcy with pride.

Elizabeth thought of Mme Rousel's eye and thought that *liked* was a strong word, but at least the beauty had not disapproved of her and had made her welcome.

'It is a good thing not all your family are against the marriage,' she said. 'Will you invite her to visit us at Pemberley?'

'Possibly. But I do not think she will leave France. Her life is here, with the glamour and amusements of Paris.'

Elizabeth was not sorry. She could not imagine Mme Rousel in England, where, in her gossamer-like dresses, she would surely catch her death of cold!

∞

Elizabeth woke late on the morning after the ball. She and Darcy had not returned home until almost four o'clock in the morning, and when she finally roused herself, it was almost midday.

'Good heavens!' she said, jumping out of bed. 'Why did you not wake me?' she asked her maid.

'The master said I was to let you sleep,' said Annie, as she placed a tray of *pain* and chocolate in front of her.

'Well, perhaps he was right. But now I must hurry,' she said, eating her breakfast. 'We are supposed to be going riding in an hour.'

Darcy had bought her a new mare and the animal was due to be delivered that morning. They had arranged to go riding by the side of the Seine if the weather was fine.

She had not brought a riding habit with her, having not intended to ride, but she had been able to buy one in Paris. The Darcy money and the Darcy name had ensured that the habit was made and delivered quickly, and it was now ready for her to wear. It lacked the artistry of London tailoring, but nevertheless, it was finer than anything she had worn as Miss Elizabeth Bennet. It was made of dark green broadcloth, with a high waist and a long, slender skirt, and she matched it with a green hat and York tan gloves. Her ruffled shirt showed white between the lapels. She glanced at herself in the mirror and then went downstairs.

As she crossed the hall, she heard a voice she recognised and she smiled with pleasure because the voice belonged to one of Darcy's English cousins, Colonel Fitzwilliam. She knew Colonel Fitzwilliam well. They had met at Rosings the previous Easter and they had spent many happy hours walking and talking together. They had got on so well that he had thought it necessary to let her know, in a roundabout fashion, that he could not afford to marry a poor wife and that he must marry an heiress if he were to have the comforts he had come to expect from life. She had not been offended, indeed she had thought it well done, and besides, she had not had any interest in him as a husband; she had not even, at that time, had any interest in Darcy.

She went into the drawing room, looking forward to greeting him, but the men did not hear her enter and she heard Colonel Fitzwilliam saying, 'Are you mad? You should never have married her. What were you thinking of, Darcy?'

Elizabeth was shocked. She had not known that Colonel Fitzwilliam objected to the match. He had liked her at Rosings but it seemed that, whilst he liked her well enough as a guest of his aunt's parson, he did not like her as Darcy's wife.

'Let her go, Darcy,' he continued. 'You can't do this to her. Send her home.'

'No,' said Darcy, turning away defiantly.

As he did so, he saw Elizabeth. He held out his hand to her and she went and stood next to him, taking his arm and presenting a unified front to his cousin.

'Well?' demanded Colonel Fitzwilliam.

'Well?' returned Darcy implacably.

'Are you not going to tell her? You owe her that much. Give her a choice.'

Darcy seemed to fight a battle within himself, then he turned towards her and searched her eyes, as if he could find the answer to his problem written there. He cupped her face with his hand.

'Well, Lizzy, what do you say?' he asked, looking into her eyes. 'My cousin would like you to return to Longbourn. I want you to stay with me. Which is it to be?'

Elizabeth knew that she had not been accepted by Darcy's family, that there had been disapproving eyes turned on her at the salon, and that she would probably never be accepted by all the Darcys, but she was not unduly concerned. She was not the kind of person to be easily intimidated, and she was certainly not going to be driven out of Europe or out of her marriage by ill will. If Colonel Fitzwilliam thought that she would crumple under a bad-natured reception, then he had much to learn about her character.

She turned to Darcy. 'Where you go, I go. If you stay, I will stay.'

Darcy slid his arm around her waist then turned to his cousin and said, 'You see?'

'I see only that she does not know what it is she should fear. If you will not take my advice, speak to your uncle,' said Colonel Fitzwilliam. 'You have always respected him. Go and see him, and be guided by him.'

She felt a relenting in Darcy and he said, 'I had already

decided to do so. Elizabeth and I are going to visit him after we finish our sojourn in Paris. Now, if you will excuse us, we are going out riding.'

'I am surprised you can find a horse to carry you,' Colonel Fitzwilliam said darkly.

'I brought my own from the Pemberley stables,' Darcy said. 'It travelled with us, tethered to the back of the coach.'

'I should have guessed,' said Colonel Fitzwilliam. Then, saying, 'Darcy. Mrs Darcy,' he made them a curt bow and took his leave.

Elizabeth looked at Darcy enquiringly as he left the room.

'What was all that about?' she asked. 'Does he disapprove of our marriage, or does he think that I am expecting your family to welcome me? Does he think I do not know that there are some among them who will never accept me, and does he really think me so poor spirited I will be afraid of a cutting remark or a cold shoulder?'

'Elizabeth—'

'Yes?' she asked.

He looked as though he was about to say something more and suddenly she felt a sense of dread, as though there were something dark lurking beneath the surface of her life, something which threatened her world, her security, her happiness. But then he stroked her hair and everything was as it should be. He relaxed, and she relaxed as well.

'No matter. The horses are ready. Let me see if I can convince you to enjoy Paris from horseback.'

They went out into the street, and there in front of the house was Darcy's impressive black stallion and the sweetest mare Elizabeth had ever seen. Although she was no horse-woman, she had lived in the country all her life and she knew that the mare was exceptional.

'She is called Snowfall,' said Darcy.

The name suited her. She was white, with a long mane and tail, no more than fourteen hands high with slender legs and nicely sloping shoulders. Her neck was arched and she had an overall air of elegance.

Darcy made a sign to the groom, who trotted her up and down the road on a leading rein, showing off her paces and her neat, small hooves.

'She looks as though she has Arab blood,' said Elizabeth, as the groom brought her to a halt.

'Yes, she has.'

Elizabeth took a carrot from the groom and gave it to the mare, feeling the animal's soft mouth nuzzling her hand as the carrot disappeared.

'Do you like her?' asked Darcy.

'I do indeed,' said Elizabeth.

He helped her to mount, holding her hand as she stepped up onto the mounting block and then settled herself comfortably on the mare's back, hooking one leg around the pommel of her side saddle before arranging her skirt and allowing the groom to adjust the straps. Then she declared that she was ready.

Darcy mounted beside her and the two of them set off towards the river.

The main city was dirty, but once they approached the Seine, it was clean and beautiful. The river was lined with grand buildings, their long elegant lines stretching gracefully into the distance. Their walls were of stone and their roofs were of a pale grey, as though a watercolourist had chosen the shade to echo the river and the sky.

They rode past the Louvre, where they had already spent a morning looking at the luscious paintings of Titian and

Rubens, and where they now saw a great many people making the most of the Peace of Amiens to enjoy the activities which had long been denied them. Elizabeth enjoyed the sights, and she took pleasure in the neat steps of her mare and the warm air and her husband beside her.

'When your cousin spoke of us visiting your uncle, which uncle did he mean?' she asked, as they rode over a bridge and came to Notre Dame. The great Gothic cathedral rose against the skyline, a concoction of spires, rose windows, and buttresses which were impressive in their artistry and their size. 'Not his father, I take it, or he would have said so.'

'No, not his father. I have another uncle here on the Continent. It is to him we will go.'

There came a cry behind them: 'Darcy! Elizabeth!'

Katrine and Philippe rode up on matching bays, both of them splendidly dressed, Katrine in a velvet riding habit and Philippe in a caped greatcoat with knee breeches disappearing into highly polished boots.

'I hoped I would find you here,' said Katrine. 'This is the place to meet everyone in Paris. They are all here to see and be seen.'

'I hear you had a visit from your cousin, Darcy,' said Philippe, as he and Katrine fell in beside the Darcys and the four of them continued together. 'He tells me that you are going to stay with your uncle. I envy you. It is many years since I visited the Alps. The clear air, the scented forests, the feel of the night wind against the face... I miss it.'

'Have you ever been to the Alps before?' Katrine asked Elizabeth.

'No, never.'

'You did not plan them as part of your tour?'

'We did not plan on coming abroad at all.'

'Ah. It has been a surprise, but not an unpleasant one, I hope?'

'Not at all. I like to see new places and meet new people.'

'*Vraiment*, it is good what you say. Without seeing new places and meeting new people we grow old before our time. We must make an effort to do new things, must we not? It is what gives life its zest.'

'But you will return to Paris?' asked Philippe.

'No,' said Darcy shortly.

Philippe raised his eyebrows but said nothing.

'At least not for a while. But later, who knows?' said Katrine.

'You must,' said Philippe, turning to Elizabeth. 'We will never forgive Darcy if he deprives us of your company, will we Katrine?'

'Me, I would forgive Darcy anything!' she said with a longing look at him. 'But come, Philippe, we must away. I have to be at the du Bariers' in an hour and you have promised to escort me.'

They rode off in a flurry of manes and hoofs.

'Why do you need to see your uncle?' asked Elizabeth, continuing their earlier conversation. 'From what you said to your cousin, it sounded as though you wanted his advice on our marriage and our reception in society. Is that so?'

'Not in the way you imagine, no,' he said.

'In what way, then?'

He hesitated, as if choosing his words carefully, and said at last, 'We are different, you and I. We belong together and yet we are not the same. My uncle is very experienced. He might perhaps have encountered the difficulties we will face before, and know how to deal with them.'

Elizabeth was silent. Darcy too was silent, and the only sound was of their horses' hooves clopping along the road.

'You're very quiet,' he said after a minute or two.

'I'm… surprised,' she said. 'I thought our differences had been resolved, at least the differences that matter, those involving our hearts and minds. The others, the differences in our social standing and the opinion of other people, I thought no longer mattered to you, as they have never mattered to me. I thought you had overcome them.'

'So I have, a long time ago. You're right, they don't matter.'

'But something matters,' she said, bringing her mare to a standstill, 'because you are not happy.'

He looked surprised.

'I am happy,' he said.

'Then you are not easy in our mind,' she persevered. 'Otherwise why would you want your uncle's advice?'

Again he thought before speaking.

'Elizabeth, there are things you don't yet know,' he said with a frown.

'About you?'

'About me, and my family.'

'You mean there are skeletons in the closet?' she asked, patting her mare's neck.

He gave a ghost of a smile.

'Not skeletons, no,' he said. 'But I think I might have underestimated the problems we will face. For myself, it doesn't matter, but for you… I want to protect you, I want to make you happy.'

'You do.'

'No, not entirely. I've seen you looking at me, puzzled, a few times since we married.'

She could not deny it.

'That's because I don't always understand you,' she said.

'I don't always understand myself.'

'You have always been a difficult man to fathom,' she agreed. 'Even at the Netherfield ball, I could not make you out. And I think that recently, you have grown more perplexing rather than less so. I hope your uncle can help.'

'I think you will like him, and I think you will like the Alps. The scenery is unlike anything you have ever seen before.' Then his eyes laughed and he said, 'Your mother would certainly like him. He lives in a castle.'

'A castle?' she asked, impressed despite herself. 'Is it finer than Pemberley?'

'Bigger, certainly.'

'Finer than Rosings?'

'More imposing, at least.'

The horses began to trot more quickly, as if sensing the lightening in their riders' moods, and before long, they reached a wider open space.

'And what of the chimney piece?' asked Elizabeth teasingly.

'It is the most impressive chimney piece I have ever seen; the sort of chimney piece that would send Mr Collins into raptures.'

'Then I beg you will not tell him about it, or he will find a way to visit your uncle, and drag poor Charlotte with him,' said Lizzy, laughing. 'What is his name, this uncle? Is he a Darcy or a Fitzwilliam?'

'He comes from… an older branch of the family,' he said. 'He is an uncle a few times removed. He is neither a Fitzwilliam nor a Darcy. His name is Count Polidori.'

'A count?' asked Lizzy, amused. 'Then we must definitely

not tell Mama about him, or she will be introducing him to Kitty!'

'He is rather too old for Kitty,' he said.

'That is a relief. Poor Kitty has had enough to cry about these last few months, with Papa saying he would keep a careful watch over her and never let her out! It took a great deal of soothing to make her realise that he was joking. When do you expect us to leave for the mountains?' she asked.

'That depends. We can go as soon or as late as you wish. Have you seen enough of Paris or would you like to stay?'

'I think I have seen all I need to see,' she said. 'It is very elegant, despite the destruction wrought by the revolution. The people too have surprised me, but...'

'But?'

'I find I do not really like it here. The buildings are all very fine, but I am longing for green fields once again.'

'Then we will make our preparations and set out as soon as they are complete.'

CHAPTER 4

THE WEATHER WAS FINE when they left Paris. It was a golden October, with plenty of sunshine and warm, drowsy days. They set out at a leisurely pace, enjoying the journey. Elizabeth travelled in the coach as it passed through the city and headed in a south-easterly direction. They stopped for lunch at an inn near Fontainebleau and then Elizabeth took to horseback, riding through the forest beside Darcy. The whitebeams were starting to lose their leaves, creating openness above them, and the air had a clarity that made the colours sing.

They passed the chateau of Fontainebleau and Elizabeth looked at it in wonder. It dwarfed Pemberley and Rosings, too.

'At least the revolution didn't destroy this,' she said.

She had seen a great deal of destruction in Paris, with buildings defaced or demolished, but the palace was still intact, rapturous in its beauty. It had graceful proportions and elegant lines, ornamented with the curve of a horseshoe staircase at its front. And surrounding the palace were the greens and blues of the gardens and lake.

'No, not the outside, but the inside has been ransacked and the furniture sold. François would not recognise it now, nor Louis, nor Marie Antoinette.'

He spoke about them as if he knew them, but Elizabeth's education, governess-less though it had been, was sufficient to tell her that he meant the French kings and queens of centuries gone by.

'Autumn was always the time for Fontainebleau,' he said. 'That was when the Court came here to hunt. But not anymore. Nothing lasts. It all fades away. Only the trees remain.' He pointed one of them out to her, an ancient tree, standing alone. 'I used to climb that tree as a boy,' he said. 'It was perfect for my purposes. The lower branches were just low enough for me to be able to reach them by jumping, if not on the first attempt, then on the second or third, and the topmost branches were strong enough to bear my weight. When I reached them, I would hold on to the trunk and look out over the surrounding countryside and pretend I was on a ship and that I had just climbed the mast, looking for land.'

'You may climb it now if you like!' she said. 'I will wait.'

He laughed.

'I doubt the branches would bear my weight. It was a long time ago.'

She liked to hear of his childhood, and as they rode on, he told her more about his boyhood pursuits. She responded with tales of her own childhood, games of chase with her large family of sisters on the Longbourn lawn and rainy afternoons curled up on the window seat in the library with a book.

Elizabeth patted her mare's neck as they came to a crossroads and turned south, the carriages rolling along behind them. Darcy, watching Elizabeth said, 'Has Snowfall won you over? Do you like riding?'

'How could I not with such a mount?' said Elizabeth. 'But—'

She shifted a little in her saddle.

'Saddle sore?' he asked.

'Yes! I am not used to it, you know.'

'Would you rather walk?'

'I think so, for a little while, anyway.'

He helped her to dismount and then dismounted beside her, and they walked on, leading their horses, until Elizabeth at last tired and took her seat once more in the coach.

As they travelled south through France, the Alps drew steadily closer.

'Twice now I have been deprived of a promised visit to the Lake District, but both times I have been glad to change my destination. I never thought anything could be so beautiful,' she said.

She raised her eyes to their summits, which were iced with snow.

'You must have seen pictures of them,' said Darcy.

'Pictures, yes, but they didn't prepare me for their scale or grandeur,' she said.

As day followed day, they left the lowlands behind and began to climb, following a winding road through the foothills of the mountains which gave extensive views at every turn. Against the backdrop of the mountains there were tall trees and shady glens, and here and there, they saw mountain goats. There were flowers still blooming in the meadows. Butterflies flitted between the gentians, harebells, and saxifrage, their iridescent blue and yellow wings catching the light.

From time to time, they came across cool, bubbling springs at which they stopped to drink.

Darcy knew the way, having travelled the route before, and as the light started to fade at the end of each day, he led them to a homely cottage where they could shelter, having them safely inside before sunset.

At the end of several days' travelling, they stopped for the night at a small inn.

'It's not like the inns in England,' said Darcy as they approached.

'It's delightful,' said Elizabeth.

It was set amidst the mountains beside a mirror-like lake. She ran her eyes over the rustic building with its gaily painted shutters, its blooming window boxes, and its overhanging eaves.

They were welcomed warmly with genuine hospitality. The size of their retinue at first caused some consternation, but the problem was quickly solved by the judicious use of outbuildings which nestled close by the inn.

Elizabeth's room was homely, with pine furniture. There was a picture over the bed, but the real picture in the room was the view. Framed by the window, it was magnificent. Elizabeth rested her arms on the window ledge and watched the sun setting. It turned the sky golden as its last rays blazed out, then flooded it with orange and red as the sky around it grew darker, changing from blue to purple, and then, as the sun sank at last, to black. The white finger of the mountain could still be seen, glowing softly in the ethereal light of the stars that pricked the sky. Elizabeth watched it still, delighting in the novelty and the splendour of its majesty, until the wind blew cold and she drew the curtain.

She washed and changed and then went down to dinner. The dining room was a simple apartment with only three tables, each flanked with benches. But the room was pretty, with long gingham cushions on the benches and gingham curtains at the windows.

Despite the remoteness of the place, the Darcys were not the only guests. A middle aged English couple, a Mr and Mrs Cedarbrook, were also staying there. They had an air of solid respectability about them and whilst her husband's expression was absent-minded, Mrs Cedarbrook's face wore a sensible aspect. They were dressed in good but unostentatious clothes, with Mrs Cedarbrook wearing a cashmere shawl over her cambric gown and Mr Cedarbrook wearing a well-tailored coat and breeches with a simply folded cravat.

The inn was so small that friendship was inevitable, and the four of them were soon engaged in conversation.

'Have you come far?' asked Mr Cedarbrook, as their host brought in a large bowl of something savoury and proceeded to ladle appetising soup into clay bowls, placing large hunks of crusty bread on the plates next to them.

'From Paris,' said Darcy.

'Ah, Paris! How I love Paris,' said Mrs Cedarbrook.

'Humph,' said her husband, tasting his soup. He made an appreciative noise and took another spoonful. 'Big cities are not for me.'

'My husband is a botanist,' explained Mrs Cedarbrook. 'He prefers the countryside. We are on a walking tour, collecting plants.'

'New species,' said her husband as he broke off a piece of bread. 'There are plenty of them in the Alps. What do you do?' he asked Darcy.

'I am a gentleman of leisure,' said Darcy.

'A man needs a hobby, even so,' said Mr Cedarbrook. 'You should take up botany.'

'My dear, not everyone wants to be a botanist,' said his wife.

'Can't think why not,' he returned.

Mrs Cedarbrook smiled indulgently, but accompanying the look was also an expression of good humour and common sense. She reminded Elizabeth of her Aunt Gardiner, who treated Mrs Bennet's foibles in much the same way as Mrs Cedarbrook treated her husband's eccentricities.

'Do you always travel together?' asked Elizabeth.

'We do now,' said Mrs Cedarbrook. 'When the children were younger I stayed at home because I did not like to be away from them for months at a time, but now that they have all married and have homes of their own, I enjoy our journeys and I like to see something of the world.'

'And what do you do when your husband is studying plants?' asked Darcy.

'I have my sketchbook and my watercolours, and I make a pictorial record of everything we see,' she replied.

'And very useful it is, too,' said her husband.

They talked of their experiences in the Alps over the meal, sharing their pleasure in the scenery. They also shared with each other information about the journey, for they had approached the inn from different directions, and so they knew what difficulties their fellow guests would face on the following day.

When they had finished their meal, their host brought in a bottle of some local spirit and Mrs Cedarbrook said to Elizabeth, 'I think it is time for us to withdraw.'

'Gladly,' said Elizabeth.

It was a long time since she had had a woman to talk to—a sensible, mature woman—and she felt herself in need of someone to turn to.

As there was no withdrawing-room, they retired to Mrs Cedarbrook's chamber and there they sat and talked. All the time, Mrs Cedarbrook watched Elizabeth and after a while she said, 'Something is troubling you, my dear. Can I help?'

'No, it is nothing,' said Elizabeth.

'I have two grown up daughters and I can tell that something is wrong. Will you not trust me?'

Elizabeth was longing to do so, but she did now know how to begin.

'You are from Hertfordshire, I think you said?' prompted Mrs Cedarbrook.

'Yes, that's right, from a small town called Meryton,' said Elizabeth.

'I do not know the town, but I have passed through Hertfordshire often on various journeys. It is a very beautiful county, but very different to the Alps. You are a long way from home. Do you not find it lonely here, where there are so few people?'

'I have my husband,' said Elizabeth.

'Of course. But sometimes a woman needs another woman to talk to.'

Elizabeth said nothing, but she had been thinking exactly the same thing. She had been troubled for some time, and she found it difficult to keep her feelings to herself, because at home she had always had someone to talk to.

'You are a long way from your mother,' said Mrs Cedarbrook.

'Yes, I am,' said Elizabeth.

She gave a rueful smile as she thought of her mother.

Mrs Cedarbrook said, 'Ah,' quietly, and added, 'And your friends.'

'Yes,' said Elizabeth with a sigh.

'You must miss them,' said Mrs Cedarbrook kindly.

'I do. But not as much as I miss my sister.'

'If you need someone to talk to, my dear, I am here.'

Elizabeth looked at her uncertainly and then came to a decision. Mrs Cedarbrook was a stranger, but she was a sympathetic woman and Elizabeth needed to confide in someone. Her friends and family were a long way away and she had no one else to turn to in her need for a listening ear and, more importantly, some advice.

'You are worried about something,' said Mrs Cedarbrook gently.

'It is only…' said Elizabeth, not knowing how to begin. 'It is just that…'

'Yes, my dear?'

'It is just that, sometimes, I don't understand my husband.'

'You have been married long?'

'No, we are only just married. We are on our wedding tour.'

'You seem very happy together. It is not difficult to see that your husband loves you very much.'

'I wonder,' said Elizabeth, looking down at her hands, which were pleating the fabric of her skirt in her lap.

'What makes you say that?' asked Mrs Cedarbrook.

'It is just that he hasn't so much as touched me in all this time. He's attentive and friendly and considerate, we have a great deal to say to each other, and the way he looks at me— you have seen the way he looks at me.'

'Yes, I have.'

'But at night, when we could be alone, he avoids me.'

Mrs Cedarbrook looked at her thoughtfully.

'You are very young. Perhaps he is just giving you time to adjust to your new life. Tempt him, my dear. You are very lovely, and there isn't a man alive who could resist you if you put your mind to it.'

'That's just it,' said Elizabeth. 'I don't know how.'

'You are a woman in love, you will know how when the time comes. Go to his room if he will not come to yours. It will not be long before you are happy, I am sure.'

'You have taken a load from my mind,' said Elizabeth. 'Just to be able to talk about it has been a help.'

There was a noise from below.

'I think the gentlemen are coming to the end of their conversation. Go now, my dear, and I am sure your problems will soon be over.'

The two women rose and Elizabeth returned to her own room. Annie helped her to undress and then, saying, 'Thank you, Annie,' Elizabeth waited only for her maid to leave the room before she went through the interconnecting door into her husband's room. She had hoped to find Darcy there, but the room was empty, save for a faint, lingering scent of him.

On the washstand, his valet had laid out his brushes and razor, and Elizabeth went over to them and ran her hands over them. These were the things he had touched, and she let her fingers linger there. Her eyes wandered round the small, rustic apartment until they came to rest on the window. It had been left open. The night air was fresh but cold, and it carried a hint of frost. She went over to the window and prepared to close it, but her hand rested on the catch for a moment and she looked out over the tranquil, moonlit landscape. The lake was shining placidly in the silver light and, far off, trees were silhouetted against the white backdrop of the mountain. Hanging above it was a gibbous moon, phosphorescent in the darkness.

Her attention was attracted by movement close at hand and she saw the dark shape of a bird—no, a bat—heading towards the window. She closed it quickly, leaving the bat to hover outside. As she looked at it she was seized with a strange feeling. She thought how lonely it must feel, being shut out, being a part and yet not a part of the warmth and light within.

Then the bat turned and flew away and the moment was

broken, and she went back to the other side of the room, warming herself by the fire.

There was still no sign of Darcy.

She returned to her own room, and to her astonishment, she found him standing on the hearthrug. She had not heard his footsteps in the corridor, but her surprise quickly gave way to a sense of anticipation. He had come to her after all. She went closer and she felt the tension in him, as though he was trying to hold back some great force by sheer strength of will. She shivered, but not with cold. She could hear his shallow, uneven breathing, and he leaned towards her…

…and then she saw his hands clench as if he had fought an inner battle and emerged in some way victorious, but as if the victory had brought him no pleasure and had cost him dear. He kissed her gently on the cheek, the faintest brush of his lips, and said, 'Good night, Elizabeth,' Then, going into his own room, he shut the door.

She could still feel the warmth of his lips on her skin, and she raised her hand to them in an effort to hold the feeling. But gradually it faded, until there was nothing left of it.

She shivered, and looking round, she noticed that the window in her room too was open. She went to shut it, then she climbed into bed. She lay awake for a long time before she at last she fell asleep.

⁊∞⁊

The morning sunlight streaming through a crack in the shutters woke her. She was confused for a moment, not recognising the room, then she remembered that she was in the Alps and she jumped out of bed. She threw back the shutters to see that the sky was a startling blue and that the mountains were rising majestically against it.

Her eyes wandered downwards, to the meadows and wild-flowers that surrounded the taverna, and then to the still and placid lake. When she looked more closely, she could see that someone was swimming there. Her heart leapt as she saw that it was Darcy. She longed to join him, and although she thought, to begin with, that she could not possibly do any such thing, she soon changed her mind and thought, *Why not?*

She slipped into a chemise and gown, then picked up a towel and went softly downstairs. There were the usual early morning sounds coming from the back of the taverna, the sizzle of cooking and the thunk of wood being chopped, but in the front of the taverna it was silent. It was still very early and the other guests were in bed.

Elizabeth slipped outside unnoticed and felt the crispness of the air, then she felt the warming of the sun as she stepped out of the shadow and began to run across the meadow. As she sped over the carpet of wildflowers she crushed them beneath her feet, releasing their scent. It rose in a cloud around her, sweet and heady. At last she came to a stop, breathless but exhilarated, by the side of the lake. It was the deepest blue she had ever seen and as smooth as glass. It reflected the mountains and the tall pine trees that surrounded it without so much as a ripple to break the surface.

She set her towel down by the side of the water and then dipped a toe into the lake. It was very cold, but by and by, her foot became used to it and she began to find it refreshing. She put her foot further into the water, first her ankle and then her calf, and then she was seized with a sudden longing to be swimming. She unhooked her dress and pulled it over her head and was about to slip into the lake in her chemise when Mrs Cedarbrook's words came back to her: *tempt him*. She hesitated for a moment, but there was no one about, nor was there likely to be so early in the morning, so she slipped out of her chemise as well and slid into the water.

She gasped as the cold liquid closed around her and struck out for the end of the lake. Gradually the movement began to warm her. She looked for Darcy and saw his head rising above the surface. She began to close the gap between them. As she drew closer she saw that his hair was wet, lying dark and sleek against his head, with rivulets of water running down his neck, over two small scars and onto his shoulders. She felt suddenly nervous, but it was too late to turn back. He had seen her. A look of surprise and delight crossed his face and then his eyes, at first joyful, darkened as his face flooded with desire. He closed the gap between them in a few strokes, his eyes roaming over her face and hair, and then down to her throat which rose, naked, above the water.

'You are so beautiful,' he murmured as he bent his head towards her. 'You are intoxicating, ravishing, exquisite.'

She felt herself growing weak with need, drowning in the overwhelming force of his desire. Her skin yearned for him and her body leaned towards him. She felt as though they were not two separate beings but halves of the same whole, which had been long sundered and longed to be joined. He put his hands on her shoulders and her body grew heavy and languorous. He bent his head to kiss her and she felt his breath whisper over her neck like warm silk. She turned her head to expose her throat as her senses were consumed by him, mesmerised by his breathing and the hypnotic beating of his heart.

And then, like a sleepwalker awakened, she heard the wheels of a carriage as it pulled to a halt by the side of the lake. She heard the opening and closing of a carriage door and then a voice which was at once familiar and unfamiliar. Darcy lifted his head and Elizabeth, turning slowly, saw the figure of Lady Catherine de Bourgh. Beside her, pale and bloodless, was her daughter, Anne.

Elizabeth thought she must be dreaming. The swim in the lake, Darcy's touch, her heavy languor, together with the strange and unsettling appearance of Lady Catherine and her daughter, all had the quality of something unreal. Lady Catherine seemed to be insubstantial and ghostly in the strong sunlight.

But as Elizabeth's senses began to return to normal, she realised that it was not a dream, that she was awake, and that everything was happening.

Darcy pulled her behind him and she was glad of his protection because there was something menacing about Lady Catherine. At Rosings she had been dictatorial, at Longbourn she had been ridiculous, but here she was frightening.

She was dressed all in black. Her long black cloak hung heavily around her and a black veil hung from her black bonnet, covering her face. She was leaning on a black parasol, which she used like a walking stick.

'How did she find us?' asked Elizabeth.

'We made no secret of our journey or our destination,' said Darcy. 'If she was in Paris, she had only to ask my relatives where I was and they would tell her.'

Lady Catherine took a menacing step forward.

'So, you have done it. Against all advice, you have married this—person. I never thought to see the day when you would do something so stupid, you of all people, Fitzwilliam,' said Lady Catherine.

'You knew I was going to marry her,' said Darcy inimically.

'I knew you *intended* to marry her, but I thought you would come to your senses in time. I told you that she would be rejected by the family, or worse—you have been to Paris, you know that I am right. But you went ahead and married her anyway.'

'I have a right to my own life,' he said.

'You have no rights! Marriage is a family matter. It is for those who are older and wiser than you to make the decision. It is not for you to indulge a whim.'

'It is too late to complain now,' said Darcy in a warning voice. 'We are married; it is done.'

'Aye, you are married,' said Lady Catherine malignantly. 'You did it behind my back, when I was out of the country. I should not have left, and I would not have done so if I had thought you would go through with this scandalous act.'

'You should not have come here. Darcy and I are happy,' said Elizabeth. 'You tried once before to separate us and you failed. You should know by now that it cannot be done. Who are you to decide what we can and cannot do? It is time for you to accept it and leave us alone.'

Lady Catherine turned malignant eyes on her and Elizabeth felt afraid.

'Be silent!' she hissed.

Elizabeth opened her mouth to speak but no words came out.

'You should have married Anne,' said Lady Catherine, turning once more to Darcy. 'Anne is your mate. She is the one you were meant to marry. She is from an old and honourable family. She is the one who will keep the blood lines pure.'

'It is too late for that,' said Darcy darkly. 'What is done is done.'

'No,' said Lady Catherine. 'It is not too late. For our kind it is never too late. I only hope you come to your senses sooner rather than later, but you will come to them in time, that is certain. You cannot doubt it.'

'Then leave me alone and let me enjoy it whilst I can,' said Darcy.

'Enjoy it?' asked Lady Catherine with a bitter laugh. 'You will not enjoy it. Every moment will be a torment to you. You know you cannot marry a woman like this and be happy. Your pride should have prevented it, pride in who you are and what you are and a pride in your place in the world. And if your pride was sleeping then your conscience should have forbidden it.'

'Enough!' said Darcy. 'You should go.'

'The sight of you sickens me, so yes, I will go, but you have not seen the last of me,' said Lady Catherine. 'You will threaten us all if you pursue this course. It is up to you, up to all of us, to ensure the continuation of our kind, lest we become extinct. You have seen your fellows hunted down and slain, you know of what I speak.'

Elizabeth thought of the revolution and the rich and titled who had fallen prey to its merciless scythe.

'That has nothing to do with me!' said Darcy.

'It has something to do with all of us,' she said.

Then, giving him one last poisonous glance, she returned to her carriage, with Anne following her like a sorrowful ghost.

When she had gone, Elizabeth realised how cold she was. She had been stationary in the icy water for the length of Lady Catherine's tirade, and she shivered.

'You're freezing,' said Darcy, suddenly solicitous. 'You need to get dressed.'

Elizabeth began to swim towards the edge of the lake.

The water was very cold and her teeth were chattering as she reached the shore. She was about to climb out when she saw her maid, Annie, running towards her.

'Ma'am, oh Ma'am, you've had a visitor,' said Annie, beaming. 'A very grand lady, a Lady Catherine de Something. I asked her to wait but she said she couldn't.'

'It is all right, Annie,' said Elizabeth. 'She found us.'

'Us?' asked Annie.

Elizabeth looked round and saw that Darcy had gone.

She had not seen him depart and she felt suddenly lost without him. She wondered why he had disappeared before realising that he had done it to spare her blushes and the blushes of her maid.

She let Annie help her out of the lake.

'This water's too cold to go swimming in,' said Annie as she handed Elizabeth the towel. 'You'll catch your death.'

Elizabeth dried herself vigorously, her teeth chattering all the while, then she slipped into her clothes, but she was still shivering when she returned to the taverna. As soon as she was back in her room, she stripped off her damp clothes and sat in front of the fire whilst Annie rubbed her hair with a towel.

'It was nice of Lady Catherine to come and wish you well,' said Annie. 'Mr Darcy's aunt she said she was. Just visiting the Alps. She must have been surprised to find you here, too.'

Elizabeth did not reply. She huddled over the fire and then she began to sneeze.

'There you are, what did I say, you've caught your death,' said Annie, looking at her with a worried expression.

'It's nothing,' said Elizabeth, 'but I would like a hot drink all the same.'

'I'll get you one right away.'

Annie left the room, and when the door opened again, Elizabeth turned towards it with thanks on her lips. But it was not Annie who stood in the doorway; it was Darcy.

'I heard you sneezing,' he said. 'I shouldn't have left you in the lake for so long.'

'It wasn't your fault,' said Elizabeth. 'I knew Lady Catherine didn't approve of our marriage, but I never thought she would pursue us on our wedding tour. Why did she do it? And why did she say all those terrible things?'

'Lady Catherine is old,' he said by way of explanation.

'Not so old that she doesn't know how to behave, and not so old that age excuses her for behaving in such a manner,' said Elizabeth.

'Things are not so simple,' he said.

'They seem simple to me,' she said.

He looked at her with a wistful smile.

'You're very young,' he said.

'I am only seven years younger than you.'

His eyes held hers for long moments, then he said, 'You break my heart.'

He sounded so sad that Elizabeth felt a catch in her throat and she reached out her hand to him, but he had already turned away, and a moment later, he was out in the corridor, issuing instructions to his valet.

Elizabeth felt low in spirits. Lady Catherine's tirade had unsettled her and Darcy's strange demeanour had unsettled her even more, so that she longed for someone to talk to. A cheerful conversation about ordinary things was just what she needed to dispel her gloom. She thought at once of Mrs Cedarbrook, knowing that a few minutes talking about Mr Cedarbrook and his botany would soon put a smile on her face. She wrote a short note requesting Mrs Cedarbrook's company, and when Annie returned with her drink, Elizabeth asked her to take it.

'I'm sorry, Ma'am, but they've left,' said Annie. 'They were off an hour since. Mr Cedarbrook wanted to get on with his plant collecting.'

Elizabeth was disappointed but there was nothing to be done about it, so she finished her drink and then started a letter to Jane.

My dearest Jane,

I wish you were here. How I long to talk to you. So much has happened that I scarcely know where to begin. We left Paris a few days ago and we are now in the Alps. Things are changing so rapidly that my head is starting to spin. First Dover, then the sea crossing, then Paris, and now the mountains—my dearest Jane, I woke up this morning and wondered where I was. But then I saw Darcy from the window, swimming in the lake, and things began to change. I went to join him and for the first time, married life started to be what I thought it would be. We were close, body, mind, and spirit, and I longed for him as he longed for me. Everything else was forgotten, until the moment was broken by Lady Catherine de Bourgh.

Can you believe it? She followed us here.

Are you plagued by Bingley's relatives? Do they pursue you?

I am beginning to think we will never be free of Darcy's family. Perhaps Lady Catherine was right. Perhaps their attitude does matter to me after all.

But no! What am I saying? How can it matter when I have Darcy? For a few short minutes in the lake we were so close, and if it happened once it can happen again. To be sure, he has retreated again, withdrawing into a cold world and gone where I cannot follow, and yet it cannot be for long. He wants me, I know he does, it is only his family and his concerns, perhaps, for my feelings—or what he thinks my feelings must be when everything is so new to me—that keep him aloof.

Writing to you is doing me good. I was despondent at the start of the letter but now things are wearing a rosier aspect. We are going further into the mountains to visit Darcy's uncle, and there, perhaps, we may grow close again. Darcy respects his uncle and wants to seek his advice, about what I am not quite sure. I only hope it sets his mind at rest and leaves him free to follow his heart which I know, Jane, leads to me.

I must go now, but I will write to you again when we reach the castle. For the moment, adieu.

She sanded the letter then put it away in her writing desk to be finished later.

Annie, in the meantime, had been packing her things.

'Master's orders are that we'll be moving on as soon as we're ready,' she said.

'Yes,' said Elizabeth. 'He wants us to reach the castle before dark.'

She dressed in warmer clothes than previously, for she was still cold. She chose a dress with long sleeves and she wore a long pelisse instead of her shorter coat. She dismissed a bonnet which perched on her head and instead chose one that covered her ears. She tied the ribbon under her chin and then she was ready.

Darcy was waiting for her downstairs. The coach was already at the door and she could tell that he was impatient to leave.

Their hosts wished them God speed and then they were off.

Elizabeth was glad to be leaving the inn behind. She could tell that Darcy was on edge and she only hoped that things would improve once they reached the castle.

CHAPTER 5

A T THE START OF their journey Elizabeth was content to look out of the window, where the smiling landscape was bathed in the warm glow of early morning, but by the time midday approached, it was replaced by a wilder view. The mountainside was becoming more craggy and they passed a number of waterfalls which dazzled with their spectacle, their waters flowing down in torrents and throwing clouds of rainbow spume into the air. Alpine plants flourished, clinging to the rocks, and chasms yawned beside the road.

As Elizabeth watched the scenery, Darcy watched her. He had seen the impressive sights many times before, but to Elizabeth they were all fresh and new. As he watched her ever-changing expressions, it revitalised his enjoyment of the scene and reawakened his lost sense of wonder.

There were very few people on the road, but here and there they saw a man carrying a pannier of logs on his back or a woman leading a donkey or occasionally a small child with a basketful of berries.

'The people hereabouts seem very religious,' said Elizabeth, as a man moved to the side of the road to avoid the coach and crossed himself; a common custom, it seemed.

'Things are very different here,' Darcy agreed. 'The people have their own traditions and their own way of doing things.'

Elizabeth, growing tired of mountains and glaciers and waterfalls, let her eyes linger on the women's rustic garb, admiring the colourful skirts with white aprons and their curious cloth head coverings.

'Will your uncle mind us calling on him without any warning, do you think?' she asked, as they found themselves on a lonely stretch of road once more. 'Or have you written to him and told him we are coming?'

'No,' said Darcy. 'There is no post in these outlying parts and a messenger travelling alone would be subject to attack. But my uncle won't mind. He is always pleased to see me and the castle is so large that he can always accommodate more guests.'

'Even with our large retinue?'

'The castle will swallow the retinue,' he said. 'It could swallow ten such retinues. It is very old and very rambling, and it is large enough to house an entire village if the need arises.'

'And does it arise?' asked Elizabeth curiously.

'It certainly has in the past. When the village was attacked by bandits, then everyone would crowd inside the castle, taking their livestock and possessions with them, and they would not come out until the danger had passed.'

'What is he like, your uncle?' she asked.

'He is a learned man. Intelligent. Charming,' Darcy said. 'He is a great thinker and something of a philosopher. He has travelled widely and knows many things. He is amusing and lively on occasion, but more often he sits and listens, or draws out his companions with interesting questions and remarks. He has a fund of wisdom at his disposal but he never seeks to dictate. I think you will like him.'

But will he like me? Elizabeth wondered.

At home, such a thought would not have occurred to her but here it was different. She had no friends or family close by to fill her with confidence and no well-loved places to reassure her. To begin with, that had not mattered, but as she moved further and further away from her own world, she found that she was becoming less sure of herself, and she hoped that her welcome would be a warm one or, at least, not a cold one.

The road began to climb more steeply, and the coach slowed until it was almost at a halt. Elizabeth suggested they get out and walk in order to help the horses, but Darcy would not hear of it.

'The horses are well conditioned. They have pulled heavier loads up steeper slopes than this,' he said.

'But there is no need for them to do so here. It will not hurt us to walk. Besides, I would like to take some exercise and feel the wind in my face,' she protested.

'At another time I would be happy to indulge you,' he replied, placing a restraining hand on hers as she moved to open the door, 'but we are not in England now.'

She was about to ask him what he meant when she glanced out of the window and saw that two red orbs, which she had taken for berries, suddenly blinked and moved, and she realised with a shock that they were eyes. She looked to right and left and saw that there were more eyes all round them.

'Are there wolves here?' she asked apprehensively.

'Wolves—and worse,' he added under his breath.

She sat back in her seat, chastened. Wolves, bears perhaps… She was a long way from Hertfordshire. She was glad of the coach and the safety it offered. It was sturdily built and would withstand an attack by wolves or any other animals which might be lurking close by. She was glad too of the outriders and the pistols they carried—a warning to predators with two legs and a protection against those with four.

She endeavoured to take an interest in the scenery again, but it had lost some of its glamour for, underneath the beauty, danger lurked.

As the coach climbed further the sky began to darken, as if to match her thoughts, turning from blue to indigo. Clouds blew up rapidly and it looked as though it would rain.

'We are going to have a storm,' said Elizabeth. 'Are there any inns nearby where we can stop until it passes?'

'No, there is nothing for miles, but no matter; in another half hour, or hour at most, we should be there.'

There was a distant rumble and the threatened storm began to make itself felt. The sky was suddenly lit from behind, glowing with a lurid brightness before quickly darkening again. Inside the coach, it was becoming hard to see, and matters were made worse when the trees began to thicken as the road went into a forest of dense trees. They cast long shadows, and Elizabeth could barely make out her husband's features, although he was sitting only a few feet away from her.

They emerged at last, but it was scarcely any brighter beyond the trees for the sky was now almost black. Another rumble, closer this time, tore the silence and a few minutes later the rain began to pour. The thunder grew louder as the storm broke overhead, and the sky was rent apart by a jagged spike of lightning which ran down to the ground in a network of brilliant veins. The horses neighed wildly, rearing up and flailing their hooves in the air. The carriage rocked from side to side as the coachman tried to hold them, and Elizabeth took hold of the carriage strap which hung from the ceiling. She clung on as she was bounced and jolted this way and that. She managed to keep her seat until the horses at last quieted, but she did not let go, knowing that another flash of lightning would scare the horses again.

'How much farther?' she asked.

'It is not far now,' said Darcy, holding onto the strap which hung on his side of the carriage.

Another flash of lightning lit the sky and revealed an eerie shape on the horizon, a silhouette of spires and turrets that rose from a rocky pinnacle—a castle, but not like those in England, whose solid bulk sat heavily on the ground. It was a confection, a fragile thing, tall and thin and spindly. And then the sky darkened and it was lost to view.

The rain was coming down in earnest, drumming on the roof of the coach, and Elizabeth was glad when the gatehouse came in sight. The coachman held the horses and guided them over the last stretch of road. There was a pause at the gatehouse, and through the wind and the rain, Elizabeth heard a shouted exchange between the coachman and the gatekeeper. Then the windlass creaked and the drawbridge was lowered, its chains clanking in the rain-sodden air before it settled with a dull thud on the reverberating ground.

The coach traversed the drawbridge and Elizabeth glimpsed a steep drop on either side, and then they were through, into the courtyard. Armed men in billowing cloaks with hats pulled down over their eyes were patrolling with large hounds, more wolf than dog, and their free hands rested on their sword hilts.

'There is no need to be afraid,' said Darcy as Elizabeth shrank back against her seat. 'This is a wild country and my uncle employs soldiers to protect him from roaming bands of villains.'

'He employs mercenaries, do you mean?' asked Elizabeth.

'If you will. Armed men, at any rate, who are in his employ.'

Elizabeth heard the drawbridge being raised behind them, and as it clanked shut on its great chains, she knew a moment of panic, thinking wildly, *We're shut in.*

Darcy touched her hand in silent support and the gesture calmed her, and the sight of liveried footmen emerging from the castle dispelled much of her fear. Darcy stepped out of the coach as the footmen unloaded it, and he handed Elizabeth out. The butler appeared, a man past youth but not yet old, with bright eyes that missed nothing as they ran with recognition over Darcy and then ran more watchfully over Elizabeth. He greeted them with a few barely comprehensible words in garbled and heavily accented English, then bowed them towards the steps that led up to the massive oak door. Darcy returned his greeting and then stood aside to allow Elizabeth to precede him through the door.

As she stepped over the threshold, there was a grating sound and one of the axes which was displayed above the door, just inside the hall, came loose of its fastenings and fell to the floor. It missed Darcy by inches and Elizabeth by more than a foot. There was an initial moment of shock, but then they quickly recovered their composure. Not so the butler, however, who cried out in a strange language and rolled his eyes in fear.

It was not an auspicious beginning to their visit. Nor was the walk across the vast, echoing hall, with its dark stone walls and its draught-blown torches and its gloomy wall hangings. But once they were shown into the drawing room things improved. The room was warm with the heat of a log fire, which crackled in an enormous stone fireplace. The carpet was old but not threadbare, and the furniture, though dark and heavy, was of a good quality. Sitting in a chair with his legs stretched out to the fire was a man whom Elizabeth took to be the Count.

The butler announced the Darcys in a foreign tongue and the Count rose, surprised, his look of astonishment quickly giving way to one of welcome. He was somewhat strange of appearance, being unusually tall and very angular, with a finely-boned face, long, delicate fingers, and features which gave him a perpetual look of haughtiness, yet his manner when he greeted Darcy was friendly.

Elizabeth let her eyes roam over the Count's clothes, which were reassuring in their familiarity, for they were the kind worn by country gentlemen in England. He wore a shabby but well-cut coat of russet broadcloth with a ruffled shirt, which had once been white but was now grey with many washings, beneath which he wore russet knee breeches and darned stockings. His black shoes were polished, but they too were shabby. The only thing she could not have seen on some of her more countrified neighbours was his powdered wig, which would have marked him out as old-fashioned, eccentric even, in Hertfordshire.

The two men spoke in a foreign tongue which Elizabeth did not recognise. It seemed to bear some resemblance to French but many of its words were unfamiliar, and she could not understand what was being said. Darcy quickly realised this and reverted to English. The Count, after a moment of surprise, glanced at Elizabeth and then, understanding, spoke in English too, though he spoke it with a heavy accent and a strange intonation.

'Darcy, this pleasure, it is not expected,' he said, 'but you are welcome here. Your guest, too, she is welcome.'

He extended his hand and the two men shook hands with a firm grip.

'Thank you,' said Darcy. 'I am sorry I could not give you warning, but I did not like to send a messenger on to the castle alone.'

'The road to the castle, it is not a safe one,' the Count agreed. 'But what does it matter? My housekeeper, she is always prepared for guests. And this so charming young woman is…?' he asked.

'Elizabeth,' said Darcy, taking her hand and drawing her forward.

'Elizabeth,' said the Count, bowing over her hand. 'A beautiful name for a most beautiful lady. Elizabeth…?'

'Elizabeth Darcy. My wife,' said Darcy with wary pride.

'Your wife?' asked the Count, recoiling as though stung.

'Yes. We were married three weeks ago.'

'I had not heard,' said the Count, quickly recovering himself, 'and that, it is not usual; *en général* I hear of things which concern the family very quickly. But we are out of the way here…' he said, looking at Elizabeth curiously before turning his attention back to Darcy. 'And so, you are married, Fitzwilliam. It is something I thought I would not see.'

'There is a time for everything,' said Darcy, 'and my time is now.' He completed the introduction, saying, 'Elizabeth, this is my uncle, Count Polidori.'

Elizabeth dropped a curtsey and said all that was necessary, but she was not entirely at ease. Though the Count was courteous and charming she sensed an undercurrent of curiosity and something else—not hostility exactly, but something that told her he was not pleased about the marriage. She wondered if he too thought that Darcy should have married Anne.

'The day, it is not a pleasant one for your journey,' said the Count. 'Alas, it rains often in the mountains and we have many storms. The darkness, too, it is not agreeable. But no matter, you are here now. My housekeeper, she will show you to your chamber at once. You will want to change your wet clothes, I think. I have already dined, but you must tell me when you would like to eat and my housekeeper, she will prepare a meal—unless you would like better to have something in your room?'

Finding herself suddenly tired, and knowing too that Darcy had something he wished to discuss with the Count, Elizabeth seized on the opportunity to retire to her chamber and said that something on a tray would be welcome.

The Count made her a low bow and rang the bell. It set up a dolorous clanging which echoed from somewhere deep in the bowels of the castle, and Elizabeth wondered how far the housekeeper would have to walk to reach the drawing room. Whilst they waited, the Count continued to ask them about their journey and commiserate with them on the difficulties of such remote travel. The housekeeper arrived at last, a dour woman, small and watchful. She seemingly spoke no English, for the Count addressed her in his own tongue. She inclined her head and then, saying something incomprehensible and yet at the same time so expected that Elizabeth had no difficulty in understanding it, she conducted Elizabeth from the room.

As the door closed behind her, Elizabeth heard Darcy saying to the Count, 'I must speak to you on a matter of great importance,' and the Count saying gravely, 'Yes. I can see it. There is much to discuss.'

What there was to discuss, Elizabeth did not know, but she was beginning to wonder if it had something to do with the marriage settlement. That would explain why Darcy was reluctant to discuss it with her, for he would not want her to feel uncomfortable that her dowry had been so small. Her parents had given up all attempts to save many years before, and what little they had possessed had been used up when they had had to pay Wickham to marry Lydia. Elizabeth knew that Darcy did not care for himself, but for their children… It was customary for the bride's portion to be settled on the children, and it might well be that Darcy needed the Count's advice on how to compensate any future offspring for her own lack of funds. It was also possible that that was partly responsible for the coldness of some of Darcy's family.

She followed the housekeeper across the hall and up a flight of stone steps. They had been worn in the middle where countless feet had trodden over the centuries, and their footsteps echoed with a hollow sound. Then the housekeeper turned along a twisting passageway before going up a spiral staircase and into a turret room.

Annie was already there, unpacking Elizabeth's things. There was a large four-poster bed in the middle of the room, hung with red velvet drapes, and assorted pieces of heavy furniture arranged around it: a washstand, a wardrobe, a chest of drawers, a writing table, and, pushed under the table, a chair. There was also a dressing table, but it was of a different type to the other furniture, a delicate piece painted in soft blues and pinks, with slender legs tapering into dainty gilded feet. Narrow windows were set vertically into the walls, which were very thick. Beside the window hung heavy velvet drapes which had not yet been drawn. In the grate was a fire. It was as yet a puny thing, having been so recently lit, but the huge logs were starting to kindle, and before long there would be a blaze. Candles were set around the room, showing it to be a perfect circle, and the stone wall above the bed was softened by a tapestry.

The housekeeper murmured something unintelligible then curtsied and was about to withdraw when Elizabeth said, 'One moment.'

The housekeeper stopped, arrested by the tone of her voice.

'There is no mirror on the dressing-table,' said Elizabeth, trying to show by a kind of pantomime what she meant. 'Will you have one sent up please?'

But either the housekeeper did not understand her, or there were no mirrors to be had, for she shook her head emphatically and then withdrew.

'Well,' said Annie, 'folks are strange hereabouts and no mistake. First, all the talk in the servants' hall, and now this. No mirror indeed! How do they expect a lady to dress without one?'

'Never mind,' said Elizabeth, thinking that she would ask the Count on the morrow. 'She probably did not understand me.' She removed her cloak then asked curiously, 'What talk in the servants' hall?'

'Nothing but idle nonsense,' said Annie. 'Saying as how the axe falling means you're to cause Mr Darcy's death. Saying that it fell once before when the Count and his wife walked through the door and look what happened to her. Will you wear the blue dress or the lemon tonight, Ma'am?'

'Neither,' said Elizabeth. 'I will be having something in my room, so there is no need for me to dress for dinner. What do you mean, the axe falling means I will cause Mr Darcy's death?'

'Well, Ma'am, they say that as the axe fell when you were both walking through the door, and it fell nearer to him than to you, that means you're going to kill him or some such nonsense. They were all shaking their heads and muttering about it when I went into the kitchen. Most of them don't speak a word of English, but Mr Darcy's valet told me what it was all about. Heathenish nonsense, all of it.'

'I don't think they're heathens,' said Elizabeth absently. 'On the contrary, they seem to cross themselves a great deal. As we came to the castle, the local people crossed themselves every time the coach passed.'

'Even so, Ma'am, they're not like the people at home.'

'No, they are not,' said Elizabeth.

She thought of all her friends and neighbours at home. Their absurdities did not seem so absurd at a distance; instead they felt reassuring. Even the memory of Mr Collins seemed endearing rather than ridiculous.

Annie finished unpacking and then pulled the curtains across the windows. The fire had blazed up and the room was beginning to feel warmer. Elizabeth slipped out of her wet clothes and into a dry woollen dress and then stretched out her hands to the fire. They were very cold, but at last she felt them beginning to thaw.

There was a timid knock at the door and a young maid entered, bearing a tray of something hot and appetising. She stayed as far away from Elizabeth as possible as she crossed the room and put the tray down on the writing table, looking at her with frightened eyes.

'What did I tell you?' asked Annie in aggrieved accents as the maid hurried out of the room. 'She's one of the day servants. They're the worst. They won't even stay in the castle overnight; they say they see things, unnatural things.'

Elizabeth walked over to the tray and looked down at the stew.

'It tastes better than it looks,' Annie said. 'I had some in the kitchen.'

Elizabeth picked up the spoon that was set beside the bowl and tasted the dish, which was a kind of chicken stew with a distinctive flavour.

'Peppers, those are the things they put in it to make it taste like that,' said Annie. 'Better than all that garlic in Paris, this doesn't taste so bad.'

Elizabeth broke off a piece of bread and ate it with the stew. When she had finished, Annie removed the tray and Elizabeth, left alone, wandered round the room. She examined the few books that were placed on a bookcase by the window and gazed at the tapestries, but instead of soothing her before she went to sleep, the contents of the room unsettled her. The books were not like those in the Longbourn library, smelling richly of leather; they were damp and they smelt of mould.

The tapestry too was unsettling. It displayed a bold picture worked in faded reds and emeralds and golds, and it appeared to be some kind of bestiary. It showed a forest populated with strange creatures: wolves of gigantic proportions, their sharp faces dominated by red, glowing eyes; bats with human faces, monstrous in size; satyrs and dragons and basilisks; and in one small corner, a wan-faced woman with flowers in her hair. The monsters reminded her of the pictures in the books of fairy tales she had read as a child. In the safety of Longbourn, they had seemed ridiculous, but here, in the castle, they did not seem so easy to dismiss. The idea of Little Red Riding Hood losing her way in the woods close at hand did not seem an impossibility; nor the idea of the Sleeping Beauty being haunted by a malevolent witch who caused her to sleep in the mouldering castle for a hundred years; nor of men who were beasts and of beasts who were men.

Her one satisfaction was that the tapestry was hung above the bed, so that she would not have to look at it as she lay down to sleep.

She wandered over to her travelling writing desk, which Annie had unpacked, and took out her writing implements. Then she sat down to finish her letter to Jane. She read through what she had written so far, ending with: *Darcy respects his uncle and wants to seek his advice, about what I am not quite sure. I only hope it sets his mind at rest and leaves him free to follow his heart which I know, Jane, leads to me.*

I must go now, but I will write to you again when we reach the castle. For the moment, adieu.

She then continued:

We have arrived at the castle and it is as remote a place as I ever hope to visit. It is also the strangest and I feel very alone. I wish you were here, Jane. I miss your calm sweet temper and your goodness and ability to see the best in everyone. Everything here is strange. We arrived at the castle in a terrible storm. It is in a far-flung part of the mountains and surrounded by woods which are inhabited by wolves. I saw them on the way here, running alongside the coach, their fur grey and their eyes shining red through the foliage. I can hear them howling at the moon as I write. The castle itself is an old building built of stone, dark and gloomy, and it is in a state of disrepair. When we arrived, one of the axes fell off the wall, narrowly missing Darcy and myself. The servants say it means I will cause his death! And yet, although I know it is ridiculous, I can't help feeling afraid. I feel shut in here; indeed, when the drawbridge was raised behind me I felt like a prisoner. Things would not seem half so bad if you were by my side. Together we would laugh at the wolves and the strange portents. But without you, my own dearest Jane, I find myself surprisingly nervous. God forbid I should end up like Mama! Write to me soon and laugh me out of my idiocy. Without any letters from home I feel strangely alone. Tell me of our Aunt and Uncle Gardiner, and the dear children. Remind me that there is a world beyond this one and that order and familiarity and calm and security exist. Tell me too of the delights of London and your beloved Bingley. I hope your fears are less and your joys greater than mine.

Oh, I wish you were here! I need my Jane to talk to, and not just about the castle. I need to talk to you about my marriage, too. Darcy has not come to me again, though the hour is late. I find I am no longer surprised by his absence. Indeed, I find now that I would be surprised if he joined me. This cannot be a good thing. But perhaps I am only thinking this way because I am tired. It has been a long and curious day. I will get some rest. I am sure things will seem better in the morning.

She sanded her letter and put it away, then, snuffing all but one of the candles, she climbed into bed. She arranged the coverlet and extinguished the final candle, then lay down. Sleep came quickly, but it was not a restful sleep, for it was plagued by disturbing dreams.

CHAPTER 6

ELIZABETH WAS GLAD TO rise the following morning. She had spent the night running through the forest pursued by wolves, or losing herself in the castle, or being tormented by other unsettling nightmares, and she was pleased to put them behind her.

She dressed warmly, wrapping her thick shawl around her, and left her room. She found her way down from the turret easily, but then she stood hesitating on the landing, uncertain which way to go. Luckily one of the Count's footmen happened to pass by. He looked at her fearfully, but she did not let him depart before she had made him understand that she wanted to eat and he led her to the dining room. Darcy was already there at breakfast. He rose with a smile on his face and she was instantly calmed. Here was reality. Here was sanity and repose—not in sleep, but in the waking world.

'Has the Count already eaten?' she asked, as she was served with a kind of thick porridge which looked unappetising but tasted surprisingly good.

'Yes, he was up before daybreak. He has gone to consult with some of his friends and neighbours on the matter which has been troubling me. They are scattered over thirty miles or so of hard riding terrain, and he will not be back until tonight.'

'Has he been able to give you any advice?'

'Not yet, but I hope that an answer will soon be found.'

She waited for the servants to leave the room and then said, 'I asked you once before if you regretted our marriage and you said you did not. I need to ask you again.' She paused, uncertain how to continue. She wanted to say to him, *Why don't you come to me at night?* But now that the moment had come, she felt tongue-tied and did not know how to broach the subject.

'No, of course not,' he said with a frown. 'You have no need to ask me and I am only sorry I have made you feel that way.'

'Are the problems anything to do with the marriage settlement?' she asked. 'Is that why you need your uncle's advice?'

'Not precisely, no,' he said evasively. 'But matters will soon be cleared up, I hope, and then we can forget it and enjoy the rest of our wedding tour.'

He took her hand and kissed it, and she felt heat radiating out from the place where his lips had touched.

A shaft of sunlight came in through the window and Elizabeth, having finished her porridge, said, 'Let us go out into the courtyard,' for she glimpsed a small garden, of sorts, through the window and longed to be out of doors.

'By all means,' he said.

The rain had abated, but despite the gleam of sunshine, the morning was sulky and promised more rain to come.

The garden itself must once have been attractive, but it was now overgrown. It was square in shape, backed by the grey stone walls of the castle, and in its centre was a stagnant pool, choked with weeds. Little light entered the courtyard and even that was sickly and pale, as if the effort to find its way down into the courtyard had depleted it of energy. Weeds sprouted between the paving stones and yellow grasses competed for space with unhealthy looking ferns. A statue of a satyr rose from the tangle of creeping plants which stalked the ground, but it was broken, its pan pipes lying beside it, coated with moss and lichen.

'What a pity it is so overgrown,' she said. 'It is protected from the wind, and it might be pleasant to walk here if the garden were cleared.'

'The castle is old and the upkeep is expensive,' said Darcy, offering her his arm. 'My uncle doesn't have enough money to attend to everything that needs doing here. His fortunes have suffered a reverse of late and he has had to let some parts of the castle fall into disrepair.' He glanced at her as they began to stroll through the garden. 'I suppose I do not notice its deficiencies because I am used to them. I have loved the place since I was a boy. But you, I think, do not.'

'No, I must confess I don't,' she said. 'It seems very forbidding to me, and it is not just the castle. The language is strange, the gossip…'

'It is not like you to listen to gossip,' he said.

'No, I know, but I feel different here, not like myself. I feel shut in, trapped.' She shuddered as she remembered the drawbridge clanging shut and she pulled her shawl more tightly about her. 'When the drawbridge was raised behind me, I felt as if I were a prisoner.'

'The drawbridge is to keep people out, not keep them in,' he said, putting his hand over her arm reassuringly. 'We are in a very remote part of the country and there are lots of bandits hereabouts. They would willingly prey on the castle if its defences weren't secure.'

'Yes, of course. But it is not just the drawbridge—it is everything. When I looked out of my window this morning, I looked down onto a terrible drop with nothing but jagged rocks below. It is not what I am used to,' she said apologetically.

'You are used to rolling meadows and winding rivers in a peaceful part of the world,' he agreed, 'but the castle is in a less hospitable country. It was built as a fortress at a time when fortresses were needed. The rocks keep it safe. They make sure that no one can climb up and assault it from behind. I know it can seem forbidding if you are not used to it, but inside the castle you don't feel afraid?'

'Not afraid, precisely, but anxious. The windows are small and the castle is gloomy. And the rumours...'

'Go on.'

'Oh, they are foolish, of course, but they say in the servant's hall that the axe falling was a portent of your death and that I will cause it. They say that the same fate befell the Count's wife. Is it true?'

He hesitated.

'After a fashion,' he said. 'The Count lost his wife, but there was nothing strange about her death. She had been ill for a long time.'

'And did the axe fall?'

'Yes, it did, but the castle is very old. Some of the wall fixings had worked themselves loose, that is all.'

'Of course,' she said, his calm words filling her with relief. 'I don't know why I took any notice of it. It is just the atmosphere here, it is oppressive.'

'A pity. I hoped you would like it. But we will not be here much longer. The Count should return this evening and we need only stay a few days. I have a hunting lodge in the area, and I would like to visit it as we are so close by, and we must stay a little while longer for politeness' sake, but by the end of the week, if you are still unhappy, we will go.'

Elizabeth was comforted.

'Do you really have a hunting lodge here?' she asked. 'It's a long way from Pemberley.'

'I own hunting lodges throughout Europe, a relic of the old days. I don't use them anymore, but from time to time, I find a tenant for one or other of them. The Count thinks that one of his friends might like to rent the nearest lodge and so I would like to see if it needs any repairs. Why don't you come with me? We can go tomorrow, and it will give you some relief from the castle.'

'Oh, yes,' she said. 'I would like that very much.'

'Very well, I will go and make the arrangements.'

Whilst he went off to the stables, Elizabeth went inside, finding the drawing room after three attempts. She had seen little of it the night before, and she hoped there might be a pianoforte but there was no instrument. She took a turn around the room, examining the portraits which hung on the walls and coming to rest in front of the fireplace. Above it hung a fine portrait of two gentlemen in seventeenth century dress. They were clothed in the fashions of the time, in satin coats and breeches, and they wore dark, curling wigs which fell to their waists.

She looked at them more closely. It was not easy to see them clearly from her low angle but something about them was familiar. She wondered who they reminded her of and then she realised that it was Darcy and the Count.

'The paintings are very good, do you not think?' came a voice behind her.

She very nearly jumped.

'My apologies, I did not mean to startle you,' said the Count, for it was he.

'I thought you were visiting neighbours,' she said.

'And so I was, but the riding, it is hard with old bones. I would have said to my servants, "Go! Do this errand for me!" but Darcy, he is a valued nephew of mine and I do not like to send a servant in a matter concerning him. When I arrive, my neighbours, they are good to me, they say, "We will go to the next castle ourselves to spare you the travelling. Your commission, it will be done in half the time and with less jostling to you of your old bones." And so it goes. One visits another and they each of them travel only a short way to the next castle. I encourage them by saying, "You are welcome to my castle. I have with me a new bride!"' he said with a twinkle in his eye. 'You had small hospitality yesterday but today it will be not the same. You will like my neighbours, I think. Some of them are family and all of them are friends. They will entertain you and make up for the castle's darkness with their humour and conversation. And they will like you. You are an ornament to my home. It is many years since such loveliness has been inside the castle. You are comfortable here, may I hope? You have everything you need?'

'Yes, thank you.'

'If there is anything I can do to make your stay more agreeable you must say, "Count! I will have this!"'

'There is one thing,' said Elizabeth.

'Only say its name.'

'There is no mirror in my room.'

He became as still as a heron. At last his hands moved and he said, 'Alas! I have no mirrors. I have been a widower for very long, you understand, and a man with no pretensions to beauty, he does not seek to fill his home with these things. Ask anything of me but this.'

'It doesn't matter,' said Elizabeth hurriedly, hoping she had not wounded him. 'Thank you, there is nothing else I need.'

'I am glad of it. The castle, it is ancient and not made for today, it is made for the old times, when my ancestors they needed a fortress from war, but I have made it my home.'

Elizabeth felt uncomfortable for a moment, wondering if he could have heard her comments on the castle's upkeep, but then dismissed the notion as impossible.

As they continued to talk, she felt herself growing more at peace with her surroundings. The Count spoke deprecatingly of the castle, but it was clear he loved it as his home, and Elizabeth began to view it with new eyes.

'The portraits are good, do you not think?' asked the Count, looking up at the picture she had been examining. 'Of them, at least, I need not be ashamed. They were painted by a local artist, a man with much talent. That one in particular is a favourite of mine. The artist has caught the fabric well. See the lace!'

'Who are they?' asked Elizabeth. 'The men in the portrait?'

'The first is of my sire, the first Polidori,' he said, pointing to the man on the left. 'It is from him I inherit the castle. And the one on the right is a Darcy.'

'Yes, I thought it must be. The family resemblance is striking,' said Elizabeth.

'*Oui*, though I think that Darcy is slimmer than the man in the portrait. And more handsome, *n'est-ce pas*?'

He dropped into French with the ease of the English aristocracy, and Elizabeth was glad he had not lapsed into his own native tongue, which, although it bore some resemblance to French, was one she did not recognise.

'When was it painted?' she asked.

'Over a hundred years ago, in 1686. Times, they were very different then. The castle was full of light and laughter. Much has changed.' He seemed to be lost in a reverie and

Elizabeth did not like to disturb him, but at last he roused himself and said, 'But we cannot live in the past. We must accept what we have in the present, and that is not so bad, with a visit from friends to look forward to. My housekeeper, she will be doing what she can to improve the castle's appearance in honour of my valued guests. If it will not discommode you greatly, will you take your meal at noontide in your room and remain there until we eat at six o'clock? We keep early hours at the castle. I believe, in England, you call them country hours.'

Elizabeth said that it would not discommode her at all and the Count excused himself. She soon followed him from the room, feeling more cheerful than she had done since arriving at the castle.

She found Annie in her room, pressing her evening gowns with a flat iron heated on the fire, and the homely scene further reassured her.

'It will be lunch on a tray today, Annie,' she said, 'and then there will be guests for dinner. I will wear my amber silk, I think, with plenty of petticoats. It's very cold away from the fires. And I will have my cashmere shawl.'

'Will you wear the amber beads or the gold necklace?' Annie asked.

'The beads, I think,' said Elizabeth, recalling the Count's shabby clothes: she wanted Darcy to be proud of her, but she did not want to look too fine.

'Very good, Ma'am.'

One of the maids soon arrived with a tray of hot, steaming stew which tasted exactly the same as the previous night's meal, and Elizabeth thought of how shocked her mother would have been at this deficiency in the housekeeping, then fell to musing about the Count's wife. She wondered what the Countess had been like and thought it a tragedy she had died, for she suspected that, if the Countess had still been alive, the castle would have been better looked after, even if the Count's fortunes had dwindled.

After her lunch, Elizabeth finished her letter to Jane, but alas, she knew she could not post it in such an out of the way place and that she would have to wait until they returned to civilisation before she could send it.

There was no dressing room, the bedroom filling all of the turret, but one of the footmen carried a hip bath upstairs and the maids brought jugs of hot water so that Elizabeth could take a bath. It was a delight to soak in the hot, soapy water and soothe away all the aches and pains caused by the jostling of the coach the day before.

By three o'clock there were already sounds of commotion from below, gusting in through the door whenever Annie opened it to fetch hot water, and Elizabeth found herself looking forward to the evening. Scented, warm, and delicately flushed, she climbed out of the bath and dried herself before the fire, then set about dressing for the evening. Her amber gown suited her complexion, and with its round neck, it complemented the shape of her face. Annie dressed her hair and then said, 'There,' standing back with satisfaction.

'Thank you, Annie,' she said.

She found it strange going downstairs without first looking in the mirror to make sure she was dressed to her own satisfaction, but there was no help for it and so, putting on her gloves and picking up her shawl, she went downstairs.

The castle looked brighter than formerly, with a profusion of candles lighting the hall and bowls of wildflowers set on the tables. There was a murmur of voices and, from outside, the sound of horses and carriage wheels. The door opened and a draught swirled into the hall. With it came the sound of laughter.

'You're looking very lovely,' said Darcy, materialising beside her. 'Shall we go in?'

She took his arm and they entered the drawing room.

It looked altogether different. Candles were set on every surface and the room had a bright and welcoming air. The fire roared in the fireplace, giving out not only heat but light, and the sound of conversation bubbled everywhere. It was in a foreign tongue, but it sounded good humoured and lively.

Gradually the hubbub died down and one by one the Count's guests turned towards the door. They were mostly men, dressed in shabby, comfortable clothes which nevertheless had the air of being their best. The few women amongst them were all dressed in woollen clothes that were shabby too, and Elizabeth felt conscious of being finer than her neighbours.

It was the first time she had had such a feeling since the start of their wedding tour. In France she had felt positively dowdy by the side of the butterfly-like creatures who flitted about the ballrooms and salons, but here she felt like an exotic bird in a room full of sparrows. She quickly saw that the Count's guests did not resent the fact, but that they liked seeing a bride in all her glory.

'So you are the woman who has captured Darcy?' said one of the men jovially, coming forward. 'It is easy to see why he has lost his heart.'

The introductions were made, and Elizabeth was made to feel very welcome. For the first time since her marriage, Elizabeth felt she was in a world she could understand. Although the clothes, the customs, and the castle might be unfamiliar, she was being given the courtesies always accorded to a bride on her wedding tour. She was the centre of attention, her every word was being listened to with great interest.

'You must tell us how you met,' said Gustav. 'We have heard nothing about it.'

'We never hear of anything here!' said Clothilde.

'Yes, do tell us,' said Isabella.

'Indeed,' said Frederique.

'We met in Hertfordshire,' said Elizabeth, 'when Darcy's friend rented a house in my neighbourhood. Darcy attended the local assembly with his friend...'

'And it was love at first sight. I comprehend!' said Louis.

Elizabeth laughed.

'Far from it!' she said.

'No? But what is this? Darcy, you did not fall in love at once with the beautiful Elizabeth?' He turned to Elizabeth. 'If I had been there, I would have prostrated myself at your so-charming feet.'

'When, then, did Darcy see the error of his ways?' asked Gustav.

'It was not until many months later,' said Elizabeth.

'No? Darcy! You are a veritable blockhead!' said Frederique.

Darcy smiled.

'Ah, yes, my friend, you can afford to smile, you have at last won the hand of the beautiful Elizabeth and you bring her to us as your bride.'

'But how did it happen?' asked Carlotta. 'You must tell us how Darcy changed his mind.'

Nothing would do for them but to hear a full recital. Elizabeth left out any mention of Georgiana and Wickham, and she passed lightly over Lydia's elopement, saying only that Darcy had come to the aid of her sister when that sister found herself in difficulties a long way from home.

They were still asking her questions when dinner was announced, and over that meal, which consisted of venison, root vegetables, and partridge, they teased out more information about Elizabeth's home in Hertfordshire. Gustav announced that he had been to England many years ago and he discussed its merits with Elizabeth.

The women were engaging and the men were attentive, so that Elizabeth felt herself charmed. For all their shabby clothes, they knew how to set her at her ease, and the men knew how to flatter her delicately and how to make her laugh.

After dessert, the port was passed round and the ladies withdrew. The Count's female guests were full of admiration for Elizabeth's gown and they were eager to hear about the Paris fashions.

'Tell me, how are the sleeves this year? Are they long or short?' asked Clothilde.

'They are scarcely there at all,' said Elizabeth. 'They are nothing but frills at the top of the arm.'

'That is all very well for a heated drawing room where the press of bodies makes one hot, but it will not do for the mountains where we have snow for half the year,' said Isabella, laughing.

'It might, if we sit close to the fire,' said Clothilde. 'I like the thought of sleeves that are nothing more than a frill.'

'Do you really want to sit close to the fire all day?' Isabella teased her. 'No, you cannot sit still for more than a few minutes at a time. You would be jumping up and going somewhere, doing something.'

'Not all the time; in the evening now and then sitting still would not be so bad if it meant I could be *comme à la mode*. And how are the skirts, are they all like your dress, with the waist very high?'

'Yes,' said Elizabeth. 'They have been this way for some time.'

'We have much to catch up with,' said Carlotta. 'We used to get the fashion journals, but since the troubles, they have not been so easy to come by.'

'Then we must go to Paris,' said Clothilde. 'We must treat ourselves. Too long have we been content to live in the forests. We will take a trip to the capital and return laden with gowns and shawls and gloves and fans. We will startle our men folk with our fashionable dress and perhaps it will prompt them to go to town themselves and get some new clothes, too. I am sure they could benefit from them. They look very clumsy, our friends, next to Mr Darcy.'

'I cannot believe Frederique will wear new clothes; his old ones are too comfortable,' said Clothilde. 'He will wear them until they fall from his back! Have you men like this in England, Elizabeth?'

'We have men of all kinds,' she said, 'some who follow the fashions closely and some who dress as they please.'

'Ah! Then it is the same everywhere, I think! But here they are now. We were just saying how we would like to go to Paris and buy some new clothes, and that you should come too,' she said, as the men entered the room.

'New clothes!' said Louis in horror. 'I cannot abide them. Always they are uncomfortable. They scratch or they are too tight or they are too loose, and they are never the right shape. A coat needs to be worn for a year before it is comfortable.'

'You see, Elizabeth, we can do nothing with them!' said Carlotta with a laugh.

A game of cards was suggested and everyone readily agreed to the plan. They were just taking their places at the card table when there came a sudden loud knocking on the front door.

Elizabeth looked up in surprise and all eyes turned towards the hall.

'Now who can that be?' asked the Count.

There was the sound of voices in the hall. The butler's voice was angry and contemptuous, and the other, a woman's voice, was feeble with age and yet at the same time resolute. A moment later the door was flung open and the old woman entered, followed by the outraged butler, who said something in his own language to the Count. Although Elizabeth could not understand his words, his indignation was clear, as was his step towards the old woman. But the Count lifted his hand and the butler stepped back, muttering.

'We have before us an old crone who asks to tell our fortunes. What say you?' said the Count.

'Let her in!' said Frederique, laying down his hand of cards. 'It would be a thousand pities to miss such sport.'

'What do the ladies say? Would it amuse them?' asked the Count.

'Certainly,' said Clothilde.

'But assuredly! I would like to discover what she makes of my hand,' said Isabella with an impish smile.

The Count, his eyes glittering in the candlelight, turned to Elizabeth. 'Do you object, Mrs Darcy?'

The old woman came forward. By the light of the fire Elizabeth could see that she was not as old as she had at first appeared. Her face was lined but not wrinkled, and her stoop was assumed. Elizabeth guessed that the woman was a friend of the Count's, someone who had agreed to pose as a fortune-teller in order to amuse his friends, and she said, 'No, I don't object at all.'

'*Alors*, then please, come closer to the fire,' said the fortune-teller.

She spoke with a heavy accent, but she spoke in English, confirming Elizabeth's opinion that she was a friend of the Count's and not the peasant woman she appeared to be.

She established herself on a stool by its side, protected from the brightness of the candles by the shadow of the mantelpiece.

Clothilde stepped forward, but the old woman said, 'Not yet, my dark lady. There is one here who must come before you; I see a bride.' She fixed her eyes on Elizabeth. 'I would give a fortune to the bride.'

Elizabeth went over to the woman and sat opposite her and the woman held out her hand.

'You must cross my palm with silver,' she said.

'Ah! Now we come to it,' said Frederique, laughing. 'The fortune is nothing, the silver is all.'

There was a murmur of laughter amongst the Count's guests and then Darcy stepped forward, placing a coin in the old woman's hand.

The fortune-teller nodded, bit it, and then slipped the coin into the folds of her cloak.

'Now, come close, *ma belle*.' She took Elizabeth's hand and turned it over so that it was palm upwards. 'I see a young hand, the hand of a woman at the start of her journey. See,' she said, pointing to lines that ran across it, 'here are the dangers and difficulties you will face. Your hand, it is the map of your life and the lines, they are the dangers running through it. They are many, and they are deep and perilous. You will be sorely tried in body and spirit, and you must be careful if you are to emerge unscathed.'

'That all sounds very exciting!' said Gustav.

'And very general,' said Clothilde with a laugh.

She had drawn closer and was now standing by the fire.

'You think so?' asked the fortune-teller sharply. 'Then give me your hand.'

Before Clothilde could react, the fortune-teller seized her hand and turned it palm upwards. She ran her finger across its lines and then let out a moan and began to rock herself.

'Darkness!' she wailed. 'Aaargh! Aaargh! The emptiness! The void! Everything is darkness!'

'She puts on a fine show,' said Frederique in a stage whisper.

'I put on no show,' said the woman, turning to him sharply. 'Never have I felt such emptiness, such terror and such darkness. The cold, it terrifies me. It turns my bones to ice. But you, *ma belle*,' she said, giving her attention once more to Elizabeth and looking at her earnestly, 'you are of the light. You must beware. There are dangers all around you. Believe this, if you believe nothing else. The forest is full of strange creatures, and there are monsters in many guises. Not all who walk on two legs are men. Not all who fly are beasts. And not all who travel the path of ages will pass through into the shadow.'

Elizabeth could make nothing of the old woman's words, but she was impressed despite herself by the woman's intensity and her glittering eye.

'*Mais oui*,' said the old woman, nodding. 'You begin to believe. You have seen things in your dreams. And you are not the first. No, assuredly you are not the first. There was a young woman like you, many years ago, who came to this castle. They called her *la gentille*, because she was kind and good, and because she loved the flower *gentiane*. She wore a spray of it always in her hair. She was young and in love, and like all young women in love, she thought she could conquer everything. And she was right, for love, it can conquer everything if it is deep and true. But when the terror came, she doubted. And when the horror came, she fled. Through the forests she ran, and the wolves, they pursued her and in the end, they ran her down. Take care! Take care! There is darkness all around you. Do not falter. Do not doubt, or you too will share her fate.'

Elizabeth stared into the old woman's eyes, chilled, despite herself, by the woman's words. Then a touch on her arm brought her back to her senses—to the drawing room with the dancing candles and the air of *bonhomie* and good cheer—and she laughed at herself for being drawn in by the fortune-teller, and she agreed with the other guests that they had all been well entertained.

The woman was paid handsomely by the Count, but as she walked out of the door, Elizabeth glanced at Darcy and she could see that he was not smiling. Instead, his look was dour.

There was much laughter as the fortune-teller's visit was discussed and then it was dismissed as attention once again turned to the game of cards. They separated into groups and played at cribbage, with Elizabeth coming second to Clothilde in her group and Darcy winning in his.

'Darcy, he always wins,' said Louis.

'Not always,' said Darcy, and a shadow crossed his face.

But then it was gone.

The evening at last drew to an end. One by one, the guests said their goodnights and withdrew to their rooms. Elizabeth excused herself and she too retired. It was cold in her room, the fire having burnt down low. She undressed quickly and was soon in bed. But as she was about to blow out the candle she caught sight of the tapestry and something caught her eye. She lifted the candle to see it better and she saw to her horror that the woman peering out from the mass of strange creatures was wearing a spray of gentian in her hair.

CHAPTER 7

I T WAS AS SHE had suspected, thought Elizabeth the following morning as she made ready to visit the hunting lodge with Darcy, the fortune-teller was one of the Count's friends. How else could the woman have gained access to the castle, and how else could she have known about the figure in the tapestry? But even so, the evening had left its mark, and Elizabeth found it difficult to put it out of her mind. There had been something uncanny about the woman, and her story had seemed out of keeping for someone wanting to entertain a group of friends.

As the coach rolled out of the gate, Elizabeth found herself glad to be leaving the castle, even for a short time. She was not looking forward to the journey through the forest, but to her surprise, she found that it had taken on a different aspect in the daylight. Gone were the dark and gloomy shadows and in their place were dancing sunbeams and sunlit clearings. The undergrowth was full of nature's bounty, with nuts and berries growing profusely, and here and there she could see patches of mushrooms, too.

'When we were children, Jane and I used to take a basket and go out blackberrying,' said Elizabeth. 'We would set out early in the morning and Hill would give us whatever she could spare from the larder, a piece of chicken pie, perhaps, with an apple and a slice of cake. We would go out into the fields and woods round about Longbourn, and we would spend the day filling the basket. We would at last return home, laden down with fruit, tired but happy. Kitty and Lydia would dance around us and Mary would look up from her pianoforte and her eyes would gleam. Mama would scold us for dirtying our dresses—or at least she would scold me, for Jane never ruined her clothes—and Papa would smile at us and say we had done well. Having shown off our spoils to the rest of the family, we would take the basket to the kitchen. Hill would say that it was the finest crop she had ever seen and she would bake a pie for tea. I well remember the taste of that first blackberry pie of the season; it always tasted better than any other.'

Darcy smiled and said, 'I used to pick fruit in these very forests. I always felt free out here in the wilds. At Pemberley I was conscious of being the master and I had to set an example to those around me. Here I could be myself. I would wander through the forests from morning to night and not go home until dark.'

'Were you not afraid of the wolves, or did you have out-riders to watch over you even then?'

'No, I didn't have outriders, and no, I wasn't afraid. I knew how to protect myself.'

She thought of the education of an English gentleman and knew that he would have learned to handle a sword and pistols, just as she had learnt to sew and paint. She imagined him walking through the forest self-reliant and unafraid.

'Were your parents happy for you to wander?'

'Yes, they were,' he said. 'They never prevented me from doing anything I wanted to do, and besides, they thought it was good for me to be out of doors.'

'Did you used to stay at the hunting lodge, or did you stay with the Count at the castle?'

'To begin with I stayed with the Count, but later I stayed in the hunting lodge.'

'Do you have many hunting lodges?' she asked.

'Five. There used to be seven but two of them were in such a poor state of repair that I disposed of them some time ago. I seldom travel to Europe now; my time is tied up with Pemberley.'

'The Pemberley estate is even bigger than I imagined and it stretches farther than I ever realised,' said Elizabeth as she reflected, not for the first time, that she had moved into a very different sphere of life. 'I knew about the house in London and Pemberley, of course, but not of anything in Europe.'

'There used to be a town house in Paris but it was destroyed in the revolution. When the storm has finally spent itself, I intend to rebuild the house, or perhaps buy another house there.'

'Do you think the wars with France will ever come to an end?'

He nodded.

'Everything does eventually, and I hope it will be sooner rather than later,' he said. 'There are other properties in Europe, too, and there are smaller properties scattered throughout England, all of which I hope to show you in time.'

Elizabeth thought of how her mother's eyes would widen at the thought of properties in Europe, as well as properties scattered throughout England. She could almost hear her mother telling Lady Lucas and Mrs Long all about it!

The coach followed the road through the trees until at last it came to a high wall running alongside the road. A little further on there was an iron gate, and through its bars Elizabeth could see a box-shaped house as high as it was wide. One of the footmen jumped down to open the gate, which creaked as it swung open, and then the coach bowled through. It went up an unkempt drive, full of encroaching weeds and tough grasses, which lay in the midst of overgrown grounds, and came to rest outside the lodge.

Although it was called a lodge, it was larger than many of the houses in Meryton, with three storeys and large chimneys. It seemed, at first sight at least, to be in a good state of repair. The steps leading up to the front door were sound, and the rooms, though smelling somewhat stale, were dry and in good condition. The floorboards felt firm as she walked over them and the window shutters were unrotted. There was no furniture and no decorations, save for the cobwebs that were strung from every corner and were hanging in festoons from every shelf or ledge. She went over to the windows and threw them wide, letting in the fresh air.

'This is better than I had expected,' said Darcy, as they wandered through the rooms, throwing windows open as they went. 'It needs cleaning and the grounds need some attention, it needs furniture, too, but other than that I see no reason why it should not be let.'

Elizabeth thought of another letting, in another neighbourhood, just over a year ago, and remembered the excitement it had brought in its wake. Her mother had thought of nothing else for weeks! She wondered if there were any similar families in the mountains who might be as delirious at the thought of a new tenant at the lodge as her mother had been at the thought of a new tenant at Netherfield Park. She imagined them dressing in their finest and going—where? Not to the assembly rooms, for there were none nearby. To a private ball, perhaps.

When they had inspected the lodge from top to bottom Darcy, having seen what he wanted to see, suggested they return to the castle. They were just about to leave the lodge when they heard a commotion outside. Elizabeth's first thought was that it was bandits, but the shouts quickly resolved themselves into friendly halloos and the sound of galloping hooves came to a halt just outside the drawing room window. Looking out, she saw some of the Count's guests leaping from their saddles and, breathless and excited, heading towards the house.

They were dressed in simple woollen clothes, suitable for hard riding through the countryside, the women wearing serviceable riding habits and the men wearing rough coats and breeches with well-worn boots. They disappeared from view and then there was the sound of the front door being flung open and Gustav's voice called, 'The Count, he told us you were visiting the hunting lodge and so we thought you might like some company. We have brought a picnic.'

The room was suddenly full of people, their faces flushed with exercise, all laughing and talking at once.

'What a morning we have had of it!' said Gustav. 'The best sort in many a long day. There is nothing to beat a bright autumn morning when the air is crisp and the blood is flowing with the thrill of the chase. We must persuade you to hunt with us tomorrow, Darcy, and Elizabeth, too.'

'Elizabeth does not hunt,' said Darcy sharply.

'Then you must teach her. There is nothing like hunting for sharpening the senses and bringing them to life. Every sight, scent, and sound is magnified. To live without hunting is to be only half alive. Well, Elizabeth, what is it to be? Will you hunt with us tomorrow?' asked Isabella.

'No, I thank you, not I,' said Elizabeth.

'A pity. But perhaps we may persuade you yet,' said Louis.

Carlotta, meanwhile, had unpacked the hamper, spreading

the contents out on a rug in the window seat. There was cold chicken and ham, breads and cheeses, game birds and venison, and to go with the food, there were bottles of wine.

'We have you to thank for this, Elizabeth,' said Gustav as the plates were passed round. 'Polidori has not invited us to the castle for years. I had forgotten how much fun it was to hunt hereabouts.'

'You have not forgotten our agreement, I hope, and been killing things you shouldn't,' said Darcy.

'Never fear, we have respected the Count's property and your wishes. We hunt to live, not to make enemies of our neighbours.'

'You must come here more often,' said Frederique, lifting a leg of chicken to his mouth.

'Yes, indeed, and bring your friends and family with you. Do you have any sisters as beautiful as yourself?'

'Yes,' said Elizabeth.

'No,' said Darcy at the same time.

'I have four sisters,' said Elizabeth.

'But none of them as beautiful as yourself,' said Darcy.

'Naturally. How is it possible to match perfection?' asked Louis with roguish gallantry. 'But if they are not all as beautiful, they are at least numerous. Four sisters is a family indeed.'

'Two of them are married,' said Elizabeth.

'Which means that two of them are not. I will have to visit England again with all rapidity.'

'And you, do you have brothers and sisters?' she asked him.

'Me, I have two brothers, but they are neither of them as handsome as me!' he said outrageously.

Frederique laughed.

'His brothers are the most handsome men you have ever seen. They quite put him—how do you say it?—in the shade!'

'Are they married?' asked Elizabeth.

'*Mais oui.* Both of them have been married for many years.'

'Do you have any nephews and nieces?' asked Elizabeth.

'More than I can count. Hundreds of them!' he said.

Elizabeth laughed. Sometimes it seemed as though her Aunt Gardiner had hundreds of children, when they were all running around noisily on a summer's afternoon!

'Do any of you have sisters?' Elizabeth asked, as they gathered on the rug and began to eat.

'I have two,' said Clothilde, between mouthfuls of game pie, 'both older than me. I am the baby of the family.'

'Do they live nearby?' asked Elizabeth.

'No, my family is scattered,' she said. 'Some of them live in France, some in Austria, and some even further away.'

'So that is why you thought that Charlotte had settled an easy distance from her family,' said Elizabeth to Darcy. 'And when compared with settling in another country, then yes, she has.'

'Everything, it is relative,' said Frederique as he helped himself to a glass of wine, and then helped Elizabeth to one as well.

'But what are you doing here?' said Isabella to Darcy. 'I hope you are thinking of living amongst us again?'

'No,' said Darcy. 'The Count thinks he might have found a tenant for me.'

'*Vraiment?* Who?'

They were all eager to know, and when Darcy mentioned the name they each had their own opinion to give.

'He will not like it. He thinks he wants to live in the country, but he would never be happy away from town,' said Louis.

'He will come here for a few months and then he will go,' agreed Carlotta.

'Is he married?' asked Elizabeth. 'When an unmarried gentleman moved into Meryton it was the talk of the neighbourhood, and he was seen as the property of one or other of the Hertfordshire daughters! I am sorry if I offend you, but it was so!'

Isabella sat up straight and looked at Louis with interest.

'Well? Is he handsome?' she asked.

'He is not handsome enough for you!' said Louis with a laugh.

'And how do you know what is handsome enough for me?' she asked. 'I might like him very well.'

'You might, I suppose. Very well, he is unmarried.'

'Louis!' said Frederique with a groan. 'You are a traitor! Why not tell them that yes, he is married, and then he can know some peace when he arrives.'

'I think he would like very much the company of such beautiful young women; it will amuse him to have them all paying a call on him as soon as he arrives.'

'But what is this you say?' asked Isabella. 'When we pay a call? It is our fathers who will call. Carlotta's father cannot call, it is true, but my Papa shall go for both of us.'

They continued to laugh and banter and tease each other throughout the meal, the women asking more questions about the prospective tenant and the men laughing at them whilst serving Elizabeth with all the choicest delicacies from the hamper. They were attentive and gallant, and Elizabeth responded in a lively fashion.

When they had finished eating, the ladies packed the remains of the picnic away in the hampers and the gentlemen carried them outside and put them on the roof of the carriage. The rug was folded, leaving a clean space where it had swept away the dust, and the windows were closed. The door was locked and then they went outside, those with horses mounting them in a flurry of skirts and boots, all except Carlotta who professed herself tired. Darcy offered her his place and handed her, together with Elizabeth, into the carriage.

The road back was full of pleasantries, and Elizabeth and Carlotta were not forgotten. Louis and Frederique rode beside the carriage, laughing and talking with them through the open window.

The castle at last loomed into sight. Against the backdrop of the late afternoon sunlight it looked less gloomy than heretofore, but once across the drawbridge, Elizabeth felt some of her apprehension return. The mercenaries were still patrolling the courtyard with their leashed hounds, and even the sight of Frederique and Gustav dismounting and talking to them did not make the sight any less threatening. Those with horses took them round to the stables, eager to make sure that the grooms rubbed them down thoroughly, and Elizabeth went back into the castle. She went upstairs to repair the damage to her hair, wrought by the elements, and to remove her outdoor apparel.

When she had gone halfway up the imposing stone staircase, Elizabeth heard Darcy calling her. She stopped and turned round. He was standing at the bottom of the stairs looking up at her.

'Elizabeth!' he said again, as he began to climb the stairs towards her place on the half landing.

Illuminated by the light from the large window she made a lovely sight. Her cheeks were aglow, her eyes sparkled, and she radiated good humour and health.

'I am glad you enjoyed the company of my uncle's guests, but it would be well not to encourage them too far,' he said in some agitation.

'I don't know what you mean,' she said in surprise.

'You were enjoying their attentions,' he said with a sudden spurt of jealousy.

She was taken aback by the injustice of his remark and flashed back, 'And why should I not? I never get yours.'

He looked startled.

'What do you mean?' he asked.

'You know full well what I mean. We have been married for weeks and yet I am still not your wife.'

'Elizabeth——' he said, and then stopped, as if at a loss.

'Why do you never come to me?' she asked him, hurt.

'I——' He shook his head. 'I should never have brought you here,' he said.

'Then why did you?' she asked.

'I didn't know how it would be. I thought it would be different.'

'Different? How?'

'Not so difficult—or yes, difficult, but difficult in different ways.'

'I don't see what is so difficult,' she said, looking at him beseechingly and reaching out a hand to touch him.

'No, I know you don't,' he said, but he did not take her hand.

'Then explain it to me. Talk to me, Darcy,' she begged him, taking his hands and looking into his eyes. 'Tell me what is wrong. I will not leave this spot until you talk to me, though sunset is already on its way. I will stand here until dark if necessary.'

He lifted his eyes but he did not look at her, he looked

beyond her, over her shoulder, to the reddening sky. Then his whole attitude changed.

'That's no sunset,' he said.

She was startled and, looking over her shoulder, she saw that he was right. The sky was not flamed with crimson, it was stained with a fire's glow.

A bell on the stables started to ring out and there was a clamour from the courtyard outside. Through the window she saw the mercenaries mount with all speed as the grating of the drawbridge's chains rent the air. The vast bridge began to lower and the mercenaries streamed across it, filling the air with the flash of their bright swords.

'There is no time to lose,' said Darcy, seizing Elizabeth by the hand and pulling her down the stairs, just as the Count appeared at their foot.

'Quickly,' the Count said, 'you must go at once. The mob, it is on the move.'

Elizabeth was at once alarmed, remembering everything she had heard about the revolution in France, when the mobs had stormed the houses of the nobility and wreaked havoc, burning and murdering as they went.

'We can't leave the castle,' she said. 'The walls are thick. We will be safe here.'

'We can and we must leave,' said Darcy.

The Count said something under his breath and Elizabeth thought he said, *Get her away from here. It is her they will not stand for*, before realising that she must be mistaken, because those words didn't make sense. Then, in a louder voice, he said, 'Do not stop for your things. Me, I will have them sent on.'

'We can't leave at night,' said Elizabeth. 'The horses—'

'We cannot ride our own horses, there is no time to have them readied,' said Darcy.

'You will find everything needful at the usual place,' said the Count to Darcy. 'Go quickly, my friend, and the wind, may he be at your back.'

Darcy nodded, then saying, 'Send our things on,' he turned to Elizabeth and said, 'We must go.'

Caught up in the sense of urgency, she ran down the flight of stairs with Darcy beside her, but when she headed for the door he caught her hand and, pulling her along with him, took her to another staircase leading down into the bowels of the castle. The steps were smooth and slippery, and the cold bit into Elizabeth's feet through the soles of her shoes. The light faded as the windows receded and they were running in near darkness, until at last Darcy pulled her through a studded door. There he took a torch from a sconce on the wall and fumbled on a shelf, striking a light with a tinder box. The torch caught fire and a light shone out, a dreadful echo of the torches of the mob.

They were in a storeroom with sacks of flour stacked against the walls. It was hewn out of the rock on which the castle stood, and the ceiling was so low that Darcy had to stoop and Elizabeth was in danger of hitting her head.

Darcy pulled aside the heavy sacks of floor and then, taking the torch in one hand and Elizabeth's hand in the other, he led her on through the door that had been revealed. Elizabeth found herself in a dark, dank tunnel with water running down the walls, and she shuddered with cold and fear. The floor was uneven, and twice she stumbled, but she quickly righted herself, wondering where they were going. She guessed they were passing beneath the castle walls and the thought of so much weight above oppressed her so that she hurried her pace. At last they came to another thick door which was barred with a stout oak log. Darcy again handed her the torch and then heaved the bar out of its housings and opened the door. Beyond was a tangled thicket of thorns and ivy, disguising the opening, and beyond that lay the forest.

A wolf howled and Elizabeth's pulse jumped at the thought of the dangers ahead and the dangers behind.

Darcy extinguished the torch and threw it aside. Then he led her cautiously ahead, pushing the creepers out of the way with his hands and making a passage for her through the thick and thorny tangle. Even so, she scratched her face and caught her cloak on a briar before she was able to stand upright in a dense part of the forest.

Through a gap in the canopy above there came the faint and sickly light of a new moon rising in the sky, floating like a ghost in the stark and terrible blackness. Beneath it was an angry red glow, moving towards the castle. But the castle was now some way behind them and Elizabeth stopped to catch her breath.

'No, we can't stop yet,' Darcy said. 'We are still not safe.'

There were far-off shouts and the dim commotion of steel on steel, but closer to hand all was quiet.

Darcy turned and looked ahead. Through the thick and gnarly tree trunks a cottage could be glimpsed, and it was to this building that Darcy headed, Elizabeth at his side. They moved quickly and quietly, their breath misting in the air and their lungs gasping with the cold.

They had almost gained the cottage when a shadow detached itself from the surrounding blackness and Elizabeth froze. She could not at first see what it was, it seemed too large for a wolf or a man, but then it split and separated and she could see that it was made up of half a dozen men or more, each holding a club.

'They were waiting for us,' said Darcy under his breath. 'We were betrayed.'

He began to back away from the men, pushing Elizabeth behind him, protecting her with his body. And then she heard a twig crack behind her and she froze. Her arm was seized and she was pulled backwards, amidst a flurry of blows and cries. And then from out of nowhere, a wind arose, circling with force and speed, and she felt a roaring in her ears. She could see nothing and hear nothing, save a confused jumble of sounds and images, and then suddenly everything went quiet. The wind dropped, the cries died, and she was standing alone in the forest. There were no hands holding on to her, no one anywhere. The forest was empty.

'Darcy!' she called, softly to begin with in case there were any enemies nearby. But then, needing to hear a friendly voice whatever the cost, she called more loudly, 'Darcy!'

'It's all right,' he said, 'I'm here.'

Somehow he was right beside her, though she had not seen him or heard him a moment before.

'What happened?' she asked.

'Some of the mob knew what we would do and tried to cut us off,' he said.

'I know, but after that. The wind, the cries, what happened to the men?'

'Gone,' he said.

He turned slightly and the moonlight fell on one side of his face. His hair was dishevelled and his clothes were awry, and she saw to her horror that he had blood on his mouth.

'You're hurt,' she said, removing her glove and lifting her hand to see to his wound.

He caught it, stopping her, and all of a sudden they were not in the forest, they were nowhere, in some strange realm where only they two existed, and where every inch of her needed him. She looked into his eyes and something shot between them, connecting them, joining them, making them one. She felt the hunger in him, she saw the longing in his eyes and her heart stopped beating. Then he wrenched himself away.

'What is it?' she begged him. 'What's wrong? Why won't you tell me?'

'I should never have let her do this to me,' he muttered under his breath, 'but then, if I hadn't, I would never have met you.'

There was a low murmur like the sea coming towards them and the red glow was getting closer.

'We must go,' he said.

He took her hand again and together they ran through the forest, snaking through the tree trunks and jumping over gnarled roots until they came to the cottage door.

Darcy knocked swiftly and quietly in a distinctive tattoo. The door was opened at once by a woman carrying a candle, which gave out only the smallest light. She said something to Darcy in a foreign tongue and he thanked her, then took Elizabeth through the house and out of the door at the other side. A barn lay ahead, and a man was leading a couple of horses, both saddled and ready to go.

Elizabeth looked at her horse with some apprehension. It was no gentle mount, but a large and restive looking creature, and it had a man's saddle on its back. There was no help for it, she had to mount. Darcy lifted her into the saddle, then mounted his own animal, and they set off. She could barely hold the horse, but she hoped it would become less restive when it had run off some of its energy.

'Where are we going?' she asked.

'Across the mountains,' he said.

'But the Count—' she said.

'—Will survive,' he said. 'He has survived worse.'

His horse shot forwards and Elizabeth's animal followed, and they were swallowed up by the dark.

CHAPTER 8

THE NIGHT WAS LONG and wearisome. The horses were strong and not used to their riders, so that Elizabeth could only hold her mount with difficulty. The saddle was uncomfortable, and it was not long before her arms and legs were aching with the unaccustomed exertion. At last her horse began to tire and she was able to relax a little, which came as some relief, but the road seemed endless and she longed for journey's end.

To begin with they rode side by side but, as the road narrowed, Darcy began to ride ahead of her, stopping at each junction to consider the way.

'Haven't you been here before?' she asked him.

'Yes, I have, but not for some time,' he said, looking down three roads. 'This way I think.'

'You think?' she asked in a dispirited voice.

He looked at her with sympathy.

'Tired?' he asked in concern.

She sat up in the saddle.

'No,' she lied, 'I have never felt better.'

He smiled at her blatant but courageous lie and there was admiration in his eyes, then he laughed, and she laughed too. It was a bright sound in the deserted forest, ringing through the trees, and it heartened them, until it was answered by the desolate howling of a wolf, and then their laughter died.

Darcy turned to the right and Elizabeth followed him.

The road now began to wind downwards until it reached a hollow, where ice was already starting to form on the shallow pools of water which had collected there, but once through the hollow, it began to climb steadily. The horses had to pick their way carefully as the road began to narrow and finally dwindled into a path.

The branches of the trees closed in on them from every side, and when the path became a track, the trees were so close that the branches reached out and groped at Elizabeth as she passed, snagging her cloak and tangling in her horse's mane. The animal whickered nervously and began to roll its eyes. For all its fatigue, it became jittery and tried to turn back, and Elizabeth had to struggle to keep it moving onwards, threading its way through a tangle of tree trunks and wading through deep undergrowth whilst she swerved and ducked to avoid the low hanging branches.

The horse's nervousness communicated itself to her and she began to start at the slightest sound. Her nerves were stretched so tight that they quivered like a plucked bowstring for the forest was full of noises. Leaves rustled, twigs cracked, and, every now and then, a wolf howled, sending its lonely ululations high into the air, wailing and crying like a tortured soul. Worse was the agony of expectation as she waited for the answering cry, so that it was almost a relief when it came, although it was quickly replaced with a new terror: the knowledge that the wolves were out in force and were hunting in a pack.

They rode on to the point of endurance and beyond, never stopping, until Elizabeth was dazed with weariness. Then Darcy took the reins of her horse and led it behind his, whilst she slumped in the saddle. The moon rose and fell, sliding through the darkness like a pallid spectre. It was only when she saw it fall so far that it almost reached the horizon that Elizabeth realised what it meant: they were coming out of the forest. Ahead of them the trees thinned out and there, right at the edge of the tree line, was a small hut. It was a ramshackle affair, but it beckoned her with all the allure of a palace.

She was so tired by the time they finally reached it that she fell out of the saddle and into Darcy's waiting arms. He carried her inside and lay her down on a bed of bracken covered with soft white goat skins, and by the time she touched the ground, she was already asleep.

⌒∞⌒

Night was followed by day, creeping into the hut like a ghost, slowly, hesitantly, but taking on strength as the darkness faded from black to grey, before mustering its courage and illuminating the small hut to reveal a cotillion of dancing dust motes and Elizabeth's sleeping form.

She was dressed as she had been for her flight, except that Darcy had removed her bonnet to reveal her soft, tangled hair, and covered her with his coat. She looked angelic. The lines of worry had gone from her face and been replaced with the smooth calm lines of repose. Her lashes lay thickly on her cheek. It had lost some of its sun-coloured brown and was now creamily golden against the dark grey of his coat. Her hand was above the loving coverlet, the nails small and well-shaped with white crescents at the tip.

As the sun touched her cheek she stirred, but then turned over and slept again.

Her sleep was lighter this time, and she stirred more often

until she emerged at last into the waking world to see Darcy sitting in front of the door, watching her.

'You look beautiful when you sleep,' he said.

There was something so tender in his glance that it went straight to her heart and she sat up, eager to meet the day. As she did so, the greatcoat fell away, and when she saw that he had covered her with it she felt warmed and cherished. Her aching limbs no longer mattered, nor the hard bed, nor the cold which set her breath misting in front of her. All that mattered was him.

She pushed the coat gently aside and stood up, shaking out her creased gown and stretching to release the cramps in her limbs.

'How long have you been awake?' she asked.

'Long enough,' he said.

She looked at him enquiringly.

'Long enough to make sure you were undisturbed,' he said.

She remembered the wolves and said, 'We were lucky not to be attacked last night. I felt sure the wolves would set upon us.'

'You have nothing to fear from them. I will always protect you and keep you safe,' he replied.

'This is not what I imagined when we set out on our wedding tour!' she said, her natural humour reasserting itself. 'I thought I would be waking up in an inn, with hot water and a good breakfast close to hand!'

'I can give you the first of those, at least. There is water heating on a fire outside.'

He went outside and returned with the water in a bucket.

'Can I drink it?'

'Yes. Here.'

He poured some into the water canister that had been

attached to the saddlebags and handed it to her. She drank it gratefully then splashed the rest of the water over herself.

His eyes followed the movement of her hands as she scooped the water out of the bucket and then watched the beads of water as they ran down her face and neck.

She dried herself as best she could on her handkerchief and then ventured outside to put it by the fire to dry. But when she saw a man by the fire she stepped back uncertainly. His face was weather-beaten and his clothes were made of the skin of the chamois which wandered sure footed in the mountains. He appeared to be a simple shepherd, but in his left hand he held a bag and, after all the alarms of the previous day, she found herself wondering if it hid a pistol or a knife. He made no threatening moves, however, and he took from the bag a loaf of dark bread and a lump of hard cheese.

'It can't compare with hot rolls and hot chocolate,' said Darcy humorously, 'but it will satisfy you, at least.'

Elizabeth took it gratefully, tasting none of it in her hunger, eating rapidly until it was all gone. She realised with dismay that she had finished it and tried to apologize, but Darcy only laughed and said that he and Jean-Paul had already eaten.

He turned and said something to the shepherd. Although they spoke in French, Elizabeth could not understand it, for it seemed to be in some kind of regional accent or dialect.

'Are you ready to go on?' Darcy asked her when the two men had finished speaking. 'We are not out of danger yet. We cannot go back so we must go on; it is a good thing perhaps, for there are many things I still wish to show you. It will mean more riding and we must travel on mules: where we are going, no coach can travel and even horses cannot pick their way.'

'Where are we going, if even horses can't walk there?' she asked.

'Over the mountains,' he said. 'Across the Alps, over Mount Cenis, where only sure-footed beasts can tread. And then down the other side of the mountains, to Italy.'

'Italy!'

'Yes, Italy,' said Darcy. 'I think you will like it, and I have many friends there.'

'You have many friends everywhere,' she said.

'When a man has lived to my age he cannot help it,' he said sombrely. Then he cast off his low mood and said, 'I want to take you to Venice. It is a beautiful city, full of treasures, and one you should see. You have had to endure much over the last few days but this is meant to be your wedding tour. I want it to be something you will always remember.'

'There is no danger of me forgetting it, I do assure you!' said Lizzy mischievously.

Darcy laughed.

'No, I suppose there is not, but I want you to remember it for better reasons than the ones you have at present. I want you to be sorry to go home, not eager for it!'

'Sorry to go home to Pemberley? I think that will never be. But I must confess, I would like to see something of Europe beyond wolves and forests! They will not believe me, at home, when I tell them of all my adventures.'

'Jean-Paul is coming with us,' said Darcy. 'He will be our guide. Are you ready to go on?'

'Yes,' she said.

'Then we should go.'

After making some attempt to tidy her hair she set her bonnet low on her head and tied it firmly beneath her chin.

She eyed her mule with misgiving but it stood placidly whilst Darcy helped her to mount.

They waited only for Jean-Paul to gather together some food for the journey and then they set off. They moved out of the last few sheltering trees, and before long they were above the tree line altogether. All around them were the purple peaks of the Alps, bathed in hard sunshine and topped with gleaming snow. Elizabeth felt the cold and was glad of her cloak and her gloves as well as her warm boots.

She felt her spirits begin to lift despite her worries. It was impossible to be downcast amidst such magnificence, where she was surrounded on every side by the majesty of the Alps. Their travels so far had not prepared her for the sublime and terrible grandeur of the views. She soon became accustomed to her mule. The stalwart animal picked its way stubbornly yet surely over the rough and rocky paths that wound to dizzying heights as they climbed the mountains.

They passed glaciers covered in snow and thundering cataracts that plunged with a roar to the valleys below. They traversed rough bridges which had been thrown over the dreadful torrents, spanning the mighty waterfalls with their fragile strength.

They picked their way through thick drifts of snow and walked by the side of sheer precipices. They climbed through the clouds until they were above them. They stopped and looked down, seeing the clouds parting in places to reveal glimpses of dwellings and churches in the meadows far below. Then they set off again and climbed even higher, up towards the dizzying summits.

The air grew ever colder until the very waterfalls were frozen, plunging downwards in huge sheets of ice that glimmered green and white in the unclouded sunlight.

They saw no one on their way, save for a stray shepherd or two and, here and there, a hunter. Of wildlife they saw little, only the chamois who ranged over the crags and occasionally some hardy mountain cattle.

At last they began to descend, going down through the clouds, where the foggy vapour closed around them like a damp hand and where they could see nothing except the whiteness all around them. But eventually, wet and shivering, they emerged, to see the mountain track becoming wider and less steep beneath them and, far below, the green and verdant grass of the plains. The air began to grow warmer, and they felt they were leaving winter behind them and entering spring. The rocks and crags were gradually replaced with trees and grasses and then bright swathes of meadow, spotted with the greens and blues and yellows of the late wildflowers.

They stopped for a rest on a grassy slope above the mountain's foot.

Jean-Paul turned to Darcy and said something that Elizabeth did not understand, but she understood Darcy's reply: he was thanking Jean-Paul for all his help and bidding him adieu. Jean-Paul nodded his head in token of leave-taking and then, catching up the reins of the mules, he began to walk back up the foothills, returning to the rocky crags amongst which he made his home.

Elizabeth watched him go with regret. He had been a stalwart presence as the crossed the Alps, sure-footed and knowledgeable, and she had been grateful to him for accompanying them and showing them the way.

'Do we walk now?' asked Elizabeth.

'No, it is too far for us to walk. We hire horses over there,' said Darcy, indicating a nearby farm.

He gave her his arm and they began to walk towards it.

'What are those places I can see in the distance?' she asked, turning her attention to the lands that lay at the bottom of the slopes.

'Piedmont,' said Darcy, 'the foot of the mountain. Beyond is Lombardy, and in the far distance you can see Turin. And beyond Turin lies Venice.'

They hired horses at the farm, hardy animals that clopped slowly through the foothills, and continued their journey with the river Doria rushing along beside them. They passed through a landscape of forests, with streams and lakes varying the view, and with castles and monasteries nestled amongst them.

At last they reached the valley, where sheep were grazing placidly. They came then to the walled town of Susa, and as they passed through the gate, Elizabeth said, 'I never thought I would be so happy to see a town.'

Though the Alps had been sublime, the joys of hot water now awaited her, as well as a soft bed and a hot and filling meal.

They were soon at the inn. As they rode into the court-yard, there were suspicious glances from the other people there, including the grooms, who looked at the farm horses askance, but then recognition dawned on the face of one of the grooms and he called out something in Italian. The innkeeper hurried out of the inn with his wife behind him, uttering a long and excited greeting of which Elizabeth understood not a word, but she understood his smiling face and his bow and his wave towards the open door.

She and Darcy were made very welcome, and the inn-keeper's wife was soon leading Elizabeth upstairs, calling the maids as she did so, and before many minutes had passed, Elizabeth found herself in a small but pretty bedroom with a hip bath all ready and waiting for her. She was surprised at the hurry, until she saw herself in the looking glass and recoiled in horror from the sight that met her eyes. She had not brushed her hair for days and it was like a bird's nest, tangled and matted with pieces of twig and leaf clinging to it. Her clothes looked as though they had been slept in, as indeed they had, and her face was streaked with dirt. If she had not entered the inn with Darcy, at a place where he was well-known, she was sure she would have been driven out as a vagrant.

She removed her clothes gratefully, sinking into the luxurious water with a sigh of contentment. At last, when her fingers began to crinkle, she washed her hair and stepped out of the bath. She dried herself on a fluffy towel and then sat before the fire to dry her hair.

When it was almost dry, the innkeeper's wife entered the room with a maid behind her, bearing a bowl of soup and a large hunk of bread, and Elizabeth ate it thankfully. It was followed by a meal that was unknown to her, with a meaty sauce ladled over something neither soft nor hard, pale gold in colour, and cut into long, thin strips. She had great difficulty eating it and was glad she had elected to dine in her room, since much of the sauce ended up on her chin! But it was tasty, and when it was finished, she felt replete.

She went over to the dressing table where she brushed the tangles out of her hair and as she did so, her mind drifted back over the strange and wonderful events of the last few days.

She had thought about little on the journey across the Alps; indeed, the way had been so treacherous and so sublime that she had had little time to think of anything but picking her way amongst the crags or looking with awe at the magnificent views. But now she recalled the danger of all those at the castle and she could not put their fate from her mind.

She tried to tell herself that they would be unharmed, and that Darcy had been right when he had reassured her that all would be well, saying that the Count had survived worse. She reminded herself of the thick walls of the castle and the drawbridge and the mercenaries, but she could not be reconciled. If there had been no danger, then why had they fled, undertaking such an arduous if breathtaking journey?

She thought of the Count's strange words, Get her away from here. It is her they will not stand for, and wondered if she could have heard them aright. Try as she might, she could not see how they made any kind of sense. And yet she and Darcy had left the castle soon afterwards. It was a riddle without an answer; *another* riddle without an answer, for her life was becoming increasingly full of them.

And yet her life was full of joys, too.

Now that she had left the discomforts of the journey behind, she could recall the marvellous and wonderful sights of the last few days with more and more pleasure, both the unexpected heights of the mountains and the unexpected depths of her husband's character. She remembered his tenderness, and with quiet wonder, she recalled the expression of pure love on his face when she had woken to find him watching over her.

∽∞∾

The next few days were busy with all the necessary activities attendant on their sudden arrival without any of their possessions.

The local dressmaker visited Elizabeth in her rooms and

promised her some new clothes *pronto*. Luckily, Susa was a stop for many of the English travellers who visited Italy, and the dressmaker was used to meeting the needs of ladies who were newly arrived in the country. She knew that they required clothes in the Italian fashion, and that they required them quickly, and so she kept a store of dresses ready cut and half sewn in a variety of sizes. She arrived with three attendants who carried boxes of such dresses, and Elizabeth spent a delightful morning trying on a multitude of garments. As she viewed each one in the mirror, the dressmaker pinned and tucked and hemmed until the fit was right, and then Elizabeth stepped out of them, taking care not to scratch herself on the pins.

At last the dressmaker left, promising Elizabeth that at least one of the dresses would be ready by the following morning and that the rest would follow soon afterwards.

Darcy too needed clothes, and he had a visit from the local tailor, who fitted him out for a new wardrobe.

As they were finishing their luncheon, which they had taken in a private parlour, there was a most welcome occurrence. The innkeeper entered the room and spoke to Darcy in a torrent of Italian. Darcy replied and the innkeeper, saying, '*Si, Signor,*' left the room.

Elizabeth looked questioningly at Darcy.

'A messenger has just arrived. He wishes to speak to me.'

'Has he come from the castle?' asked Elizabeth.

'We will soon find out,' said Darcy, throwing down his napkin.

He left the table and walked over to the fireplace, where he stood with his hands clasped behind his back.

The innkeeper returned and behind him was the messenger, a dishevelled young man of vigorous aspect who turned his hat in his hand.

'Ah, Signor Darcy!' he said, as he entered the room, adding something which Elizabeth could not understand.

He handed a letter to Darcy.

'It is from the Count,' said Darcy to Elizabeth as he broke the seal and tore the letter open. 'The messenger has travelled night and day over the mountains, accompanied by two of the Count's mercenaries, to bring it to us.'

Elizabeth went over to him and stood at his shoulder, eager to see what the letter had to say, but when Darcy unfolded it she saw that it was written in Italian. The handwriting was thin and spidery, and covered many pages.

'Well?' she asked impatiently as Darcy's eyes scanned the first page.

'The castle is safe,' said Darcy, still reading.

'Thank goodness!' said Elizabeth with a sigh of relief.

She had feared the worst, and the message was a great comfort to her.

'There was a brief skirmish when some of the locals managed to swarm through the postern gate and started setting fire to the flags and carts in the courtyard,' Darcy continued, 'but the mercenaries dealt with the situation quickly and the danger was soon past. The fires were doused and no lasting damage was sustained.' He put the first page to the back of the sheaf and continued to read the second page. 'Several of the mercenaries were injured, as well as one of the Count's footmen, similarly some of the villagers took hurt, but there were no deaths and no serious injuries.'

'And Annie?' asked Elizabeth, looking over his shoulder and trying to see Annie's name somewhere on the page.

He turned to the third page, and Elizabeth pointed to her maid's name.

'Annie is safe,' said Darcy. 'She begs the Count to inform

you that she will pack your dresses carefully and give your letter to the messenger to post.' He stopped talking, the better to read, and then when he had finished the letter, he folded it and gave his full attention to Elizabeth. He smiled. 'They will all be with us soon, I think. The Count has already made arrangements for our retinue to be escorted over the mountains.'

'The coach will not be able to follow us,' said Elizabeth, remembering the precipitous paths and the narrow bridges across the ravines.

'No, the coach will have to be sent round by sea, as will some of the larger and heavier items, but the Count's men will carry most of our things across the mountains.'

'Will we wait for them here?' asked Elizabeth.

'I think not,' said Darcy. 'They will travel more slowly than we have done because there are more of them and also because they will be carrying baggage, which will slow them down. I do not want to delay our journey. We can hire outriders here to accompany us. I will tell the Count what route we will be taking so that our entourage will be able to find us more easily when they cross the mountains. Perhaps they might even find us before we embark for Venice.'

He said something to the messenger and then went over to the side of the room where there was a writing desk. He sat down and, dipping the quill into the ink, he pulled a piece of paper towards him and wrote a note in a flowing hand.

'How even your writing is, Mr Darcy, and how fast you write!' Elizabeth teased him.

He smiled.

'On the contrary, my writing is uncommonly slow!' he replied.

'It is a world away from Netherfield, is it not?' asked

Elizabeth, as she looked around the inn, with its homely pine table and pine benches, and to the view of the mountains beyond.

'Yes, it is,' said Darcy, pausing to look around him before continuing to sand his letter. 'But not an unwelcome change, I hope.'

'No, not at all. I am enjoying seeing more of the world.'

Darcy folded the letter as soon as the ink was dry and then he sealed it, pressing his ring into the wax to leave the Darcy imprint. He gave it to the messenger, who tucked it into a pocket inside his tailcoat, then he said something to the man in Italian, to which the messenger replied before bowing and departing.

'There is no reason for us to stay in Susa,' said Darcy. 'Once our clothes are ready, we will travel on. I am longing to show you Venice and the *palazzo*.'

'*Palazzo?*' asked Elizabeth. 'Do you mean a palace?' she asked in astonishment. 'We stayed with a count in the Alps, are we now going to stay with a prince?'

'No, we are not going to stay with anyone. We are going to stay in one of my Italian properties, the *Palazzo Darcy*.'

'Do you mean to tell me you have a palace?' asked Elizabeth.

'No, I mean to tell you that *we* have a palace,' said Darcy, laughing. 'It is on the Grand Canal, and I think, indeed I know, you will adore it.'

❧

After the splendours of the mountains, Elizabeth took pleasure in the quieter beauties of the lowlands as they travelled through northern Italy towards Padua, where they intended to take the barge to Venice. They stayed overnight at an inn and the following morning Elizabeth was delighted to find that their retinue had caught up with them. Annie was amongst them, looking none the worse for her adventure, and Elizabeth soon heard an account of the fateful night, with all its alarms and violence, and then at last its peaceful conclusion.

'I am so glad you are safe,' said Elizabeth. 'When the castle was attacked I feared the worst.'

'It was nothing really,' said Annie, with all the bravery of one whose ordeal was over. 'It was a nasty moment when the mob broke through the postern gate, I don't mind telling you, and when they ran into the courtyard setting fire to things as they went I was frightened, but the Count's mercenaries soon took care of things. I must say, when we arrived at the castle, I didn't like the look of them, but I was grateful for them that night and it was all over very quickly in the end.'

It had left its mark, however, for two of the Darcy footmen had left for England, saying they could take no more. The Count had tried to persuade them to remain by offering them more money, but when it became clear that no amount of money would make them stay, he had made up for their absence by sending two of his own men in their place.

From Padua they travelled on by river, taking the barge along the Brenta. Now that she knew that everyone was safe, Elizabeth's spirits were in a state for enjoyment and she saw much to be pleased with. The villas of the Venetian nobles slid past in an ever-changing view of splendour, overhung with poplars and cypresses, and with willows dipping their branches into the river. And then the miraculous city of Venice came into view, rising from the waters like a dream.

'I've never seen anything like it,' said Elizabeth as they drew near. 'I had no idea anything could be so wonderful and yet somehow it seems unreal. How are the buildings supported? Why don't they sink?'

Darcy's education had fortunately been wider than her own and he said, 'Their foundations are built on great timbers driven into the water and embedded in the mud.'

'Could they not find anywhere more hospitable to build?'

'They could, and did, but they were driven out of the southern lands many centuries ago. They fled north and settled on the outskirts of the lagoon where the marshland kept them safe. When danger threatened them again, this time from the sea, they took refuge in the middle of the lagoon where the waters were shallow and where their attackers' boats would run aground. There they found themselves to be secure and so they set about creating their city.'

They floated into Venice, travelling always by water, for there were no roads and no broad boulevards echoing with the whirr of carriage wheels and the clop of horses' hooves. Instead there were canals running through the city, changing colour with the play of the wind and the movement of the clouds and the reflections of the buildings on either side of them.

They came at length to the Grand Canal, which snaked its way through the heart of the city. There they left the barge to travel on by gondola. The narrow waterways were full of the slim vessels, their raised prows slicing through the waters. On a platform at the back of the boat stood a gondolier, his long oar clasped firmly in both hands. Darcy helped Elizabeth to step down into the gondola and take her place on the cushions that were scattered inside. She lay back, reclining as she saw other people doing, and gradually accustomed herself to the rocking motion of the boat.

Gone was the snow of the mountains, gone was the cold. Here was warmth and colour and light. And what colour! The blue of the sky reflected in the water, the pinks and greens of the silken clothes, all made it a dazzling sight. They floated past *palazzos* of glorious beauty, adorned with balconies that hung suspended over the waters, decorated with Gothic arches and surmounted with a delicate lacework of stone. The facades were of varying colours, rising up from the dark green waters in a marvel of strength and pride.

They came to rest outside the Darcy *palazzo*. Elizabeth looked up at the impressive building, with its dusky pink frontage. Its piercings of elaborate arches led onto a shady terrace where dark shadows contrasted starkly with the brilliant patches of light. As she let her eyes travel upwards, she saw that it had three storeys, each one with its own colonnade.

The gondolier tied the gondola to one of the brightly coloured poles that rose from the water next to the steps and then Darcy disembarked, stepping out of the vessel and mounting to the landing platform with the sure-footedness of one used to such activity. He held out his hand to Elizabeth. She stood up cautiously and, lifting the hem of her skirt, she stepped out of the gondola, feeling it rock beneath her. She ascended the steps and then took Darcy's arm and together they walked under the Gothic arches.

Elizabeth felt the coolness close around her as she went from sunlight to shadow, and walked through into a shady courtyard before climbing a flight of stone steps to the *palazzo*'s door.

They were met by the housekeeper who greeted Darcy respectfully and with warmth. Elizabeth was reminded of

Mrs Reynolds, the Pemberley housekeeper, as both women clearly had a great deal of admiration for Darcy.

After welcoming them, the housekeeper showed them to a vast apartment. It was cool and softly lit by the ribbons of light drifting in from the cracks around the closed shutters. When the housekeeper opened the shutters, sunlight flooded in.

'Well? Do you like it?' Darcy asked.

He watched Elizabeth joyfully as she spun round in the centre of the room, her head titled back to admire the magnificent paintings on the ceiling. She had seen many grand houses in England but nothing had prepared her for the sheer size and magnificence of the drawing room, with its historical and allegorical paintings on the ceiling. Even Rosings had not been so grand.

'It's breathtaking,' she said.

She wandered out onto the balcony and looked at the teeming life below: the gondolas going up and down the Grand Canal, the people going to and fro.

'I could look at this view for ever and never grow bored,' she said. 'How long have the Darcys owned the *palazzo*?'

'For a hundred years,' he said, coming up behind her. 'Venice is still beautiful but she is not what she once was. You should have seen her, Elizabeth, in all her glory, when she was at the height of her powers.'

His voice was hypnotic and as he spoke she could see it all in her mind's eye: the early settlers taking refuge on the myriad tiny islands in the middle of the salt lagoon, taming the tidal waters to form a thoroughfare of canals; the city that grew up around it; the pride of the Doge and the splendour of the Doge's palace; the building of the basilica of St Mark; the travelling Venetians who explored the seas, bringing back treasures for the front of the basilica; the great explorers who discovered new lands. He spoke of the clearing of the buildings around St Mark's and the paving over of the great square; he told her of the Campanile, with its great bell; of the building of ships to send out into the world for exploration and trade; the rise of the Rialto, with its varied shops selling goods from all over the world; and the merchant princes who grew rich on the profits of trade. And he spoke of all the wealth and pride and love for their city being poured into their art, of the great artists, Titian and Bellini and Canaletto, and he spoke of the masked balls and the Carnivale.

She saw it all before her eyes, so vivid did he make it, and as he spoke she felt the soft whisper of his breath on her neck. It hovered there, delicately caressing her.

'You don't know how good you smell, or how ravishingly appetising you are,' he said as his mouth moved closer, his breath trailing seductive and tantalising pathways across her skin. 'Your neck is so delicate, so precious, so fragile. You are so tempting, Lizzy.' He brushed away the tendrils of hair that curled in the nape of her neck and kissed it reverently. 'So white, so pure, so alluring. You are ambrosia to me. I have tried to resist you, but it is so hard... so hard...'

She was almost swooning with rapture.

He kissed her again, his lips brushing with exquisite sensitivity over her skin.

Her heart began to quicken, sending the blood pulsing ecstatically through her veins and making her dizzy with pleasure. There was a change in him, too, as her rapture enticed him beyond endurance. She felt his heart leaping in his breast, growing louder and stronger as he held her close, catching her to him as his lips touched her neck. His kiss was full of fervent desire and something more, something dangerous and deadly. She was held by some great power, suspended in a moment of exquisite anticipation, poised between safety and danger, the known and the unknown, the natural and the supernatural.

'Darcy!' she breathed…

… and with a sudden roar of frustration he let her go, wrenching himself savagely away from her, his face livid with emotion, and walking to the other side of the room where he stood with his back to her so that she could not see his face.

The strange power that had gripped her began to dissipate and she felt her pulse begin to slow and her senses return to normal. She watched him uncomprehendingly until at last he turned towards her and with a tortured semblance of a smile he said, 'I will give you an hour to rest and then I will take you to see the sights for yourself.'

When he had gone, Elizabeth retired to her room, feeling exhausted. It had been confusing but exhilarating, frightening and yet blissful, to be held by him.

At last she grew tired of trying to understand the perplexing feelings flowing through her and instead she changed her clothes, removing her travelling clothes and putting on one of the new gowns she had bought in Susa. Then she went downstairs, where she found Darcy waiting for her. He made no mention of what had just happened and, still feeling shaken by it, she made no mention of it either. Instead she smiled at him and told him she was ready, and together they went outside. Light was everywhere. It poured from the sky and it danced from the water. It leapt from the gilding and twirled from the stones.

They explored the city like lovers, riding in gondolas or walking arm in arm through the narrow streets and crossing the humped bridges which spanned the canals. They emerged into brightly-lit squares where fountains played. Darcy seemed light-hearted and carefree. He was attentive and affectionate, showing her all his favourite corners of the city.

At last, Elizabeth thought with a happy sigh, *this is what I always expected my honeymoon would be.*

CHAPTER 9

THE DARCYS WERE NOT the only English people in Venice. Many of their compatriots, tempted by the easier travel occasioned by the break in hostilities with France, had chosen to travel to Italy too. Elizabeth's table was soon full of cards left by English men and women known and unknown to them, for, when travelling, all English people became entitled to friendship. It was as Elizabeth examined the new cards one morning when she and Darcy had just returned from seeing the Campanile that she gave an exclamation of pleasure.

'What is it?' asked Darcy.

'This card is from the Sothertons.'

'I don't believe I know them,' he said.

'But you have a reason to be grateful to them, all the same, and so do I, for they are the owners of Netherfield Park. It was Mr Sotherton's debts that forced them to leave Netherfield and rent it out to Mr Bingley. I had heard they were travelling abroad, but I never expected to find them here.'

'Everyone comes to Venice in the end,' said Darcy. 'We must invite them to our *conversazione*, and I must try not to thank Mr Sotherton for managing his affairs so badly that he had to leave his home, though I will be tempted to do so, for it he had been a more capable man of affairs, I would have never met you!'

'I will send the invitation at once,' said Elizabeth.

They went through into the drawing room. She glanced, as she always did on entering the room, at the ceiling, amazed at the artistry of the painters who had produced such a masterpiece and had produced it on a surface so high above the ground.

Going over to the writing table at the far side of the room, she wrote the invitation and then gave it to one of the footmen to deliver.

'Is everything prepared for tomorrow evening?' asked Darcy.

'Yes.'

'Nervous?' he asked her.

'No,' she said, though it was not strictly true.

It was the first time she had hosted a social gathering and she wanted everything to be perfect. If she had been hosting an evening at Longbourn, it would have come naturally to her; if she had been hosting an evening at Pemberley, it would have been more of a trial, but still she would have known what was expected of her, and also what she hoped to achieve; but here in Italy, there were different ways and customs, as well as different food and drink, and complicating everything was the problem of the language.

Darcy had been a great help to her, speaking to the servants on her behalf and translating where necessary, but Elizabeth, realising that her lack of Italian was a handicap to her, had started taking lessons from a genial master. It would be some time before she could understand and make herself understood and until that time Darcy's help was invaluable. Together they had managed to arrange everything to Elizabeth's satisfaction and now she was looking forward to the *conversazione*.

Whilst Darcy went to speak to the butler in order to make the final arrangements for the wine, Elizabeth pulled a sheet of paper towards her and wrote a long overdue letter to her sister. She recalled the last letter she had sent, when she had been in the castle, and it all seemed very strange. Here, with the view of the Grand Canal outside her window, where gondolas glided past and where the buildings dazzled in the sunlight, the alarms of the forests seemed a long way away.

My dearest Jane,

The first thing she had to do, she knew, after the alarming tone of her last letter, was to reassure her sister that everything was well.

I sometimes think I must have dreamt the last few weeks, when everything was dark and frightening, and I pray you will forget about them too, for they are over now. Indeed, I am beginning to wonder if they were ever really as dark and frightening as I imagined. The castle was in a lonely spot and I think this must have preyed on my mind, making everything seem worse than it really was. The appearance of the mob was alarming, it is true, but the danger was soon past and no one was hurt, save for a few minor injuries which will by now have healed.

Here in Italy, it is very different. There are no gloomy castles and no sinister forests. Everything is magical. You must tell Bingley to bring you here, Jane. The buildings, the people, the shops—ah yes, the shops! The Rialto is an Aladdin's cave and I have bought you a fan. I have also bought some music for Mary, a new gown each for Kitty and Lydia, a shawl for Mama, some books for Papa, and a pair of gloves for Charlotte. Darcy has bought me a parasol to protect my complexion from the fierce sunlight.

Tomorrow night we will be hosting a conversazione here at the Darcy palazzo—in France the gatherings are called salons whilst here they are called conversaziones, but they are much the same thing: evening gatherings where people can meet with friends and amuse themselves. The night after that we will be going to a dinner party hosted by a group of Darcy's close friends. I am looking forward to it, as it will give me a chance to meet more of the people who are important to him

The Italians I have already met have been charming. They have the most musical voices and they move their hands a great deal when they talk. They are very expressive people, the gentlemen as well as the ladies. In this they are very different to the gentlemen at home, who mostly keep their hands clasped behind their backs.

There are some of our countrymen here as well, so at least I will be able to understand some of our guests, although my Italian is improving!

Darcy returned and Elizabeth laid aside her letter for the time being, and together they went through their list of things to do, making sure that all their preparations were in place for the *conversazione*.

∽∞∽

The landing platform, the colonnade, and the courtyard were full of blazing flambeaux as the guests began to arrive on the following evening. Elizabeth stood in the drawing room to receive them with Darcy by her side. He spoke flawless

Italian to the Italian guests whilst Elizabeth greeted them with several carefully rehearsed phrases; both she and Darcy were able to make their English guests feel at home.

The drawing room was abuzz with conversation in a variety of languages, for there were some guests from Switzerland, Austria, and other European countries, too. The *ton* had their own set of friends, as Elizabeth was discovering, and Darcy knew people from many countries. With all of them he was easy and assured, and she reflected that Darcy, with those he knew, was not the same as the more formal and reserved man who found it difficult to converse with strangers. Although he had made some efforts in that direction since knowing her, he was still not entirely at ease unless he knew people well. With strangers or mere acquaintances he always held something of himself back.

'Elizabeth!' cried Susan Sotherton as she appeared in the doorway.

She was small and plump with an abundance of fair hair which curled naturally round her face and she was dressed in a modish gown of ivory silk.

'Susan!' said Elizabeth, welcoming her warmly. 'This is Miss Sotherton,' she said to Darcy.

'Not Miss Sotherton anymore, Mrs Wainwright,' said Susan. 'I was married in the summer. Mama and Papa asked me to send their regrets, but Papa is not well and Mama did not think it wise to leave him.'

Elizabeth nodded in quick sympathy. Mr Sotherton's illness was more accurately described as drunkenness, and it was this propensity to drink, coupled with a propensity to gamble wildly, that had led to the Sothertons' difficulties.

'You must let me introduce my husband,' said Susan. 'Ah, here he is.'

Mr Wainwright came forward. He was not handsome, but he had an agreeable countenance and he seemed good humoured. He was also, by the look of Susan's clothes and jewels, wealthy. But a quick glance at Susan's face showed Elizabeth that the marriage had not been contracted for mercenary reasons and she was glad. She had found it difficult to forgive Charlotte for making a practical marriage, and she was pleased that Susan had not succumbed to the same fate.

'How long have you been here?' Susan asked.

'We are newly arrived,' said Elizabeth.

'I thought you must be, or I would have seen you before now. It is good to see a familiar face; we have been travelling for months. But more of that later, you have other guests to greet.'

The Wainwrights moved on and Elizabeth and Darcy greeted the rest of their guests.

Once everyone had arrived, Elizabeth was free to join in the conversations. There was much talk of the political situation, and the recent invasion of Venice by the French was spoken of at length with sadness and regret. When the mood seemed in danger of becoming too dark, Elizabeth turned the conversation to art, a subject sure to energise the Italian guests, who were great patrons of all the arts.

The ceilings in the Darcy *palazzo* were much admired, as were the sculptures and statues which adorned the rooms.

Elizabeth found many of the guests charming and agreeable, but it was when she met Susan by chance in the ladies withdrawing room that she really began to enjoy the evening.

'I never was more surprised or delighted to hear that you had married Mr Darcy,' said Susan, as she examined herself in the mirror and patted her hair into place. 'I am glad that something good came out of poor Papa's follies. I always thought you would find it difficult to marry anyone in Meryton. You were too clever for the local men, you know. Mr Darcy seems very much in love with you. He can scarcely keep his eyes away from you.' She separated the curls around her face and wrapped them round her finger one by one to refresh them. 'And what do you think of my Mr Wainwright?'

'I like him,' said Elizabeth.

'Yes, so do I. I was lucky to find him. I thought I would have to stay with Mama and Papa in boarding houses for the rest of my life, for Papa gambled away all my marriage portion, you know. It was not tied up as tightly as it should have been, and it soon slipped through his fingers. I am only glad that Netherfield is entailed, otherwise he would have gambled that away, too. Mama wanted me to marry Papa's heir, some distant relation by the name of Mobberley, so that when Papa died I would be able to return home, and of course, she would have been able to return home with me.'

'That is exactly what Mama wanted me to do,' said Elizabeth. 'She wanted me to marry Mr Collins, Papa's distant relation, and she was very angry when I refused.'

'Your Papa, I suppose, gave you his support,' said Susan.

'Yes, he did. He said that I must be a stranger to one of my parents, for Mama had already declared that she would not see me again if I refused him, and he would not see me again if I accepted!'

'Dear Mr Bennet! How lucky you are to have such a father, though even he has not been very sensible where saving is concerned. At least we will not have any such problems when we grow older, for we have both had the good fortune to love wealthy men.'

'And yet you did not marry for money. It is easy to see you love your husband.'

'You are right. The odious Mobberley is richer than my dear Arthur, but I could never have married him for I have never liked him, but I love my Wainwright very much. Perhaps too much,' she said mischievously, resting her hand on her stomach. 'There is already another little Wainwright on the way. To begin with, Wainwright used his discretion so that he would not risk giving me a child whilst we were travelling, but his discretion could only last so long! So now we have to delay our return to England. It is not safe for me to travel over the Alps in my condition, and I have no fancy for a long sea voyage. I am sick very often and I do not want to risk sea sickness in the moments when the other sickness gives me some peace.'

As she spoke, an idea came to Elizabeth. She had thought of many reasons for Darcy avoiding her during their wedding tour, but here was one she had not thought of. He had wanted to show her Europe, knowing she had never been out of England and that there might not be another chance to see it because the political situation was so volatile. He might have then decided it would be a good idea to delay any possibility of her suffering from sickness or other complaints until they returned to England.

If he had not been so restrained, their travelling would have had to be much curtailed if she had become *enceinte* like Susan, and their flight from the castle would have been difficult indeed. The magnificent journey over the Alps would have been vastly unpleasant for her if she had been suffering from sickness and, moreover, it could have been injurious to her or the child, or both. But they would not be in Europe forever, and besides, Darcy's restraint might not last for any longer than Mr Wainwright's! As she went downstairs, she tried to weigh the advantages of it lasting until they returned to England against the pleasures of it breaking whilst they were still in Europe, and it was in a more cheerful frame of mind that she rejoined her guests.

'You look happy,' said Darcy, joining her.

'I am,' she said with a radiant smile.

He put his arm around her waist and led her to meet some of the more dignified guests, who professed themselves charmed to meet her. The evening was further enlivened by impromptu musical performances, so that it was with great regret that Elizabeth saw the evening come to an end. As the guests left, they expressed their thanks for one of the most agreeable evenings they had spent in a long time, and Susan whispered to Elizabeth as she said goodbye, 'It was a great success.'

Darcy and Elizabeth watched their guests from the window, seeing them climb into the gondolas that waited for them in the way that carriages would have waited for them in London. Elizabeth laid her head on Darcy's shoulder and gave a happy sigh as she saw the flotilla of graceful boats gliding away, to the accompaniment of the softly lapping waters of the canal.

∽∾

There were a great many congratulatory calls the next day, and Elizabeth was glad to know that her first party as hostess had been a success. It made her eager to give more such parties when they were back at Pemberley.

After basking in the glow of all the congratulations, she turned her attention to their next engagement, this time an engagement at which they were to be guests. It was to be held by a Venetian friend of Darcy's. The friend had not been able to attend their own *conversazione* and Elizabeth was looking forward to meeting him.

'How exactly did you come to know Giuseppe?' asked Elizabeth, who was eager to learn more about her husband and about his life.

'I was walking home from a ball one night when I heard cries and I saw that a young man and woman were being attacked by cutthroats,' said Darcy. 'I went to help them, and together the young man and I drove off the assailants. He thanked me and introduced himself, then introduced his sister. They invited me back to their *casa* where I met the rest of their family. I was welcomed warmly, and they made it their task to show me the city, helping me to see it not as a tourist but as a native. They took me to all the famous sights, but they also took me to the less famous places, and they opened doors for me that would otherwise have remained closed.'

'Did you not have letters of introduction when you arrived?' asked Elizabeth.

She knew that this was the custom for young men of social standing on their Grand Tour.

'Yes, I did, and I had a guide as well, but they could only do so much for me. Giuseppe and Sophia did so much more. They took me to visit the best painters' workshops and they showed me where the best sculptures could be bought. They taught me how to appreciate art in a way that my tutors had not been able to do. For the Venetians, art is in their blood. It is a part of them, a part of their lives. Giuseppe, who loves all things beautiful, once said to me that, if he was cut, he would not bleed blood, but paint.'

'Let us hope you never have to put it to the test!' said Elizabeth.

Darcy grew silent, but then, rousing himself, said, 'They helped me choose many of the works of art which now adorn Pemberley's walls. A great number of the paintings in the gallery and most of the sculptures in the hall and elsewhere came from Venice.'

He spoke of his friends so warmly that Elizabeth found herself eager to meet them, but when they were in the gondola the following evening, on their way to the *casa*, Darcy said, 'You may find Giuseppe morose at times. Venice's recent troubles have rendered him gloomy. When Napoleon invaded the city it hurt him deeply, and when the city he loves was then given to the Austrians, as though it was nothing more than a bargaining chip, he felt the insult keenly. Many of the customs and traditions he loves have been stripped away. The great horses that used to decorate the basilica have been taken to Paris, the carnivale is outlawed, and now French banners hang from the windows of the Doge's palace.'

'I understand,' said Elizabeth.

And indeed, she could understand Giuseppe's feelings at having his beloved home invaded. England had also faced the threat of invasion, and although it was suspended for the moment by the signing of a peace treaty, it might one day return.

When the Darcys arrived at the Deleronte's *casa*, Elizabeth found it to be as splendid as any palace on the Grand Canal. The landing stage was brightly lit, and the mooring post was painted with gay colours. There were many more gondolas coming and going, and the Darcy gondola had to wait before it could approach.

Darcy stepped out of the boat first, then offered his hand to Elizabeth and she followed. She was now used to the bobbing of the boat and she could judge its movement towards and away from the landing stage exactly, so that she stepped out at exactly the right time.

They went under the colonnades and into the courtyard, which was brightly lit with flambeaux, and then went up the steps, where they found their hosts waiting to receive them.

It was to be a small party, and so there was not the ceremony that prevailed at larger gatherings. The atmosphere was more informal—a gathering of friends—and Giuseppe and Sophia's welcome reflected that informality. They greeted Darcy warmly and expressed themselves delighted to meet Elizabeth.

As they drew the Darcys into the room, Elizabeth was reminded of Charles and Caroline Bingley, for Caroline had been her brother's hostess at Netherfield, just as Sophia was Giuseppe's hostess here. But there the similarity ended. Sophia was not the cold and superior woman Caroline was; Sophia was warm and passionate, moving her hands expressively as she talked. Her brother was quieter, and Elizabeth remembered Darcy's words and thought she could discern an air of melancholy about him.

To look at, the brother and sister were very much alike. They had black hair and black eyes with smooth, translucent skin. Their clothes were old fashioned, as were the clothes of their other guests. Not for them the Grecian styles which had swept England and France in the last five years. Instead they wore sumptuous clothes in jewel-coloured fabrics, the women's dresses sitting on their waists.

Elizabeth was introduced to the other guests, a dozen in all, and saw that they all shared the Italian dark hair and dark eyes, with smooth, translucent skin. Elizabeth found it hard to guess at their ages. Their faces were unlined, but their eyes were full of experience.

They made much of Elizabeth and made her feel at home. They demanded details of the Darcys' wedding tour and teased Darcy, telling Elizabeth that it was obvious she was good for him.

'I have never seen him looking so happy,' said Sophia, who, as the hostess, took the lead in the conversation.

'Who would not be happy, married to a woman as beautiful as Elizabeth?' asked Giuseppe gallantly.

'And what do you think of Venice?' asked Alfonse, who was there with his wife, Maria. 'Is she not the most wondrous city you have ever seen?'

Elizabeth was only too happy to share her appreciation of Venice and the dinner guests nodded sagely at each compliment to their home.

They asked if she had been to the great cathedrals and if she had walked in the squares and when she said that yes, she and Darcy had seen a great deal and all of it miraculous in its beauty, Sophia smiled and replied, 'You have said just the right thing to please my brother. He loves our great city.'

'I can see why,' said Elizabeth.

'Alas, Venice is not as great as she once was,' said Giuseppe, 'before Napoleon put his boot on her beautiful neck.'

'You must forgive my brother. He feels things very much,' said Sophia.

'Who would not?' he cried. 'Elizabeth will understand, she is English. She lives on an island and so she can enter into some of our feelings. It was a terrible moment for us when Napoleon's soldiers marched into Venice.'

At the mention of Napoleon, the atmosphere in the room subtly altered, becoming awash with fierce melancholy. Elizabeth imagined Napoleon's troops marching through the streets of Hertfordshire and she shuddered, but for her it was only in her imagination, a second's vision, no more. For those around her, the invasion of their homeland was real.

'Ah, yes, I knew you would understand,' said Giuseppe, seeing the shudder. 'The English and the Venetians, we have much in common. We are both great island nations, we are daring and bold, we are explorers and adventurers, we have a great love for our country, and we have a great pride in all our achievements. We sail the seas in search of new lands and new goods to trade... but I am forgetting,' he said, with a comical smile, 'the English, they look down on trade. Darcy is horrified at the very word!'

Contrary to his statement, Darcy was smiling, aware that he was being teased. But underneath the teasing lay something more real. Elizabeth realised that Giuseppe was exploring her beliefs, and she was aware that, although Darcy's friends had told her how good she was for Darcy, they were still assessing her and wondering if she was good enough for their friend: not good enough in terms of social standing or wealth, but in terms of making him happy.

'What will Elizabeth make of us, whose fortunes came from great mercantile adventures?' Giuseppe continued.

Elizabeth smiled.

'I am sorry to disappoint you, but I do not look down on trade. One of my uncles is in business in London, and even if that were not so, I would not hold it in contempt, for it is trade that supplied Darcy's friend, Bingley, with the money to rent Netherfield, and without it I would never have met my husband.'

There was general laughter, and Darcy looked at Elizabeth with admiration and approval.

'*Excellente!* Well said! Then we have a great deal in

common, as was to be expected, for we both love trade and hate Napoleon,' said Alfonse with a laugh.

'Napoleon!' said Giuseppe, and he became sorrowful again. 'That upstart! What gave him the right to march into our city, destroying in days what it took us centuries to build, robbing us of our greatest treasures? What gave him the right to drive something wonderful from the world?'

The mood was becoming melancholic and the men were becoming morose. The women were uncomfortable, turning their fans in their hands or arranging their skirts to hide their disquiet.

Sophia proved her worth as a hostess by immediately lightening the mood and hitting upon the one thing that could rescue them all from their melancholy: a celebration.

'Let Napoleon have his edicts,' she said, dismissing him with a wave of her hand, 'let him give Venice to Austria. Let them all conspire to control us. They will not break our spirits. Let them say what they will, we will have a ball, a great masked ball in honour of Elizabeth and in honour of the splendours of Venice. Let us show Elizabeth how we Venetians used to live.'

The idea caught hold at once.

'But yes, let us show Elizabeth some of Venice's former splendour. A masked ball for Elizabeth!'

The mood had altered. The melancholy had disappeared, to be replaced with pleasure and excitement. Everyone had their own suggestions to make and the details of the ball began to take shape.

'Let it be a costume ball,' said Maria.

'Yes! A costume ball! And let it reflect one of our greatest centuries, let us wear the clothes of a bygone era. We will dress in the clothes of the thirteenth century,' said Alfonse.

'No, the fifteenth,' said Maria.

'The sixteenth,' said Giuseppe, 'the time of the great artists, of Titian and Tintoretto.'

'Very well,' said Sophia, 'the sixteenth century.'

'I have no suitable clothes,' said Elizabeth with regret, for
the ball sounded exciting.

'You shall take from me, I have plenty, and masks, too,
with which to surprise the gentlemen,' said Sophia.

'But of course,' said Lorenzo. 'That is all part of the excitement, trying to guess what face lies behind the mask.'

'We will let the others make the arrangements whilst we
do something more interesting: I will help you to choose
your clothes. Come, Elizabeth,' said Sophia. 'We will enjoy
ourselves!'

She led Elizabeth upstairs, through corridors lined with
great works of art, and took her into a grand apartment with
high ceilings and huge mirrors all around. She rang for her
maid and soon the room was ablaze with light as candles
blossomed into life.

'Here!' said Sophia, throwing open a huge pair of doors
and walking through into an antechamber full of clothes. They
were of all styles and colours, some new and some very old.
'These are the ones we will wear at the ball, from here,' said
Sophia, showing Elizabeth a collection of gowns at the back of
the anteroom. 'These are from the days of Venice's glory.'

As Elizabeth looked at the clothes, she saw that they were
very old, the glorious fabrics faded with age, but exquisite in
their beauty.

'Do you never dispose of gowns in your family?' asked
Elizabeth, amazed at how many there were.

'In my family,' said Sophia pensively. 'No. They remind
us of other times, other balls, other lives, other loves. And

that is what we live for, is it not, to love? You, who are so newly married, know that it is true. See, this dress, it is the one I wore when I met Marco Polo.'

'When you met Marco Polo?' asked Elizabeth in amusement. 'That would make you 500 years old!'

Sophia's hands stilled on the fabric of the dress. She said, 'You are laughing. Then Darcy has not told you?'

'Told me what?' asked Elizabeth.

Sophia became so still that she looked like a portrait, extremely beautiful but somehow unreal. Then, just as Elizabeth was beginning to be unnerved, she gave a slight shrug of her shoulders and said, 'It is not important, only that he has not told you my English, it is not very good. You will forgive me if the things I say do not always make sense?'

'Of course,' said Elizabeth. 'Your English is, in any case, far better than my Italian.'

They laughed and then Sophia turned back to the clothes and said, 'Now, which dress is for you?'

Elizabeth looked through the glorious gowns made of rich fabrics in blues, yellows, and scarlets. She took out a dress of deep blue velvet, which was criss-crossed with a latticework pattern in gold, matched by the slashes in the sleeves which allowed the gold silk of the undersleeve to be seen. She held it up, the candlelight winking on the gold thread woven into the latticework.

'Ah, yes,' Sophia said, 'That is very beautiful. It is well chosen. Try it on!'

Sophia helped Elizabeth to slip out of her own gown and into the antique costume. As Sophia fastened it, Elizabeth looked at herself in a mirror and was surprised at what she saw.

'I look quite different,' she said.

'Already the transformation, it takes place,' said Sophia, standing behind her.

The dress was fitted at the waist, showing Elizabeth's figure, which was usually disguised beneath her high-waisted gowns, and the fuller skirts flowed in folds to the floor. The dress was cut low at the neck with a square neckline, and it was richly embroidered with more gold thread.

Elizabeth was reminded of her childhood, when she and Jane had dressed up in Mrs Bennet's old clothes for a game of charades. They had loved the rich fabrics and hooped skirts, and they had taken great pleasure in trying on a variety of wigs.

'And now, you must choose a mask.' Sophia showed Elizabeth a collection of masks of all shapes and styles, saying, 'We Venetians, we love our masks. We have worn them always, until Napoleon; he banned them. But they are a part of us, a part of our heritage. We love mystery and the thrill of the unknown. It is a good thing for a nation of explorers! So much do we love it that even at a ball, we must explore: we explore each other.'

She picked up one of the masks.

'See, here, we have a mask that covers the whole face; the features, they are richly moulded. And see,' she said, picking up another mask, 'here we have the flatter masks. This one, it has no fastenings, only a bar at the back to be held between the teeth.'

Elizabeth looked at it curiously, saying, 'It must be very uncomfortable.'

'But yes, it is true, that mask is not comfortable at all, and it makes conversation impossible. You will not wear that one. Perhaps you like this one?'

She held up a full face mask which was supported on a stick, but after holding it in front of her face for a few minutes, Elizabeth realised it would soon make her arm ache.

'I think this one,' she said, choosing a half mask that was held on by a band passed round the back of the head.

'*Si*, that is a good one. It is still possible to eat and talk with the mouth being uncovered, but the nose and eyes are obscured, as well as the cheeks and forehead, so the mystery, it is preserved. You will set the others guessing! Your hair, it must be changed too. The styles of the day were similar but not the same. It must be parted in the middle and smooth over the top, with waves down the side of the face and the fullness pulled back into a—' She broke off and said something in Italian. 'No, it is no good, I do not know how to say it in English, but no matter, my maids, they know how to arrange such styles and I will send one of them to help you on the day of the ball. It is very important to make it right,' she said, 'otherwise it spoil things.'

At last they went downstairs, to find that dinner was being announced. As they went into the dining room, the talk of the ball became interspersed with other topics of interest, and to the Italians one of the greatest topics of interest was their art. Alfonse declared that Titian was a better artist than Canaletto, and Giuseppe declared that No! No! Canaletto was the better of the two. Darcy's opinion was sought and, as they ate, a lively discussion ensued.

It was with a light heart that Elizabeth stepped into the gondola at the end of the evening as she and Darcy travelled back to their own *palazzo*.

∽∞∾

Elizabeth was so caught up in the novelties of Venice that it was some days before she finished her letter to Jane, but when she found herself with a free hour, she took up her quill and finished the letter she had begun on arriving.

Darcy and I have been all over Venice, to the Doge's palace and the Arsenale and a dozen more such wonderful places. We have crossed the Rialto bridge and wandered through the square of St Mark's. The Venetians tell me that the city is not what it was before Napoleon ransacked its treasures, but there are still great beauties everywhere.

Tonight we are going to a masked ball. It is to be held in my honour and I am very much looking forward to it.

Perhaps we could try holding something similar at home, though I think such clothes and masks would look very strange in Hertfordshire! Here in Venice, they seem somehow right. The mask feels surprisingly comfortable, although I cannot see to the side very well when I am wearing it. It is beautiful, a work of art, as everything is in Venice. It is sculpted into the shape of a human face and it is decorated with jewels at the top.

There is time for no more or else this letter will never be sent! Adieu for now, my dearest Jane,

Your affectionate sister,
Elizabeth

'Are you writing to Jane?' came Darcy's voice as he entered the room.

'Yes.' She folded the letter and addressed it.

'Have you told her about the ball?'

'Yes, or at least, I have told her we are going to the ball. I will write again tomorrow and tell her all about it.'

'Is your costume ready for tonight?' asked Darcy.

'Yes. And yours?'

'Yes, it is.'

'What are you wearing?'

'That would spoil the surprise,' he said. He looked down at her with a smile. 'I love to see you like this, happy and excited. I knew you would love Venice.'

The clock, an ornate work of art made of ormolu and heavily gilded, struck the hour.

'It is time to get ready,' Elizabeth said.

She returned to her room, a large and airy apartment ornamented by frescoes and furnished with gilded marble furniture, and she began the leisurely process of preparing herself for the ball. As she bathed in scented water, she thought of all the times she had dressed for a ball at home, with the noise of the Longbourn household ringing in her ears: Lydia running round the house in search of a missing shoe or ribbon, Mary moralising, and their mother scolding everyone in turn, before complaining about her nerves. She did not miss their noise and chatter, but she did miss Jane. What fun it would have been to dress in her costume with Jane by her side!

But such thoughts did not last for long; there was too much to think about and too much to do.

Sophia had been as good as her word, and she had sent one of her maids to help Elizabeth. Annie had at first been suspicious of the Italian woman, but her suspicions had soon been overcome. Elizabeth sat at her dressing table so that Sophia's maid could arrange her hair and Annie paid close attention, helping to smooth Elizabeth's hair over the crown of her head and arrange the waves around her face, then catch the remaining hair up in a chignon pinned at the back of her head.

They helped Elizabeth to put on the heavy, unaccustomed dress, fastening it at the back with deft fingers and then standing back to admire the effect. Elizabeth scarcely recognised herself in the cheval glass, and when she donned her mask, her disguise was complete.

'Oh, Ma'am, you will fool them all!' said Annie.

Sophia's maid let forth a volley of Italian which neither Elizabeth nor Annie understood, but she seemed to be pleased.

'Is Mr Darcy still here?' asked Elizabeth.

'No, Ma'am, he's already gone,' said Annie.

'Then I must go too,' said Elizabeth.

They had arranged to travel to the ball separately because it was part of the challenge of the ball to see how long it would take them to recognise each other.

Elizabeth put on her cloak, for the nights were cold, and ran downstairs in high spirits, prepared to enjoy herself at the ball. She went through the courtyard and down to the canal, where she stepped lightly into a gondola. She was so used to the gondola that she did not falter, even when it rocked beneath her, but sank gracefully onto the silken cushions that lined it as the gondola moved out into the canal. The waters were dark, shot through with rippling gold as they reflected the many torches that challenged the night. They lapped against the boat and their music mixed with the voice of the gondolier as he began to sing in a rich tenor voice, brimming with passion.

'What is your song about?' she asked when he drew breath.

'About love, Signora. What else is there to sing about? The man and woman in my song, they cannot see a way to be together and so she drowns herself in the canal. It is very tragic and very romantic.'

'But much more romantic to live,' said Elizabeth.

'The beautiful signora is right,' he said. 'The living have pleasures the dead know nothing of.'

They came to rest outside Sophia's *palazzo*. The gondolier

jumped lithely out of the gondola and tied it to one of the gaily coloured mooring posts. Elizabeth stepped out of the gondola as sure-footedly as he and then ascended the steps to the *palazzo*. It was ablaze with light, which spilled from the windows and illuminated the night.

She went into the courtyard and was greeted by a hub-bub of noise and laughter as she climbed the stone steps to the door. As it opened for her, she heard the sound of violins playing and the chatter of many voices.

Guests turned to look at her as she entered, taking an interest in the new arrival, with faces made strange by their masks. Some of them wore half masks like her own, covering only the eyes, cheeks and foreheads, others were full face. Some were sculpted to fit their wearers, with well-shaped holes for eyes and mouth, and some were distorted, so that the wearers' heads had a strange, animal like appearance. Long noses, hooked up or down like beaks, changed the features and added a touch of the bizarre to the scene. She tried to find some familiar faces, but either the masks were doing their job very well or the people she knew were not near the door.

She slipped through the throng, drawing appreciative glances from the men as she passed, and went into the ball-room. It was full of people in costume, the full skirts of the women competing in their brilliance with the velvet tunics of the men.

Some of the guests were already dancing, but the dance was strange and the music was strange also. It seemed to come from an earlier time, and Elizabeth guessed that it too was a celebration of Venice's glory centuries before. The men were leaping athletically, and then lifting their partners and spinning them round before putting them down again on the floor. The guests knew the steps, and she thought that they must have hired dancing masters especially to teach them. Alas, she did not know the dances and she wondered if there would be some with which she was familiar later in the evening.

As her eyes ran over the other guests, hoping to recognise someone, she saw a strange figure watching her through a gap in the crowd. He was dressed in the colour of dead leaves and his mask was of dark cream with touches of old gold. He was not Darcy, of that she was sure, but she found him oddly compelling. His mask was moulded into the semblance of a smile, but the smile was distorted so that it looked almost malevolent. There was something gleeful about the grin and something cruel. She tried to look away but found she was held by some power she did not understand. It was only broken when someone stepped between them.

'Might I have the honour?' asked the gentleman who had blocked her view.

He spoke in a disguised voice, but there was no mistaking him.

'Are you sure it is acceptable to dance with your wife?' she asked mischievously.

His mask was only a half mask, like hers, and he smiled ruefully.

'You knew me,' he said.

'Yes,' she said, thinking, I would know you anywhere, no matter how you were dressed. 'And you recognised me too.'

He had evidently followed her train of thought for he looked at her lovingly and said, 'Always. No mask could ever disguise you from me. I know the feel of you, Lizzy, and nothing can ever change that.'

He offered her his hand, but she said, 'I don't know the

dance. I don't even know its name. Though I don't suppose it can be difficult,' she added with an arch smile.

'No?' he asked.

'No. After all, every savage can dance!'

He laughed.

'I was in a bad humour that night. How could I have been so rude to Sir William? The poor man was just trying to make me feel welcome.'

'As he was trying to give consequence to a young woman who had been slighted by other men!'

'Will I ever be forgiven for such a remark? Probably not, nor do I deserve to be.'

'Oh, I think, now that you have given me a palace, I might consider it,' she teased him.

'Only might?' he asked.

'Very well, if you teach me the dance, you may consider yourself absolved. Is it a uniquely Venetian dance?' she asked, as he gave her his hand and led her onto a quiet corner of the floor.

'No, the galliard is danced everywhere—or was, a long time ago.'

The dance was a strange one, full of lifts and leaps and twirls, but by watching the other dancers and by listening to Darcy, she was able to catch the steps.

'And now I lift you,' he said.

He put his hands on her waist and lifted her from the floor, then turned around whilst lifting her. She leant back against him, feeling the heat of his hands through her gown before he put her down again.

'You smell wonderful' he said, inhaling deeply.

'I should do, I am wearing the finest Venetian perfume!' she said.

'No,' he said intensely, 'not the perfume. You.'

They had moved into a world of their own, having eyes for no one but each other, wrapped up in the scent and the sight and the feel of each other, and they did not leave it until the music stopped.

Elizabeth felt a sense of loss, and she struggled to regain that world of heightened senses. She resented the other guests for taking her husband away from her, as they exclaimed over his dancing and introduced him to more of the guests. And then she too was claimed, and her hand was sought by one of the gentleman, who begged her to dance with him. He was gay and good humoured and to her delight she recognised him as Giuseppe.

'Ah! But how did you know?' he asked.

'I recognised your voice.'

'Then I must disguise it if I am not to spoil the surprise for others. Have you recognised Sophia yet?'

'No,' said Elizabeth, looking round the ballroom. 'Is she here?'

'Yes. You must guess which one she is.'

Elizabeth made two false guesses before finally guessing correctly, for Sophia was wearing a full face mask. In the end, Elizabeth recognised her because she recognised Sophia's gown as one of those she had seen in the dressing room, when she and Sophia had been choosing their clothes.

'Are you enjoying yourselves?' asked Sophia as she crossed the room to join them when the dance ended.

'Very much,' said Elizabeth.

'It is different from your balls at home?'

'Yes, it is entirely different.'

'You do not wear masks, I think?'

'No, we don't, but it isn't just the masks,' said Elizabeth. 'The clothes, the dances, the music, everything is different.'

'Ah, yes, you have very stately dances in England,' said Alfonse, joining them. 'I know, I have been there. You turn up your noses and you look at no one, then you walk down the ballroom in silence and you turn round at the end.'

Elizabeth laughed at his description of the English dances.

'In some private balls it may be so, but at an assembly it is very different, with a lot of lively country dances,' she said. 'There is a great deal of chatter and laughter, I assure you.'

'An assembly? I do not believe I have ever been to an assembly.'

'Then you must go,' said Elizabeth.

'Darcy, have you ever been to one of these assemblies?' asked Giuseppe, as Darcy joined them.

'I have.'

'But he disliked it excessively,' said Elizabeth teasingly.

Darcy raised his eyebrows and the others exclaimed, begging to know more.

'Not excessively,' said Darcy.

'Confess it,' Elizabeth said, laughing. 'You thought it was insupportable!'

'But how is this, if it is full of lively country dances?' asked Sophia. 'To me, it sounds fascinating.'

'I had only just arrived in the neighbourhood and didn't know anyone there,' said Darcy.

'And, of course, no one can ever be introduced in a ballroom!' said Elizabeth.

Giuseppe laughed.

'I can just imagine it,' he said, looking at Darcy. 'Darcy striding in with his nose in the air. You look horrified, my friend, but it is so! I have seen it.' He turned to Elizabeth.

'You have married a proud man, Elizabeth, from a noble line. He has ever been thus.'

'But Elizabeth has made him more human. And now he must dance,' said Sophia. 'Darcy, you must partner me.'

'And the lovely Elizabeth must be my partner,' said Alfonse, bowing.

They took to the floor again. Elizabeth found herself becoming more used to the galliard, and she could soon dance it without having to watch the other dancers. It was an energetic dance, and the room resounded with the sound of the gentlemen landing on the floor as they leaped and twirled.

Other dances followed, all equally strange, and Elizabeth had to concentrate on the steps of each one in turn so that she was glad when it was finally time for supper.

As she was going into the supper room, she felt a frisson of some strange emotion and her eyes turned, almost against her will, to the shadows in the corner, where she saw the man in the strange mask again.

'Who is that?' she asked.

'Who?' asked Giuseppe.

Elizabeth turned back to the man in the strange mask, but he had gone.

'Never mind,' said Giuseppe, 'you will see who he is at the unmasking after supper.'

Elizabeth enjoyed the food as she enjoyed the company. There was noise and good humour and laughter. The food was good and plentiful and the wine was very fine. The Italians took it seriously, pronouncing on the flavours and discussing the vineyards and even the grapes from which it was made.

Everyone ate, though those in full face masks found it more difficult than others. They lifted the corners of their masks carefully and ate sparingly, so as not to reveal their faces. There were many guesses as to the identity of the different guests, and by the end of supper, there was a buzz of excitement as it would soon be time for the unmasking.

They moved through into the ballroom, where the musicians played quietly, forming a background to the chatter, until, at the stroke of midnight, there was a loud chord from the violins and Sophia and Giuseppe demanded everyone's attention.

'You have all been very patient...' began Sophia, raising her voice so that she would be heard above the hubbub.

Shushhhing sounds ran round the room and the hubbub quieted.

'You have all been very patient,' said Sophia again, speaking more quietly now that she did not have to compete with the general noise, 'but now the moment has arrived. *Signore e Signori*, remove your masks!'

There was a rustle as the guests, as one, removed their masks to reveal smiling, excited faces. There were cries of surprise, as well as cries of recognition, with many voices saying they had already guessed the hidden identities, some truthfully, others less so.

Elizabeth was congratulated by those around her, and Darcy moved to her side, saying, 'Did you enjoy it, your first masked ball?'

'Yes, very much,' she said. 'We might think of holding something similar at Pemberley. It would be fun and I am sure Georgiana would like it.'

'Whatever you wish,' he said.

The evening was drawing to a close. Some of the guests were leaving, thanking Sophia and Giuseppe for a marvellous evening, and thanking Elizabeth too, for the ball had been in her honour. Elizabeth and Darcy added their thanks, and once the other guests had left, they too went down to the canal.

It was only as she was stepping into the gondola that Elizabeth realised she had not seen the strange man at the unmasking, but she forgot him as soon as she lay back in Darcy's arms. The gondolier was singing as he began to ply his oar, moving the boat forward along the Grand Canal, and their way was lit by moonlight.

The romantic atmosphere exerted its charm: once back at the *palazzo*, when Darcy escorted Elizabeth to her door, and he kissed her on the lips: no tortured token this, but one of deep longing.

'Good night, Lizzy,' he said softly, and as he left her there, she shivered with anticipation, thinking: *soon, soon*.

She undressed slowly for she was tired, and when she had put on her nightgown, she gave a yawn and climbed into bed. She blew out the candle and lay for some time in a hazy state between sleeping and waking as she relived the evening, until at last the sound of the water lapping the stones beneath her window lulled her to sleep.

She moved from the waking world into the sleeping world with scarcely any boundary between them. Memories of Venice, with its exotic clothes, strange masks, narrow streets, dark canals, glittering palaces, and romantic gondolas, all whirled together in the landscape of her dreams. She dreamt she was with Darcy, dancing with him at the ball. Then the scene changed, and she was laughing and talking with him as they walked through St Mark's Square. There were people all around them, laughing gaily and gesticulating with their hands as they talked in Italian, French, and English, their languages merging into one great murmur. Flocks of birds fluttered into the air as they passed and then settled down again when they had gone. The sun shone above, and from far off came the sound of the gondoliers' song.

They crossed the square and turned down a narrow street, emerging into a smaller square with a fountain playing, and then entered another narrow street, still noisy, still happy. But as soon as they entered it, something changed. The noise stopped as though it had been cut off with a knife and the light altered, going from the golden light of sunshine to the cold, hard light of moonlight in the blink of an eye. Elizabeth felt a rising tide of panic and had to fight the urge to run. The world was no longer a reassuring place; it was ominous. The buildings towered above her like cliffs, and the narrow street made her feel trapped and shut in. The canals running at the side of the street no longer seemed romantic; they were dark and forbidding, their deep waters hiding dark and deadly secrets.

She reached out for Darcy's arm but it was not there. She turned towards him and saw to her horror that he had gone. She ran down the street looking for him and calling his name but there was no reply. On she ran, through the maze of streets, until she knew she would have to turn back or become hopelessly lost. She began to retrace her steps, only to find that the streets had changed, and that she had changed with them. She was no longer dressed in her pale blue muslin, instead she was holding onto wide skirts made of scarlet silk which flowed around her like liquid flame.

'Darcy?' she called, afraid, but her voice dropped into the silence with the deadness of a stone. 'Darcy!' she called again.

But there was no reply.

And then, just as she was longing for the sound of another human voice, she heard something. It was at the very edge of her hearing and at first she could not tell what it was, but then she recognised it as music. Its faint strains were coming from somewhere in front of her. Violins were playing a jaunty tune.

It sounded strange in that dark and gloomy place, but she began to run towards it. As she drew closer, she could hear voices too, faint but unmistakable, and she followed them, running over the bridges and down the narrow passageways with her skirts flowing out behind her.

She saw light ahead, the brightness of many torches. She could see people in the square, dressed in brilliant costumes and friendly masks. She felt a rush of relief and began to run more quickly, seeing them turn towards her in surprise as she ran over the final bridge—and then they disappeared, the lights blinking out in a heartbeat, the voices abruptly silenced in mid-sentence, and with a feeling of horror, she found herself in the dark square and it was empty and she was alone.

She sped across the square, looking for the revellers, but they had gone. She looked down every narrow street, hoping to see some sign of them, but there was nothing—except, at the end of the last one, a man in costume, wearing a mask that was shaped into a curiously distorted grin. He turned to face her and she felt the power slipping out of her, as though her will was leaking out through holes in her side and flowing into him.

He beckoned and she moved forward, like a puppet with no control. She felt a brief stirring of her will as the last dregs of it resisted, and for a moment, she remained motionless, fighting his pull. But then he beckoned again and her legs began to move of their own accord.

'No,' she said, and then, ruthlessly,' No.'

And suddenly the streets were full of people again, running past her wildly, shouting, '*Incendio! Incendio!*'

There was panic in the air and a red glow on the horizon, growing brighter and brighter by the minute, and looking up she saw that the *Palazzo Ducale* was burning. The wickedly triumphant flames were leaping high into the sky where they crackled and burned across the nightmare black. She ran forward to help but before she could reach the *palazzo*, everything changed again and she stood still, bewildered and uncertain, not knowing which way to go. Without the fire, she could see nothing save a dark silhouette of buildings.

And then the hairs rose on the back of her neck. She felt her flesh crawl with horror as she knew with all her senses that there was someone—some *thing*—behind her. It was waiting in the shadows, biding its time, taunting her, playing with her like a cat with a mouse. It was a frightening thing, a glorious thing, a wonderful thing, a terrifying thing. And *old*. She was drawn to it, but she mustn't go to it, she mustn't, she mustn't…

She resisted its pull and backed away, crying, 'No!' as she did so.

She felt it laugh and then grow stronger, exerting more pressure, bending her will.

'No!' she cried again.

She picked up her skirts and turned and ran, through the streets, across the canals, pursued by its relentless force, dark and malign.

On she went, past the Doge's palace, with the ghosts who haunted its bridge clutching at her. She put her hands to her ears in an effort to stop the sound of their sighing, their terrible sighing.

'No! No! No!' she cried.

'Yes,' came a whisper in the wind. 'You are mine, my love, my bride, my *Serenissima*.'

On she ran, with the waters rising all around her, creeping out of the canals, oozing and alive, crawling into the streets, following her, pursuing her, and giving chase.

'*Acque alte!*' she called.

'Elizabeth!'

'*Acque alte! Acque alte!*'

'Elizabeth,' said Darcy again, shaking her. 'Elizabeth, wake up. It's a dream, my love, it's nothing but a dream.'

The waters stopped and listened to him, and then slunk back, slithering into the canals like supple snakes, and Darcy was there beside her, a gateway back to the real world. He was bending over her and shaking her gently, his tousled hair falling into his eyes and onto the white fabric of his ruffled nightshirt. As she emerged from the strange dream world, he sank into a chair and pulled her onto his lap, cradling her to him, and she was in her bedroom once more, where the candles blazed and the fire glowed and all was peaceful and secure.

'Ssshh,' he said soothingly, his arms around her and his warmth wrapping her round.

'Oh, it's you, it's you!' she sobbed in relief. 'I was so frightened! The streets were awash, the *Palazzo Ducale* was burning, and I had lost you, I had lost you... I looked and looked but I couldn't find you anywhere.'

'Hush, my love, it was nothing. Nothing but a dream.'

She put her arms round his neck and rested her cheek against his shoulder. Her heart began to slow and to resume its steady beating. She rubbed her cheek against the soft fabric of his nightshirt and gave a sigh as the last of the dream flowed out of her, then turned her face up to his. She was surprised to see that he looked troubled.

'What is it?' she asked, lifting her hand and stroking its back across his cheek.

Now that she was safe, the dream was receding and she felt foolish for having been so frightened.

'Nothing,' he said, taking her hand and kissing it, then turning it over and kissing her palm and then her wrist. 'It is just that I am surprised, that's all. How did you know about the floods? And how did you know that the Venetians called them the *acque alte*?'

'I don't know,' she said. 'Someone must have told me, Giuseppe perhaps,' although she could not recall his having done so.

'And the fire? How did you know about the *Palazzo Ducale* catching fire?'

'I didn't. I thought it was just in the dream. Did it really burn?'

'Yes, it did, a long time ago. Centuries ago.'

'Then someone must have told me about it, or perhaps I read about it somewhere.'

'Yes, perhaps,' he said, but his mood was sombre.

'It was nothing, my love,' she said, and now she was comforting him. 'A nightmare, that is all.'

'Of course,' he said with a distant smile.

But he put his arms around her and he did not let her go.

CHAPTER 10

THE NEXT MORNING SAW a change in the weather. The last of the summer sunshine had disappeared, to be replaced by a misty, eerie fog. When Elizabeth stepped onto her balcony, she saw not the glorious blue sky and the glowing colours of late summer, but the white and ghostly miasma of autumn, which wrapped itself around the palaces and bridges like a choking vine. Gondolas loomed out of the mist like wraiths, appearing and disappearing beneath her with a sepulchral air, and the dolorous tolling of the Campanile's bell seemed to come from a vast distance.

Elizabeth and Darcy were both subdued at breakfast. They ate, not in the courtyard as they had done when the weather was sunny, but in the dining room, an imposing, formal room ornamented with classical frescoes. Darcy ate little and left as soon as he had finished, saying that he had an appointment with his boot maker. At any other time, Elizabeth would have shown an interest, but she was thinking of her arrangement to meet Sophia at the *Venezia Trionfante* with some misgiving. It had been made on the previous evening, so that they would have an opportunity to talk over the ball, but she had no desire to go out into the fog. She consoled herself with the thought that it might clear by the time she needed to leave, but when the appointed hour came, it was as heavy as ever.

With great reluctance she donned her cloak, her bonnet, and her gloves, and she left the *palazzo* with Annie beside her. The courtyard seemed sad and cheerless without the sun to brighten its stones, and she noticed for the first time that the steps were crumbling and that there was green slime on the landing stage. She hesitated under the colonnade, thinking that the gondola was missing, and only realising that it was tied up in its usual place when the gondolier spoke to her. She took his hand and was glad of his assistance. It no longer seemed such an easy thing to climb into the flimsy little craft, now that the landing stage was slippery with moisture and the gondola itself was obscured by the fog, and she sat down and reclined with relief, only to sit up straight again because the cushions were damp and clammy. She looked at Annie and the two women pulled faces, then wrapped their cloaks more tightly around themselves, and peered ahead through the fog.

'Where do you go to, Signora?' asked the gondolier.

'To the *Venezia Trionfante*,' she said.

'The *Venezia Trionfante*?' he asked with a frown. 'I do not know this place.'

There came a cry through the mist as another gondolier shouted a warning and a few seconds later another boat appeared.

'Ayee! Carlo! Where is the *Venezia Trionfante*?' cried her boatman.

He spoke in Italian, but Elizabeth was pleased to find that she could understand him.

'The *Venezia*...? I know of no such place,' said the other gondolier, resting on his oar and thinking.

'It is a café,' said Elizabeth.

'A café!' called out her boatman.

'There is no such café in Ven—ah! you mean Florian's! It has not been called the *Venezia Trionfante* for many, many years, not since it was first opened, I think, and that is eighty years ago! These English, they are crazy, they know nothing!'

'Ah! *Si!* Florian's! I know where it is! In the square of San Marco!' cried Elizabeth's boatman, thanking him, and straight away he was plying his oar, sending the gondola through the swirling mist and into the hidden waters beyond.

Buildings loomed up in front of them every time the mist parted for a few seconds, but instead of seeing the warm colours and the splendid proportions, Elizabeth saw the crumbling corners and the exposed brickwork where the plaster was falling off. The gilding was chipped and looked tawdry in the dull light. The water too seemed darker and dirtier, full of murky secrets.

The fog had still not lifted by the time she arrived at St Mark's square. The great basilica was hidden and so was the towering Campanile. She could not see Florian's anywhere, but she found it at last by walking all around the square, her head down and her cloak pulled firmly round her with its hood up, covering her head and face.

She went in, glad of Annie's company, for the people looked at her with hostility and she felt awkward and out of place. When she discovered that Sophia was not there she felt even worse and she stood by the door for a moment, deciding what to do. The customers were still looking at her, some appraisingly, some suspiciously, and the waiters surveyed her with stony faces. She wished there were some women there, for Sophia had said that women were admitted to the café, but there were none at the tables; they were all men.

'We will wait a little,' said Elizabeth to Annie, taking a seat at an out of the way table. 'I am sure Sophia will be here presently. I think we are perhaps rather early.'

The waiter came and Elizabeth ordered coffee.

In England she would have enjoyed looking at the people who sat and talked or watching the world go by, but some of those in the café carried with them an air of danger, and she looked down, not wanting to meet their eyes. She looked instead at her coffee, stirring it with its silver spoon. It was with relief that she heard Sophia arrive at last. Looking up, she saw Sophia being greeted warmly by the waiters and many of the customers, and the café, at once took on a more cheerful air.

'Ah, Elizabeth, I am sorry I have kept you waiting, I was delayed,' Sophia said. 'Maria and I, we have been to the see the sick and the dying, to give them succour, and we were delayed on our return by the fog. Nothing is moving quickly in Venice this morning, not the people in the streets nor the gondolas in the canals; it is all travelling warily, hesitantly, and with good reason, for a misstep can lead to disaster in such weather, with the city so full of canals. It is the change of season. In summer we have the sun and this year it has lasted long, but now, today, it is autumn and the mists they have come down like a shroud.'

'Is it often foggy here?' asked Elizabeth.

'But yes, and in the winter it is worse; we have snow. The cold winds, they blow down from the mountains, and the canals, they freeze. But never mind, we are in the *Trionfante*, what care we for fog or ice or snow? You did not have any trouble finding it, I hope?'

'To begin with, yes. My gondolier had to ask where the *Trionfante* was. He couldn't find it until we realised it was called Florian's now,' said Elizabeth.

Sophia paused.

'Ah, yes,' she said. 'Florian's. Of course. He was the patron many years ago, and the café became known by his name, I had forgotten. It is a wonderful place, is it not?'

'Ye—es,' said Elizabeth.

'You do not like it? But ah, I see it in your eyes, you are afraid of some of the people. They whisper in the corners do they not?'

'Yes. They look like they are plotting,' said Elizabeth, with a smile to show that she knew such a thought was ridiculous.

But Sophia treated her remarks seriously.

'Yes, they are plotting. They want to put an end to the French; they want Venice to return to what she once was. But how can we return to what has gone?' she asked sombrely.

Elizabeth had the feeling that she was speaking of something more personal than the fate of Venice and did not interrupt her thoughts by a reply; indeed, she was sure that Sophia wanted none.

'The glory, it has passed,' Sophia went on, looking round the room. 'The great days, they have gone. There is no place in the world now for our kind,' she said, turning suddenly to look at Elizabeth. 'Not unless we will take it, and take it with much blood. There are those who will do so, but me, I find I love my fellow man too much and I cannot end his life, not even to restore what has been lost. But without great ruthlessness, glory fades and strength is gone.'

Elizabeth's mood, already low, became lower still. There was a darkness lurking beneath the gilding of the city and Venice had lost its appeal. She did not quite know how or when it had happened, but now, instead of beauty, she saw only decay. Sophia's face, so bright the day before, now seemed tired, and her conversation now seemed more macabre.

Seeming to sense something of Elizabeth's drooping spirits, Sophia made an effort to lighten the conversation and she began to talk about the ball.

'You were a great success last night. "The English bride" was spoken of everywhere. We Italians, we have a passion for romance, and your marriage to Darcy is just the sort of thing we like: two people separated by a great gulf coming together with love triumphing over all. It is a thing that does not often happen, and when it does we celebrate it, no matter how hard the future might be. Your dress, it was remarked upon, and how well it suited you, and how surprised everyone was when you removed your mask.'

Elizabeth did her best to respond but could not recapture her enthusiasm for either Venice or the ball, and she was glad when both she and Sophia finished their coffee so that they could say goodbye. She set out again with Annie, returning to the Darcy *palazzo* in no better spirits than she had left it.

The fog had lifted a little by the time she and Annie arrived, but the cloud was still low and the light was dim. Elizabeth went up the stone steps in the courtyard with Annie behind her and then into the great hall, to find that Darcy had returned from his own morning appointments.

'Did you enjoy yourself?' he asked, as she entered. 'Was Sophia full of talk of the ball?'

'Yes, she was,' said Elizabeth, ignoring his first question.

She thought how different it was, talking of the ball with Sophia, instead of talking over the balls at Meryton with Jane and Charlotte. In England, there had been pleasure in reliving every moment, good or bad, whereas here there had only been weariness.

As she removed her cloak, Elizabeth felt a long way from home. The sights which had so delighted her only a few weeks before were now unsettlingly foreign, and she could muster little enthusiasm when Darcy reminded her they would be attending a *conversazione* that evening.

'You are not feeling ill?' he asked, looking at her searchingly. 'Because if you are, we don't have to go.'

'No, of course not, I am perfectly well. I am a little tired, that's all. I will have a rest this afternoon and then I am sure I will enjoy myself.'

Her hopeful pronouncement did not in fact come to pass. There was a crush at the *conversazione* and the air was stale. In warmer weather the windows had been open, but now that the weather had changed, the windows were firmly closed. The noise grated on her ears and the atmosphere was oppressive. She saw Giuseppe, who bowed to her across the room, and she caught sight of Sophia and Alfonse, but there were a lot of faces she did not know. The thought of meeting so many more new people was daunting and, for the first time on her wedding tour, Elizabeth wished herself back in her room with the curtains drawn. She withdrew to a corner, where Darcy soon found her. He noticed at once that she looked pale, and when she confessed that she had a headache, he said, 'It's hot in here. I will fetch you something to drink.'

She watched him threading his way through the throng whilst she sank down gratefully on a sofa. One of the gentlemen happened to glance in her direction at that moment and walked over to her, saying, 'Forgive me, Signorina, but you seem to be unwell. Is there anything I can get for you?'

She managed a smile of sorts and made an effort to speak cheerfully.

'No, thank you, I am quite well, I assure you.'

'You do not look it. You are overcome by the heat, I think. You will allow me to fetch you some refreshment?'

'That is very kind of you, but it won't be necessary. My husband has gone to fetch me a drink.'

'Your husband? Ah, Signorina—I beg your pardon, Signora—you cut me to the quick. Such a vision of loveliness should not be married, she should be as free as the air to inspire all men with her beauty.'

Elizabeth laughed.

'You are amused rather than flattered?' he asked in surprise, but then his eyebrows lowered and he smiled. 'But, of course, you are English! They are very prosaic the English, and not at all romantic.'

'I assure you we are very romantic, with the right man.'

'And your husband is the right man? He is a thousand times fortunate.'

'You must meet him,' said Elizabeth, seeing Darcy coming towards them. 'Darcy, this gentleman noticed that I was out of sorts and he was good enough to offer to fetch me some refreshment.'

She took the drink that Darcy held out to her and sipped it slowly.

'Darcy?' enquired the gentleman in surprise. 'Not Darcy of Pemberley, in Derbyshire, in England?'

His accent made the familiar names sound strange and exotic, and Elizabeth wondered if her country would seem as exotic to the Venetians as their city seemed to her.

'Yes,' said Darcy.

He did not seem surprised that even here his name was known to strangers.

'But this is wonderful. Never did I think to meet you, but here you are! We have friends in common. Your cousin—I think?—Colonel Fitzwilliam and I have known each other for many years. Permit me to introduce myself. I am Prince Ficenzi.'

Elizabeth did not know how she should respond to the introduction, whether she should make some special mark of recognition of his title, but she was saved from her ignorance by the Prince saying to her, 'Do not, I beg you, rise from your seat; you must recover yourself.'

He complimented Elizabeth on her newly married status, saying that Colonel Fitzwilliam had mentioned the wedding to him, and he complimented Darcy on his beautiful wife. Then he talked engagingly about the occasion on which he had met Colonel Fitzwilliam.

'It was near my home in a more southern part of Italy, close to Rome. It is a beautiful place, better than Venice, I think, though I would not say so to any of my friends here! We have the great loveliness of the sea, but we have other things besides. There is water, which my friends in Venice have, but also we have hills and mountains, which my friends in Venice do not. We have walks through the countryside— Ah!' he broke off, seeing Elizabeth's reaction, 'you like to walk through the countryside?'

'Yes,' she said, 'I do.'

At that moment, the thought of walking along a country lane had a great appeal and she longed even more for home.

'Then I beg of you, you will visit me,' he said. 'I have a villa there. It is so beautiful now. My garden is one of the finest in Italy. The seasons they are kinder to us near Rome than they are in Venice. We do not get such cold winds or fogs or the snows of winter. Our flowers are all blooming still and our air is full of the scent of them; not like here, where the air is not so good. The canals, they are intriguing, but the smell sometimes it is not of the best,' he said, pulling a comical face. 'I think you will enjoy the countryside. It is magnificent and yet at the same time it is—how do you English say it?—homely.'

He could not have said anything more calculated to appeal to Elizabeth at that moment.

'I would love to come, if…?' she said, turning to Darcy.

'Then it is settled,' said the Prince with a gallant bow, 'for who can refuse a lady?'

Darcy, at least, could not, and the arrangements were soon made.

Whether it was the refreshing drink or the thought of leaving Venice, Elizabeth did not know, but her headache had all but disappeared by the time the Prince left them in order to mingle with the other guests, and she found that she was able to take part in the conversations and show an interest in the lives of her fellow guests, which would have been impossible for her half an hour earlier.

❦

The *palazzo* was full of bustle as the Darcys made their preparations for departure. Elizabeth's room was awash with boxes, and as Annie packed her clothes, Elizabeth assembled her paper, ink, and quills and put them into her travelling writing desk. Downstairs, Darcy made sure that the travelling arrangements had been carried out to his satisfaction and at last they were ready to go. As Elizabeth stepped into the gondola for the last time, she thought how glad she had been to arrive, but also how glad she was to be leaving Venice behind.

The Darcy coach had been sent round to Italy by sea and it was waiting for them outside the city. It was a welcome sight, with its sleek black exterior, its shining carriage lamps, and its four matched carriage horses. As soon as she saw the horses, Elizabeth realised how much she had missed them. Horses were a large part of her everyday life in Hertfordshire, even though she herself did not choose to ride. They were used to pull the plough on the home farms, her friends and neighbours rode them as they went about their daily business or used them to pull their carriages, and the officers proudly showed off their animals' paces. In Venice she had not seen a single one and she had missed the smell of them, the sight of them and the sound of them, both their familiar snorting and the comforting clop of their hooves.

The boxes were soon loaded and Darcy handed Elizabeth inside. She took her place on the forward-facing seat with pleasure, inhaling the welcoming smell of leather and seeing all the familiar details, from the silk of the window blinds to the loops of the hanging straps, with the delight of someone meeting old friends.

The coachman clicked to the horses and the coach began to move. Behind it, the coach containing Darcy's valet, Annie, and many more boxes also began to roll forward as the whole entourage headed south. The weather gradually improved, becoming warmer, and the view from the window was of a softer, rolling countryside. After the constant sight of buildings and squares and streets and canals, how welcome it was to Elizabeth! The olive groves and citrus trees, some with a few last fruits on their branches, were a reminder of a slower pace of life, and the views were of space and distance. No longer was the horizon a few feet from her face, but miles and miles away across acres of rolling hillsides, fields, and valleys.

'You have been to Rome before, I suppose?' asked Elizabeth.

Her spirits had risen since leaving Venice and Darcy seemed in a happier mood, too.

'Yes, I have.'

'Is there anywhere you have not been?' she teased him.

'China!' he said, and then added, 'yet.'

'Perhaps we will go there one day,' she said.

'Would you like to go?'

'I think, for the moment, I am content to remain in Europe. It has enough new sights to satisfy me, sometimes too many! I am glad to be in the country again.'

'Would you like to ride?' he asked.

Elizabeth's mare had made the sea voyage with the Darcy coach and was now trotting along behind them, together with Darcy's own mount.

'Yes, I think I would.'

Darcy knocked on the roof of the carriage and it began to slow, pulling up before it had gone much further.

'I should have worn my habit,' said Elizabeth as he handed her out.

'There is no one to see you here, only me, and I cannot fault your appearance,' he said with a smile.

Her mare's reins were untethered from the back of the coach, as were the reins of Darcy's horse, and he helped her to mount before mounting himself. The coach set off again and they rode beside it, keeping to the highway when it was bordered by walls but riding over the fields when they could, enjoying the freshness of the wind as it blew past their faces.

They rode intermittently as they travelled south, returning to the carriage when Elizabeth was tired or when showers made it unenjoyable, until at last they neared Rome. They passed by a pine forest that filled the air with a clean, sweet scent and beyond it they could see the Mediterranean Sea. The water was a deep and vibrant blue, changing shade where the water grew deeper, and stretching into the distance, where it met the horizon in a barely perceptible line of differing shades of azure.

The coachman had been given directions to the villa but even so he had to stop a number of times and ask the way.

The Prince had called it a villa, and Elizabeth had no idea what to expect, whether it would be a small gentleman's residence or a vast estate, but at last they saw it in the distance. The villa was three storeys high, but it gave the impression of being a low building because it was so vast. It was symmetrical, with tall arched windows and balconies adorning the façade. As she and Darcy turned into the gates, they found themselves travelling through formal gardens. On either side of the impressive driveway there were flowerbeds laid out in rectangles and squares. The flowerbeds were edged with low hedging and filled with flowers which bloomed as profusely as if it were August and not November. The whole was a riot of colour: pink and red and orange, backed with splashes of green.

The flowerbeds were divided by gravel walkways which were raked to a smooth surface. Where the paths crossed, fountains played. They were adorned with statues of mythical figures, mermaids and griffins and satyrs, which threw water into the air. The statues' faces were turned towards the spray, and they seemed to watch it as it hung at its exuberant apex for a moment before descending as a shower of brilliant diamonds, winking and sparkling in the sunlight.

'I never knew anything like this existed,' said Elizabeth, as she let down the window in order to get a better view. 'Last November I was looking at the rain in Hertfordshire and now here I am, in the midst of all this beauty, at the same time of year.'

Darcy smiled with the whole of him. His joy in her pleasure was tangible, filling the carriage with energy, like the after effects of a thunder storm.

And indeed, Elizabeth felt as though she had weathered a storm. The dark dreams were behind her and a few weeks of light-hearted pleasure in the villa were just what she needed.

The carriage wheels crunched over the gravel drive and they drew nearer and nearer to the villa with every turn of the wheels. When Elizabeth could tear her eyes away from the gardens she turned her attention to the villa itself. Its entranceway was on the first floor, and it was approached by two flights of steps, one leading up from the east and one leading up from the west and then meeting on a terrace in the middle.

The carriage came to a halt and liveried footmen flooded down the steps to form a living avenue of purple and gold, through which came the Prince. He was dressed in cloth of gold and looked at home amongst all the splendours of his home, but he welcomed them warmly, without ostentation, and led them up the east flight of steps to the front door.

As they reached the terrace, Elizabeth saw that its roof was supported by marble columns, around which sculpted sirens were entwined. Elizabeth was reminded of her first visit to Rosings with its many splendours, though Rosings paled beside the villa, and she wondered what Mr Collins would make of it. She imagined him walking in front of her and telling her about the weight of the columns, the size of the sculptures, the number of windows, and reciting an account of what the glazing had originally cost.

'Something has amused you?' asked the Prince.

'Not really—well, yes. I have a friend whose husband is impressed by large houses. I was just imagining his reaction to the villa.'

'Ah! Yes, we have such people in Italy. You, yourself, are not impressed.'

'On the contrary, I am,' said Elizabeth, looking around

her as they entered the hall and admiring the frescoes, the marble statues, and the paintings. 'It's a truly remarkable home and very beautiful.'

'But you do not admire it as vocally as your friend. Nor, I think, as obsequiously?'

There was humour in his voice.

'No,' she admitted, thinking, *That would be impossible!*

'Besides, you have a beautiful home of your own. I hear that Pemberley is very fine.'

'Yes, it is,' said Elizabeth, with a glance at Darcy. 'And full of memories.'

'Already? But how can that be? I understood that this was your wedding tour? But ah! You visited it before your wedding, of course.'

'Elizabeth came there with her aunt and uncle,' said Darcy. 'Not very often, but they are days that neither of us will ever forget.'

Elizabeth smiled at him and they shared a private moment as they remembered the occasion when she had unexpectedly met him again. It had been a moment full of awkwardness and embarrassment but nonetheless exquisite for all that—full of apprehension and yet full of hope, too.

'I pray you will treat the villa as your home,' said the Prince. 'There is a fine library and a music room, and I beg you will use them at any time. You will find a great deal of company in the villa, for I have many guests, and I hope you will find them amusing and entertaining. You will meet some of your countrymen here, as well as people from all over Europe and beyond.'

Having made them thoroughly welcome he left them to the housekeeper, who inclined her head respectfully and then showed them to their apartment. The rooms were elegant and fresh, with marble-topped furniture everywhere and huge ornate mirrors on every wall. Elizabeth saw that her dress had become disordered and she repaired the damage before going downstairs.

She found the other guests, as well as Darcy and the Prince, in the garden. The heat of the day had gone and there was a cooling breeze which made walking out of doors a delight.

Elizabeth soon felt at home. The Prince gave her a glass of wine, which he took from the tray of one of the footmen who wandered the grounds with refreshments, and introduced her to a dozen English guests, several of whom knew Hertfordshire. To her surprise, one of them, Sir Edward Bartholomew, knew Sir William Lucas, as they had been knighted at the same time.

'I remember it well,' he said. 'These very knees have knelt before the King, and these very shoulders have felt the touch of his sword as he dubbed me Sir Edward Bartholomew. I have never known a prouder moment than when he invested me with my insignia. I was nothing but a humble shopkeeper until my knighthood, Mrs Darcy, I never thought I would rise to such heights.'

'But we all thought it,' said his wife loyally. Turning to Elizabeth, she said, 'Sir Edward has made a great contribution to our neighbourhood and his mayoralty was exemplary. Everyone said so.'

Sir Edward smiled modestly and said that it was nothing, adding, 'Sir William Lucas feels as I do, that it is an honour to serve our country and that we are amply rewarded by this recognition of our services. His family are well, I hope? His wife and his charming daughters?'

'We met them all in London,' Lady Bartholomew explained, 'or at least we met the older children. The others were felt to be too young to understand the honour being bestowed on their father.'

'Yes, they are all well,' said Elizabeth, as she sipped her wine. 'His eldest daughter, Charlotte, is now married. She married a relation of mine, a Mr Collins, who is a clergyman in Kent.'

Lady Bartholomew looked surprised, but quickly hid her astonishment and said, 'I am very pleased to hear it. She was a most sensible and agreeable young woman. She is not settled too far from home, I hope?'

'My husband thinks it is an easy distance, but I think not, for it is nearly fifty miles,' said Elizabeth.

'Little more than half a day's journey on good roads,' said Darcy.

'Ah, good roads, how I long for some!' said another Englishwoman, Mrs Prestin. 'We seem to have been jolted this way and that ever since leaving England.'

The other guests joined in the conversation, the French and Italians declaring that travelling was far easier in their own countries than anywhere else, and one, a Monsieur Repar, claiming humorously that he had been overset three times in his carriage when visiting England.

'It is good to hear you laughing,' said the Prince, coming up beside Elizabeth. 'I knew you would love my home. I am honoured to have you here, and your husband, too. I like very much the English, and any friend of Colonel Fitzwilliam is always welcome here.'

In the warm, balmy air, Elizabeth felt her spirits revive. She and Darcy were able to take advantage of a lull in the conversation to drift away from the different groups and walk by themselves through the gardens, where the whiteness of the gravel paths contrasted with the scarlet flowers and the sea's clear blue.

'Happy?' asked Darcy.

'Yes, very,' said Lizzy, taking his arm.

'I thought, when we were in Venice, that you might want to go home.'

'Perhaps I did, but I feel differently now. I don't suppose we will ever come so far again so let us make the most of it whilst we are here.'

As one of the footmen walked past she attempted to put her glass, now empty, on his tray, but he turned away at the last moment and the glass fell to the ground where it broke into pieces.

Elizabeth gave an exclamation of annoyance and bent down to pick up the glass before one of the other guests should tread on it, but Darcy, bending down beside her with preternatural speed, said urgently, 'Don't!'

He caught her hand and jerked it back, but the action pulled her fingers over the jagged edge and a spurt of blood gushed from the wound in a fountain of brilliant scarlet. She felt a terrible energy in him, and he began to tremble.

'Go inside at once!' he said, standing up and backing away from her. 'Have your maid bind your wound. Now!'

'It's nothing,' she said, perplexed, as she stood up. 'Only give me your handkerchief, that is all I need.'

'Come,' said Lady Bartholomew, who had seen the accident and who had approached to help. 'Your husband is right. In this hot climate any wound, no matter how small, can soon go bad.' In a lower voice she said to Elizabeth, 'It often happens this way, many gentleman cannot stand the sight of blood. They are often very squeamish. Humour your husband in this. He will not want to appear weak in front of the other guests.'

Elizabeth allowed Lady Bartholomew to lead her away, but as she went into the villa she felt a sense of alarm and profound unease, for the look on Darcy's face had not been squeamish. It had been ravenous.

Chapter 11

My dearest Jane,

We are now in the south of Italy, near Rome, and the weather is so warm that today I did not even need to wear my shawl when I went outside. You, I suppose, are wrapped up in your pelisse and cloak! The days here are long and move at a leisurely pace. There are impromptu balls almost every evening, and if we are not dancing, then we are playing at cards or backgammon, and if not that, then we play the piano and sing. In the daytime we walk in the gardens. I am just about to go outside and play at croquet. I am becoming quite a proficient!

My dear Darcy remains an enigma. Sometimes when he looks at me I feel a sense of expectation, but sometimes I am filled with an unaccountable unease. I am longing to talk to you again, and yet I am not longing to return home. I have not yet had my fill of Italy. And so, for the moment, adieu.

The game of croquet was about to begin when Elizabeth joined the rest of her party on the lawns behind the villa. Sir Edward and Lady Bartholomew were there, as well as Monsieur Repar, Mrs Prestin, and Darcy. Darcy looked up as she joined them, and there was something hungry in his look.

'There you are, Mrs Darcy! You are just in time to start us off,' said Sir Edward jovially.

Elizabeth took her shot, knocking the ball cleanly through the hoop, and she was then succeeded by Lady Bartholomew and Mrs Prestin. The gentlemen praised their efforts then took their own turns. There was a friendly rivalry between Sir Edward and Monsieur Repar, and Monsieur Repar smiled broadly when Sir Edward struck the ball poorly, only to be repaid when his own shot went wide and Sir Edward laughed in a friendly fashion.

Darcy played well, but it was Lady Bartholomew who excelled. Every shot she made was clean and the ball went wherever it was meant to go, not too far but just far enough. It sailed through hoops and rolled smoothly across the grass.

She was just about to take her final shot, which would win her the game, when clouds appeared suddenly in the sky and a storm blew up from nowhere. The light dimmed and turned purple, changing the single cloud from a bright puff of gossamer into a dark and swollen mass that throbbed like a livid bruise.

'Poor fellow, he isn't seeing the place at its best,' said Sir Edward as a coach rolled up the drive and disgorged a new visitor. 'He can hardly see it in this light.'

Lady Bartholomew took her last shot and won the game just in time as a strong wind whipped the ladies' dresses round their ankles and the rain suddenly threw itself from the sky. They all ran inside, being soaked by the time they reached the sanctuary of the hall. The group dispersed, the gentlemen arranging to meet again once dry and play a game of billiards whilst the ladies announced their intention of writing letters or otherwise occupying themselves in their own rooms.

Elizabeth, once she had changed out of her wet clothes, retired to the library, where she hoped she might find something in English she could read in order to pass the time before dinner. The library was an impressive room, and one she had discovered soon after arriving at the villa. It was very large, with high ceilings, and it was lined with books. But today, despite the tall windows, she found it hard to see, for outside it was almost as dark as night, almost dark enough for her to need a candle. Thinking she would rather not light a candle so early in the day, no matter how dark it was, she persevered without one.

The books were bound in leather with the most exquisite tooling on the covers. Gold lettering spelled out the titles and the authors' names, which were written in flourishing scripts. She thought of the library at Longbourn, with its well-worn books, and she thought how much her father would love the Prince's collection.

As she wandered round the room she tilted her head to one side, the better to read the titles, although most of them were in Italian and barely comprehensible to her. But here and there she recognised a few English books: *Tom Jones*, *Robinson Crusoe*, Shakespeare's plays.

She found herself curiously drawn to one corner, where the books were more densely packed than elsewhere, and one book in particular seemed to call to her.

She took it out and looked at it. It was bound in old, deep red leather and it was ornamented with script in gold lettering, which had been handled so often that it was beginning to flake. She could still see the title, however, *Civitates Orbis Terrarum*.

Opening the book, she saw that it had been published in 1572 in Cologne and that it was a book of engravings. It contained maps and prospects and birds' eye views of various cities around the world. There were people in the engravings too, dressed in sixteenth century costume, the women wearing long dresses which flowed into trains behind them and the men wearing short cloaks.

It was fascinating to see views of various cities in times gone by, and as she turned the pages she found herself looking at images of places she recognised. She knew at once when she had arrived at engravings of Venice. There was a view of San Marco and the *Palazzo Ducale*, and—she felt a creeping fear crawl over her—the *Palazzo Ducale* was on fire. She had seen it before, that fire, in her dream. It had frightened her, and it frightened her again, so badly that she tried to thrust the book away from her, but somehow the book seemed to be stuck to her fingers and she felt compelled to look at the image.

I must have seen it before, she thought. *I must have seen this engraving somewhere and that is why I saw it in my dream. It must have been a memory.*

But she knew she had not seen the book before, and that, even if she had, it could not be the source of the image in her dream: the view in the *Civitates* was looking at the burning palace from the direction of the canal, but in her dream she had seen it from the other direction.

I didn't dream it, she thought, with a terrifying realisation. *I was in the past. I was there.*

She dropped the book, letting it fall from numb fingers. Despite its great antiquity and obvious value, she felt only the vaguest sense of relief when it was caught by other hands which stopped it plummeting to the floor, for one of the Prince's guests had entered the room and had saved it from its fall.

'My dear young lady,' he said in concern, 'you are as white as a ghost. Are you unwell?'

She turned towards him and had difficulty in making out his face. It seemed ageless: unlined and yet old, sympathetic and yet devilish. It floated before her in silent mockery, completely at odds with his words and behaviour, and she felt very strange.

'Here,' he said, offering her his arm.

She did not respond, only looking at him, and he pulled her hand through his arm himself, saying, 'Let me escort you to a seat.'

As he touched her, she felt her will altering, flowing, and merging with his. She moved with him to one of the window seats. She was ensorcelled by him. Her body was light and ethereal and her thoughts were unclear, as though her mind was filled with mist.

She was aware of a peculiar sensation as the room around her began to alter, distorting and changing like a wet portrait in the rain. The green wallpaper began to melt and run down the walls and a deep ochre ran down in great rivulets behind it and took its place. The curtains too began to change, their dark green velvet dropping away to be washed over with rivers of gold silk. Pictures were appearing and mirrors disappearing; beneath them the console tables were altering, their legs narrowing and their tops flowing with marble; the vases of flowers were being replaced with porcelain and ormolu clocks. The carpet was giving way to polished floorboards and the sound of unearthly laughter filled the air. He seized her in his arms and waltzed with her around the room, whispering to her in some unintelligible language.

'I am not well,' said Elizabeth, her heart beating strangely and her mind trying to hold on to reality.

'No?' he asked. 'I think you are very well.'

Strange faces peered at her as the room was suddenly full of people, laughing and chattering and looking at her through their masks.

She put her hand to her head, feeling it throb, and then, through the mist, she heard something familiar. It was Darcy's voice.

The gentleman was saying to him, 'It is nothing, never fear, the lady is feeling unwell that is all, but I am caring for her. Please do not let us detain you.'

'No,' she wanted to say. 'I don't want you to care for me, I want to be with my husband.'

But nothing came out.

She turned beseeching eyes to Darcy and she saw him as if from a great distance, through a distorting glass, but his words were firm and clear.

'She has no taste for your company,' he said.

'No?' said the gentleman. 'But I have a taste for her.'

Hers, thought Elizabeth. He should have said *hers*.

'Let her go,' said Darcy warningly.

'Why should I?' asked the gentleman.

'Because she is mine,' said Darcy.

The gentleman turned his full attention towards Darcy and Elizabeth followed his eyes.

And then she saw something that made her heart thump against her rib cage and her mind collapse as she witnessed something so shocking and so terrifying that the ground came up to meet her as everything went black.

∽∞∾

When she came to, she was in her bed and her maid was sponging her brow with cool, scented water.

'What happened? Where am I?' asked Elizabeth, looking round the room and finding it unfamiliar.

'You're safe, Ma'am. You're in your own room in the Prince's villa. You fainted, that's all,' said Annie.

'But I never faint,' said Elizabeth, struggling to sit up.

'Lie back,' said Annie, putting gentle pressure on her shoulder.

Elizabeth, seeing the room beginning to spin, had no choice but to comply. As she lay back, she realised that she was still in her gown but that her stays had been loosened so that they did not constrict her breathing. She tried to recall exactly what had happened. She had been playing croquet, there had been a storm, she had gone into the library, and then... she could remember no more.

'It was the weather,' said Annie. 'When the clouds blew up it turned sultry. It's a wonder more people haven't fainted.'

'Yes, I suppose so,' said Elizabeth. 'Only I'm sure there was something...'

She struggled to catch the elusive memory, but it had gone.

She waited until she felt her strength returning and then she tried to sit up again, this time with more success. Although the room had stopped spinning, she still found it hard to catch her breath and a glance out of the window showed her why. The sky was black and low, trapping the heat like a blanket. The landscape looked strange beneath the dark sky, the colours transformed and the light unnatural.

Annie was still mopping her forehead, but the water, cool to begin with, was now unpleasantly warm, and Elizabeth pushed her hand irritably away.

'I'll fetch some fresh water,' said Annie.

As the door closed behind her, Elizabeth sat up and

swung her legs over the edge of the bed. After sitting thus for a few minutes and discovering that she no longer felt faint she got up and walked about the room. She was restless, unable to settle to anything, and when the door opened she was about to send Annie away when she saw that it was not Annie standing there, it was Darcy, with a look of torment on his face.

She held out her hand to him, hoping for the comfort and reassurance of his touch, but he did not respond to her gesture and he made no move to enter the room. Instead he stood by the door, watching her.

'You don't remember, do you?' he asked.

'Remember what?' she said, ceasing her restless pacing.

'You don't remember what happened.'

'No,' she said, 'but Annie told me. I fainted. It was the heat, she said.'

'The heat.'

His voice sounded strange and Elizabeth felt a long way away from him, although they were separated by no more than ten or twelve feet. All the difficult and disturbing incidents of the past few weeks, together with the distance from home and her estrangement from Darcy—for she could no longer pretend that they were not estranged—together with the agitation and tears which these things occasioned, threatened to overset her again. She dropped her hand and sank down on the edge of the bed.

She had told herself it was only a matter of time before things were well between them. She had made excuses and invented countless reasons for his absence from her room, but she could deceive herself no longer. He simply did not want her. He had mistaken his feelings and now they must face the consequences.

'Are you still feeling unwell?' he asked, looking at her with concern.

'Yes.'

'Elizabeth, it was an unpleasant morning, but—'

'It is nothing to do with the morning,' she said. 'It is us. We should never have married.'

He looked stunned.

'I have been trying to pretend to myself that it was just the newness of our life together, or that you were being considerate, or that it would not be long before you came to me, but I cannot go on pretending. I know now we should never have married. I will not stay here to embarrass you and distress myself.' She thought of Longbourn and a wave of homesickness washed over her. She wanted to be amongst familiar sights and familiar people. 'As soon as I feel well enough, I will pack my bags and go back to England.'

'No! You cannot go! I forbid it!' he said, striding into the room but then hesitating and stopping before he reached her, with lines of pain etched clearly across his face.

'There is nothing else to be done,' she said. 'This is not a marriage. I am not your wife.'

His complexion became pale and she saw some great emotion wash over him as he struggled for composure, but composure would not come and at last he said in agitation, 'I can't come to you. There are things about me you don't know...'

'Then tell me!' she cried, jumping up. 'That is what men and women do when they are in love. They talk to each other. They share their thoughts and feelings. They share their problems. They share their secrets, they share everything.' She stopped and sighed, making an effort to master her overwhelming emotion, and then she continued in a calmer manner. 'Will you not tell me what is worrying you? We are married, Darcy. We took an oath to love each other for better, for worse, for richer, for poorer, in sickness, and in health. Those words mean something. They mean that we stand together in times of trial and we share our burdens as well as our joys. There is nothing so terrible that we cannot face it if we do so together.'

His face was ashen.

'I can't share this with you,' he said.

'Why not? Don't you trust me?' she asked.

'It's not that—'

'Then what is it?' she cried.

He shook his head as though he were being goaded beyond endurance and said, 'It is for your own good.'

'How can it be for my own good?' she cried in astonishment. 'Whatever your secret, it cannot be more terrible than the pain I am feeling at this moment.'

He started, but then he let out a cry and he said, 'If I tell you, then there will no going back. Once you have the knowledge you will never be rid of it, and if you decide you were happier without it, it will be too late.'

'Then if you won't tell me, there is no hope for us,' she said with a droop of her shoulders.

'Don't say that.'

'What else is there to be said?'

She saw his expression change slightly and she thought that he was weakening. She held out her hand to him and he moved as if he was going to take it. His fingers reached out to her but then he drew them back.

'No! I can't. But I can't go on like this either,' he said in agony. 'I have to think.'

He sprang towards the door.

She had a sudden and terrible fear that if she let him leave the room she would never see him again.

'Darcy!' she called, but it was too late, for he had already gone.

CHAPTER 12

A NNIE SOON RETURNED WITH a bowl of fresh water and sponged Elizabeth's brow. Elizabeth felt nothing except the emptiness of her own heart. When Annie had finished sponging her brow, Elizabeth got up and went over to her writing desk and finished her letter to Jane.

I can conceal from you no longer the true state of affairs, for I can no longer conceal them from myself. My husband does not love me. I have fought against it but I can deny it no longer. I never thought, when I married my beloved Darcy, that I would return home a few months after my wedding, alone, but I can see no other choice. I cannot live with him and be with him when he constantly rejects me. I don't know what I will tell Papa, and with Mama it will be even worse. I believe that being the mistress of Pemberley is my only claim to her affection, and without it, I fear she will not welcome me home. I dread her constant admonishments, but with you, dear Jane, I know there will be solace. I shall visit you at Netherfield everyday. Or, at least, not everyday, I shall give you and Bingley some time alone. How wonderful it must be to be loved by your husband! Write to me, Jane, I have not had a letter since leaving England, and although it might not find me as I travel home, what bliss if it does. To hear the sound of your voice, even in a letter, will be a comfort to me. And I need comfort, I fear. How

am I to live without him? And will I even be allowed to try?
It is scandalous for a married woman to leave her husband, and
yet to live with him is beyond my strength. I am in need of love
and comfort and sound advice and I am longing to be at home,
where you and my Aunt Gardiner will help me.

Your loving sister,
Elizabeth

When she had finished the letter, she handed it to Annie, saying, 'Give it to one of the footmen at once, I want to make sure it goes to the post today.'

'Very good,' said Annie.

Elizabeth looked out of the window and saw that the weather had improved. The sky had lightened and the storm had blown over. From the window came a fresh breeze, luring her out of doors. There was a collection of people by the door, laughing and talking, but further along the house, by the French window leading out of the morning room, there was no one. Being disinclined for company, she decided to make her way out of the villa through this route.

As she entered the morning room its opulence both attracted and repelled her. The gilded mirrors, marble-topped tables, and damasked chairs were beautiful but soulless. They were perfect, with no signs of age or wear, unlike the furniture at Longbourn which was scuffed and worn with years of family living. There was something unnatural about the villa, as though it had been artificially preserved, caught in time and unable to age. It was like a museum, not a living, breathing home.

There was a soft footfall behind her and Elizabeth's heart leapt, but it was only the Prince. His closeness startled her, for she had not known he was there. Even though she was standing by a mirror, which gave her a clear view of the door, she had not seen his reflection.

She turned round to see him bowing before her. Although he was handsome and courteous and dressed in the finest clothes, she had a longing for friends and family, people she had known all her life, for what did she know of the Prince, after all?

'You have not been well, I hear?' he said in concern. 'I am sorry for it. So much beauty should never be distressed. You have everything you need, I hope?'

'Yes, thank you, I have.'

'And you are feeling better?' He looked at her searchingly. 'Forgive me, but you still seem very pale.'

'I am much better, thank you.'

'It is this heat; it is beautiful, certainly, but it is overpowering sometimes. There is a cool breeze in the garden. I think it will do you good. Will you walk with me there? We will not go in the sunshine but will walk along the shady paths and rest, if you will, in the summer house.'

She was still feeling somewhat unsteady on her legs and she thought she might have need of his arm, and so she said, 'Yes. Thank you.'

They went through the French doors and into the garden. They were soon walking down an avenue at the back of the house where the shadow of the tall trees made the way pleasant, and the breeze was as refreshing as she had hoped it would be. The Prince seemed to sense her mood for he was not demanding company. He talked to her gently of the vistas, stopping here and there to show her some delightful view, but he did not expect her to answer him and she felt herself begin to relax.

Halfway down the avenue, they came to a fountain and Elizabeth, feeling in need of a rest, sat on its brim.

He sat beside her and then, taking her hand, looked at her kindly.

'There is something that makes you unhappy, I think,' he said. 'No, do not trouble to say it is not so, I can see it. In English society it is not always polite to discuss affairs of the heart but here, in Italy we think differently. You have no one to confide in here, but I am an experienced gentleman and you are a young lady a long way from home, and as your host, and your friend, too, I hope you will confide in me.' His voice was soft and soothing, and it was balm to her troubled spirit. 'It is Darcy, is it not?' he asked.

'Yes,' she admitted reluctantly, and then she could hold the words back no longer and they came out in a torrent, pouring out of her like long pent-up waters breaking through a dam. 'I don't know what's happened to him—to us. I thought we were in love... we *were* in love... When we were newly engaged, it was settled between us that we were to be the happiest couple in the world!' she said, smiling suddenly at the remembrance. Then her smile faded. 'But once we were married, everything changed.'

'When did you notice it, this change in him?' asked the Prince gently.

'It's difficult to say,' she said, trailing her hand in the fountain and letting the cool water slip through her fingers. 'Although no, perhaps not. It started on our wedding day. It was just after the ceremony. We were returning home from the church when I caught sight of his face in the carriage window and I saw that he looked tormented. I thought I must have been imagining it at the time and so I dismissed it, but now I think differently. I am sure that was when it began.

I wondered if he had read something that troubled him but now I think that was not the case.'

'Ah.' He paused, thinking. 'It was love at first sight, your affair?' he asked.

'No, far from it,' she said. 'In fact, when we first met each other we took an instant dislike to each other.'

'No one could dislike you, I think,' said the Prince.

'Well, perhaps he did not dislike me, for it is true that at that point, he did not know me and so he could scarcely have any opinion regarding me, or at least regarding my character, but he thought me not handsome enough to dance with: "only tolerable",' said Lizzy, with a laugh, and then her laughter faded as she thought that, perhaps, he had returned to his first opinion.

'And you were intrigued by this, yes? And challenged by it. So you tried to win his favour. I see how it must have happened. He is a rich and powerful man and you did not like to be dismissed by him, so you set out to charm him and win his favour.'

'Quite the opposite,' said Elizabeth. 'I had no interest in him, and I certainly had no interest in charming him. What was he to me?'

'A man with a large estate and a handsome income, and you ask, "What was he to me?"' he said in surprise.

'He was not my friend or my neighbour, and as for having a large estate and a handsome income, what of it?' said Elizabeth. 'How can it matter, when set beside rudeness and arrogance and disdain for the feeling of others?'

'And did you tell him that he was rude and arrogant and disdainful?' asked the Prince.

'Yes, I did,' admitted Elizabeth with a rueful smile.

'I see,' he said, becoming thoughtful.

Elizabeth turned enquiring eyes towards him.

'What do you see?' she asked.

'I see how it happened,' he said, looking at her with sympathy. 'With some men it is so. They do not want the easy conquest; they want the challenge. That challenge is hard to find for a man like Darcy. Women seek him out. They flatter him and praise him, they throw themselves in his path. I see you smile. You have seen it, no?'

'Yes,' said Elizabeth. 'I have. There was a woman in England, the sister of his best friend; she was always trying to attract his attention and win his approbation, and in Paris there were women like that too.'

'But you were different. You were not charmed by his name or his fortune, you demanded something more from him, some proof of his worth as a man. His interest, it was aroused. There are men like this. Once their interest is caught they will pursue a woman with passion and dedication, they will do anything to win her, they will make friends with her friends, they will make friends with her family, they will offer them help—ah! You start!'

'He helped my sister,' said Elizabeth. 'And he made friends with my aunt and uncle, even though at first he had dismissed them as being beneath his notice.'

'So will a determined man proceed. He will stop at nothing to win the object of his interest. But once he has her, then what will you?' he asked with a shrug. 'It is the chase that matters. They are hunters, these men, predators. To claim a woman, it challenges them, and to succeed in their quest, it brings them to life. But once they have gained their object, once they have caught their prey, then their interest, it wanes, until it is no more.'

Elizabeth took her hand out of the fountain and rested it on the warm stone of the rim.

'And is that what you think has happened to Darcy?'

'I can think of no other reason for him to neglect you.'

'He says there is a reason, but that he cannot tell me what it is.'

'Ah,' said the Prince.

That one word spoke volumes.

'You think that, if he had a reason, he would tell me,' she said.

'I think nothing.'

'Perhaps not. But I do.'

He looked at her with compassion.

'You are very young,' he said. 'You are a novice in these matters. He has wounded an innocent and that was very wrong of him.'

'He didn't mean to hurt me.'

'No?' He sounded disbelieving, but then said, 'Perhaps it is as you say. But you have been hurt all the same and if you stay with him, you will be hurt again and again. Will you listen to some advice?'

'Perhaps,' she said cautiously.

'Then I advise you to go away from here, right away. You are not alone; you have friends and a family who care about you. Go to them. Go back to England. Tell Darcy you have made a mistake. If he knows you are truly unhappy with him, he will let you go. You will live again and love again—'

'No!'

'Ah,' he said delicately. 'Well, perhaps not. But perhaps—who knows? You are very young and time, it is a great healer. But whatever the future holds, one thing is certain: there is nothing for you here, only unhappiness, rejection. and loss.'

'I know,' she admitted.

It was the same conclusion she had come to herself no more than an hour before, and with the Prince's advice leading in the same direction, she had nothing to lift her out of her low thoughts.

'It is difficult, I know, but it is for the best,' he said. 'Once the break is made, you can start to live again.'

She thought how pleasant it would be to sit by the fountain forever. The thought of moving even a step, let alone going into the villa and giving the orders for packing, as well as dealing with the hundred and one arrangements that would be attendant on her return to England, was wearisome. But she knew it must be done. Making an effort, she stood up. She shook her hand, sending droplets of water sparkling through the air, and as she moved her hand to and fro her wedding ring caught the light. It had been a symbol of all her hopes and dreams, but now it seemed to mock her, and yet she could not bring herself to take it off.

The sound of footsteps crunching on gravel aroused her from her reverie and looking up she saw that Annie was hurrying towards her.

'Ma'am—' Annie began breathlessly.

'What is it?' asked Elizabeth.

'Yes, why do you disturb your mistress?' asked the Prince, standing also and resting a hand protectively on Elizabeth's shoulder. 'Is it a matter of urgency?'

Annie looked awkward and she said, 'No, not really.'

'Then do not disturb your mistress now,' said the Prince.

Annie hesitated then bobbed a curtsey and turned back to the villa, but then she turned again to Elizabeth and said, 'I just came to tell you that I've finished hemming the new handkerchiefs as you asked, Ma'am, and I've put them in your valise.'

'Thank you,' said Elizabeth absentmindedly.

The Prince waved Annie away with an imperious gesture and Annie departed, but Elizabeth still lingered.

'Do it now,' said the Prince. 'You will not have the strength if you wait, and there can be nothing for you here, only pain. Do it whilst your husband is not here. He has taken his horse and gone riding. Write him a note and I will see that he gets it. My coach is at your disposal. I will have word sent ahead to the inns along your route so that they will be expecting you, and I will send a courier with you to guard you on your journey and to make all the necessary arrangements for you as you travel.'

'You are very kind.'

'It is nothing,' he said. 'I could do no less for beauty in distress. Take heart, you will recover. You think not, but a few weeks in the warmth of your family will do much to ease your pain.'

'Yes,' she said, 'my family.'

She thought of Jane and her Aunt Gardiner and she longed to be at home.

'You need only to see that your things are packed and you may leave the rest to me,' he said.

The Prince offered her his arm and he escorted her back to the villa, talking to her gently of inconsequential matters until they reached the door.

Once in her room she rang for Annie, then sat down to write her note to Darcy. The words would not come, but at last she managed to say what needed to be said.

My dear Darcy,

I cannot stay here any longer. I am not making you happy and the gulf between us has destroyed all my peace and happiness. I am going home to Longbourn. The Prince has kindly given me the use of his carriage and he is sending a courier with me to smooth my journey. I hope you find what you are looking for. I can see now that it isn't me.

Elizabeth

She rang the bell again for Annie, but when her maid didn't come she went downstairs herself in search of the Prince. She found him in the music room with his other guests. She thought how strange it was that they could continue with the house party as if nothing had happened. Sir Edward and Lady Bartholomew, so plump and happy, Monsieur Repar and Mrs Prestin, and all the other guests. For them it was a day like any other.

As soon as the Prince saw her he slipped away, leaving his guests singing and talking together, and joined her by the door. He took the note from her, promising to make sure that Darcy received it, and told her that the carriage was ready for her.

'I will send one of the footmen upstairs to carry your boxes,' he said.

'They are not yet packed,' said Elizabeth, adding with a glimmer of humour, 'I seem to have mislaid my maid.'

'Ah! See, a burden it has been lifted from you, it is always the way. A decision, once made, no matter how difficult, frees the shoulders from the weight of indecision, and that is a heavy weight indeed. Already you are happier, your humour returns. It is good to see you smile, even if only for a moment,' he said genially. 'But now, we must find your maid.'

He beckoned to one of the footmen and told the man to go to the servants' hall and look for Mrs Darcy's maid.

The footman looked uncomfortable.

'Well?' demanded the Prince. 'What is it?'

The footman said something in Italian and although Elizabeth did not understand every word, she was able to make out that he had just been to the servants' hall and that Annie had not been there. He looked as though he could say more but did not know if it would be welcome.

'Say everything,' commanded the Prince.

The footman said, haltingly, that Annie was a friend of one of the gardeners, and that it was the gardener's afternoon off, and that the footman had seen them heading for the forest.

'Ah!' said the Prince, with a wry smile. '*Amore!* It is very wrong of her, of course, but what will you? No matter.' He turned to Elizabeth. 'I will send one of my maids to help you and to accompany you to the nearest inn, and I will send Signorina Annie to you when she returns.' He said to the footman, 'See to it.' The footman bowed and withdrew, and the Prince continued to Elizabeth, 'I am sorry you have had this inconvenience.'

Elizabeth said, 'It doesn't matter. At least someone's love is prospering. I am only sorry that I am taking her away.'

'But you will return,' said the Prince. 'You are welcome here at any time, you know that, I hope, and you must bring your charming family with you the next time you come to Italy. They will all be very welcome here. Your mother will like it, do you think?'

'I am sure she would,' said Elizabeth, smiling again as she thought of her mother exclaiming over the furniture, then trying to persuade every gentleman at the villa that either Kitty or Mary would make him a charming wife.

Whether the Prince would enjoy the visit as much as her mother she very much doubted!

'Then you must visit me again soon, and stay with me for as long as you like,' he said with a bow.

Elizabeth thanked him for his generous invitation and returned to her room, where her spirits once more drooped. To leave this place where she had been happy, for in the first days at the villa she had still hoped that she and Darcy would become one, was a trial to her. Once gone, she would have to admit that hope was dead.

The arrival of one of the Prince's maids at least gave a new turn to her thoughts as she instructed the girl, and very soon Elizabeth's things were packed and a footman arrived to convey them to the carriage. With one last, lingering look around the room, she followed the footman downstairs.

The carriage was waiting for her by the side door. It was an elaborate affair with a florid coat of arms emblazoned on the side. Two footmen flanked it –'For your protection,' said the Prince—both dressed in the Prince's scarlet livery, and the courier stood by its side. He was a handsome young man, charming and respectful, and he took his place next to the coachman on the box, where he was joined by the maid.

'Until we meet again,' said the Prince, bowing over Elizabeth's hand.

'Thank you for your hospitality,' she said, 'and thank you for your kindness and your advice.'

'It is nothing,' he said. 'Take courage, you will soon be with your family and then your happiness, it will recover.'

He handed her inside and she arranged her skirts around her on the sumptuous silk-upholstered seat.

The footmen took their places, standing on the runners on each side of the carriage, then the coachman called to the horses and they began to move, the heavy carriage going slowly forward until it began to pick up pace and bowl down the drive.

The fountains, which had been singing on her arrival, now seemed to be weeping, and Elizabeth was weeping too. Tear after hot tear, held back until now by pride, came freely, and in the solitude of the carriage, she gave way to her emotions.

'This will not do,' she told herself after a while.

She sought out her valise, in which Annie had stowed her newly hemmed handkerchiefs, and found it under the seat. She pulled it out and opened it—and then her heart stopped beating, for there, on the top of her clothes, was a bundle of letters, all in her own hand, and addressed to her family and friends.

She lifted them up with disbelief.

There must be some mistake, she thought, scarcely able to believe the evidence of her own eyes, and with trembling hands she untied the bundle and tore open the top letter.

My dearest Jane,

You will be surprised when I tell you that we are not going to the Lake District after all, we are going to France…

She picked up another one:

My dearest Jane,

…We are now established in Paris, and it is the most beautiful city…

And another:

My dearest Jane,

I wish you were here. How I long to talk to you. So much has happened that I scarcely know where to begin. We left Paris a few days ago and we are now in the Alps.

All of them, every letter she had written since leaving England, they were all there. Her mind raced. What were they doing there? Who had put them there? Why had they never been sent?

And then she thought of the strange incident when Annie had found her in the gardens and told her that her handkerchiefs had been hemmed. It wasn't urgent news, it could have waited. But then with a creeping feeling running down her spine, she realised that Annie had not sought her out to tell her about the handkerchiefs; she had sought her out to tell her about the letters, but, on finding that Elizabeth was not alone, she had given nothing but a veiled warning instead.

Then if Annie had known about the letters, had she put them there? If so, where had she found them? And who had stopped them being sent?

Elizabeth remembered Annie's strange behaviour when she had first noticed the Prince and she wondered if Annie suspected him of stealing the letters. But a moment's thought showed her that, whatever Annie might or might not have suspected, the Prince could not have been involved because most of the letters had been written before Elizabeth had visited the villa.

But who, then? The only people to touch the letters, apart from herself, were Annie and the footmen who took them to be posted. Annie she could exclude, which left the footmen. But why should any of them do such a thing? They were all loyal to Darcy. They had been in his family's employ for years. Except…

She remembered an incident in Paris when one of the footmen had fallen ill and had been quickly replaced. He had had excellent references but they had not known anything of the man personally. It seemed ridiculous to think that he was involved, but the fact remained that the letters had not been sent. *Could he have been paid to suppress the letters?* she wondered. But, if so, why? And by whom?

It might be possible that Annie knew, but Elizabeth could not ask her because… she shivered… because Annie was missing. What had happened to Annie? Where was she? Was she really in the forest with a lover or had something happened to her?

'Stop the coach!' called Elizabeth, rapping on the floor of the carriage with her parasol to gain the coachman's attention. 'Stop the coach at once!'

But the carriage did not slow its riotous pace.

She wound down the window and called out, 'Stop! I command you, coachman, stop this instant!'

But his only response was to whip the horses and drive them faster. She felt a rising tide of panic as she realised that she was in the Prince's carriage, driven by the Prince's coachman, and surrounded by the Prince's servants.

She looked out of the window and wondered if she could jump out of the carriage, but it was going too fast. It passed farmers on their way to market and she called out to them as they crossed themselves and stood back to let the carriage pass. Their faces were sullen and hostile, but when they heard her cries, their expressions turned to horror or pity. One woman, moved to action, ran forward when the carriage slowed to take a corner, and thrust a necklace of small white flowers through the window. She said something unintelligible, but her gesture was clear: put it around your neck.

Elizabeth, frightened by her look and by the tears in her eyes, did as she said.

As she did so, she smelt the pungent smell and recognised the flowers as wild garlic.

Strange tales began to come back to her, folk tales she had read in the library at Longbourn, stories of strange creatures that preyed on the living and haunted the forests of Europe, half men, half beasts, mesmeric, and seductive, but evil and dangerous, creatures who bit their victims, piercing their skin and drinking their blood; beasts which could be held at bay by garlic.

'No, I will not think of it,' said Elizabeth aloud. 'It is nothing but a story, a myth, a folk tale. There is no such thing as a vampyre.'

But she held on tight to the necklace, crushing the delicate flowers and leaves with the tightness of her grip.

The coach sped on and she saw that it was heading for the forest. A terrible dread seized her and a fear of the looming trees.

There must be something I can do, she thought.

She looked wildly around the carriage and saw that her travelling writing desk had been packed beneath the opposite seat. As quickly as she could she pulled it open and dipping the quill into the ink she began to write.

My dearest Jane,

My hand is trembling as I write this letter. My nerves are in tatters and I am so altered that I believe you would not recognise me. The past few months have been a nightmarish whirl of strange and disturbing circumstances, and the future...

Jane, I am afraid.

If anything happens to me, remember that I love you and that my spirit will always be with you, though we may never see each other again. The world is a cold and frightening place where nothing is as it seems.

It was all so different a few short months ago. When I awoke on my wedding morning, I thought myself the happiest woman alive... but of what use are such thoughts now? I wanted to spare you but I am in terrible danger. I have nowhere to turn and you, my dearest Jane, are the only person I can trust. I am being abducted by Prince Ficenzi's servants and I am writing this letter in desperation because I can think of no other way to help myself. I mean to throw it out of the window when it is finished, for I am at this moment in the Prince's carriage, in the hope that one of the local people will see it. I think they will make sure the letter is sent, for, thank God, I have reason to suppose they will help me if they can.

If this letter reaches you, then please have my father make enquiries about my whereabouts, starting at the Villa Ficenzi near Rome. Tell him he must not be put off, whatever he is told, for the Prince surely knows where I am being taken and he just as surely knows my fate.

When I think of the vast distances that separate us I fear my father will be too late, but he must try and, God willing, my dearest Jane, we may yet see each other again.

There is time for no more, we have almost reached the forest, I must go.

Help me, my dearest!

Elizabeth

She folded the letter and wrote the direction on the outside, then winding down the window she threw the letter out. And not a moment too soon, for the carriage was entering the forest and soon the trees closed about it and there were no more people to be seen. The world became dark and mysterious, with green shadows closing in around the carriage, eerie and malevolent. The sounds were muted and the atmosphere was heavy and thick.

They came at last to a clearing where ferns grew dense and lush, and from above came the faint glimmer of the sky, just enough to show Elizabeth that it was dusk, the nebulous time when worlds collided, night with day, dark with light.

The carriage came to a halt.

Elizabeth, who had been wanting the carriage to stop for miles, was now filled with a terrible sense of dread.

'Drive on!' she called in panic. 'Don't stop! Drive on!'

But the carriage did not move.

Chapter 13

E LIZABETH LOOKED WILDLY ABOUT her and there, in the hazy light in the centre of the clearing, she became aware of a figure, a man, who was standing still and silent. He was dressed in satin, wearing a green coat trimmed with gold lace and green breeches sewn with gold thread. On his head he wore a feathered hat and over his face he was wearing a mask. She had seen that mask before, at the ball in Venice and she had seen it again in her dream. It belonged to the man who had taken control of her and who had propelled her into the past.

She felt a sense of horror overwhelming her. The fear crawled up and down her spine and paralysed her will. She could not move; she could only watch as, with dreadful ceremony, he made her a low bow and then removed his mask.

She knew him now, not the Prince as she had feared, but the Prince's guest. He had been with her in the library when she had found the book of engravings, when the walls had started to melt.

She stared at him with awe-filled dread. He was terrible in his beauty, his face shining with a dreadful radiance. His features were as smooth as if they had been carved from marble, rigid and full of cold perfection.

He lifted a hand and beckoned her and the door opened of its own accord. Like a dreamer she stepped out of the carriage and crossed the forest floor until she reached him. He took her hand and kissed it in a mockery of a courteous greeting.

Strains of unearthly music began to reach her ears and the forest began to dissolve. The trees were replaced by marble columns and the clearing gave way to a ballroom floor. He took her in his arms and whirled her round in a waltz, and then the ballroom dissolved and they were on the streets of Venice, with revellers laughing and running past them amidst torchlight and gondolas and canals. And then the streets of Venice winked out and they were in the forest again, just the two of them, with the carriage and the servants vanished.

'Please allow me to introduce myself,' he said, bowing low over her hand. 'It is an honour to meet you, Mrs Darcy. But what is this? You do not return my greeting.'

'I do not know your name,' she said, finding that her mouth, at least, was her own.

'Then I must tell it to you. I am called many things by many people, but you may call me *husband*.'

'I already have a husband,' she replied.

He gave an unnatural smile.

'You have nothing. You have a man who is afraid to touch you. He has married you but he has not bedded you. He is no husband to you.'

'What do you want with me?' she asked.

'I want nothing but to make you happy,' he said in a whisper as he walked round her, trailing his hand across her shoulders. 'I want to give you your heart's desire. You are so beautiful,' he said as he stopped in front of her, lifting his cold white hand and stroking her hair, then running his fingers down her cheek and across her lips, trailing rivers of ice down her spine.

'Who are you?' she asked, appalled.

'I have already told you,' he said, resting his hand on her shoulder and bending his head towards her throat.

'*What* are you?' she asked.

'I am vampyre,' he said. 'Oldest of the old, most ancient of an ancient line. I am fear and dread.'

She began to tremble. She wanted to run but she could not move. She was held rigid by his will.

'So beautiful,' he said reverently, as his head moved ever nearer her throat. 'So ripe, so rich, so full of life; so vital, so healthy, so *bloody*.'

He bent his head and his teeth grazed her skin...

...and a voice rang out threateningly across the clearing.

'Step away from her.'

Elizabeth turned to see Darcy springing into the clearing with a look of fury on his face.

'Let her go,' Darcy snarled, 'she is mine.'

The vampyre was amused.

'Yours?' he said mockingly. 'She is not yours. You have not had the strength to take her. There is no smell of you in her blood, there are no signs of you on her body.'

'Step away from her,' said Darcy, threateningly.

The vampyre's mockery left him, to be replaced an accursed and sinister manner.

'Do not attempt to come between me and what is rightfully mine,' he said.

His voice was full of menace and with the menace came the storm. Black clouds blew up from nowhere. They sped across the sky at a ghastly rate, boiling and rolling with hideous malevolence as they ate up the sky and consumed the stars and a terrible power was revealed. It roared around the clearing, unspeakable in its dreadfulness, an appalling, unnameable entity; something vile and grotesque and *old*.

Darcy recoiled from the tumult and the vampyre smiled.

'Oh, yes, you know me now,' he said, and his voice was as vile as the storm.

'No. It can't be,' said Darcy in fear and loathing. 'You're dead! The mob ferreted you out of your ruin and destroyed you.'

'A creature of my age does not die lightly, whatever your *friends* might think.'

'But they came on you with torches when you were too weak even to feed—'

'They came upon me in my helplessness and they laughed at me,' he said. 'They knew that my children had abandoned me and that I could not defend myself. They drew near me, fearful and wondering, and when they took no hurt they grew bold.

'"Send him to the guillotine!" they cried. "Let him see that she too has fangs!"

'And therein lay their mistake. They took me to a place of carnage and it fed me through the skin. When I grew strong I rose above them, borne aloft on mighty wings. They froze before me in horror, afraid at what they had done, and then I fell amongst them, drinking with greedy pleasure. Long I drank, slaking my thirst, and as I did so my skin revived and my bones returned to strength until I was restored to some semblance of youth and vigour.

'At last I had done. I left that place of carnage and returned to life in all its glorious wonder. To Paris I went, and to my familiar haunts, partaking of all my familiar pleasures. And what did I find? That there had been a bride in our family, but she had been kept from me, instead of being sent to me, as was my right. You see, I still have some friends who will tell me of these things. My first thought was to take her; but I longed for the thrill of the chase. So I watched her and I followed her. My good friends, who are loyal to me, helped me in my endeavours. And now I am here to claim my rights. I am here for my *droit de seigneur*.'

'No!' said Darcy.

'No? You say it as though there is a choice. Every vampyre bride must come to me. She must be mine before she can feel her husband's touch.'

'Never!' said Darcy. 'Let her go.'

'Why? So that you can enjoy her?' he said with a diabolical smile. 'You do not know how. You are weak, Darcy. She was eager for you, wanting you, needing you, but your conscience forbade you to taste of her. Mine has no such qualms.'

'You have no conscience,' said Darcy with a snarl, leaping forward and baring his *fangs*.

Memories cascaded through her mind: of her time in the library when the room was changing, and the door was opening and there was Darcy—surprised, at first, then angry, and then terrible.

Now she knew why she had fainted: because when he had let out a snarl, she had seen him for what he was. She had discovered his terrible secret and the shock of it had been too much for her. But it was not too much for her now.

She ran to the side of the clearing and stood, out of the way, amongst the trees as Darcy lunged forward. A wind blew up from nowhere and he had to struggle to move, but he fought it steadily and moved inexorably forwards, towards the ancient vampyre. Then the wind intensified and he could no longer force his way against it; it was all he could do to stand. There was a moment of stillness when he could not go forward and the wind could not push him back, then he began to move forward again. But the wind suddenly gusted, whipping him from his feet and flinging him back across the clearing until he crashed into a tree. It cracked and splintered with a tearing sound and he slid down the trunk, dazed. The vampyre leapt towards him, carried aloft by the terrible wind, and, seizing him by his coat, picked him up in one hand whilst reaching for his throat with the other.

'No!' cried Elizabeth, as the vampyre's hand found purchase... and then suddenly the ancient vampyre screamed, a hideous sound, and he dropped Darcy to the ground as his hand began to burn. Clouds of black smoke billowed upwards and spiralled into the heaving sky.

'Aaargh!' he screamed in horror, folding in on himself, his hand still pouring forth clouds of smoke.

Elizabeth ran to Darcy, who was picking himself up rapidly from the forest floor, and hand in hand they ran to his horse, which stood rolling its eyes in fear. He lifted her into the saddle and mounted behind her, untangling the reins from the branch of the tree and giving the beast its head.

It needed no urging. The hate and horror filling the clearing was driving every living thing away. Birds rose from the trees, screeching and screaming as they darted off in hectic flight; animals scuttled from their burrows; worms left their holes in the earth. The ground was alive with living things swarming out of the clearing.

The horse ran, jumping streams and ditches, weaving between trees, lacing in and out of hollows. On it went, until the trees fell behind and the lanes were ahead; then on through fields and olive groves, on to the sea and along the coast; on until it came to a valley that nestled between green hills, with the sea on one side and the countryside on the other. And there, nestled in a hollow, was a small, square house, and for this, Darcy made.

They approached it via a quiet country lane and went in through wrought iron gates which swung open to Darcy's touch.

'A hunting lodge,' said Elizabeth, as the horse slowed to a trot and they rode up the drive. 'Is it yours?'

'Yes,' he said.

Elizabeth let out a sigh and leaned back against him as the fear rushed out of her.

They came to a halt in front of the lodge. Darcy dismounted and lifted Elizabeth out of the saddle, and she slid gratefully to the ground. Neither of them spoke of the revelation; it was as yet too terrible to be discussed. Beside her, the horse trembled. It had carried them for many miles and it was covered in sweat.

'I will have to take care of the horse,' said Darcy, 'I have no grooms here who are capable of seeing to his needs.'

Elizabeth nodded in understanding.

'Go in,' he said, then added, with a smile, 'There is someone inside you will be pleased to see.'

Elizabeth climbed the steps and went through the heavy front door. As she entered the hall, a woman was running down the stairs and to her delight she saw that it was her maid.

'Annie!' she exclaimed.

'Oh, Ma'am, you're safe!' said Annie.

'And you!' said Elizabeth. 'I have been so worried about you. When I found the letters I feared the worst.'

'And I you… but you look fit to drop. Here is the sitting room,' she said, going over to the door and opening it, 'I will bring you some tea. I never thought to find any in Italy, but the master has it specially brought here. It was his valet who told me.'

Elizabeth went into the small but cheerful sitting room. There was little furniture, only a threadbare sofa and a few battered but comfortable-looking chairs. She did not sit down, having spent a great deal of time in the saddle, but stood by the window, letting her eyes wander as her mind tried to make sense of all it had learnt.

Annie returned with the tea.

'It doesn't taste as good as at home, but it's hot and will put new strength into you,' she said.

Elizabeth took it gratefully. After two cups she felt sufficiently refreshed to ask, 'What happened to you, Annie?'

Annie needed no second bidding.

'It was when you gave me the letter to post, just after you had fainted, that's when it all began,' Annie said. 'I took it downstairs and gave it to one of our footmen and he said that he would see it was posted, but I happened to turn back a minute later, meaning to ask him when it would go to the post, and I saw him tucking it into his coat. I was about to say, "What do you think you are doing?" when I stopped short. He was looking round him all furtive like and I thought to myself, there's something going on. I shrank back so he wouldn't see me, then I followed him to see what he'd do with it so as I could get it back. He went to his room with it and a minute later he came out again. Well, it wasn't difficult to see he must have hidden it there, so I waited until he'd gone and then I went into his room and looked through his cupboards until I found it. I'll never forget seeing it lying there, because it wasn't on its own; it was on top of a pile of your other letters, all tied up in a neat bundle.'

'Was it the footman we hired in Paris, when our own footman was taken ill?' said Elizabeth.

'That was him. One of our own men would never have done such a thing. Well, I put the letters in my apron pocket and came to find you to tell you all about it, but then I saw you were with the Prince I hesitated. I didn't trust the Prince, Ma'am. There were rumours about him in the servants' hall. They said he'd inherited the villa from a cousin of his, but the cousin had died suddenly. One minute he was hale and hearty and the next he was dead. It was given out he'd met with an accident, but no one saw the body and no one saw the accident either, and they should have done, for there were villagers on the road at the time. Then the Prince showed up and claimed everything. There was talk he'd murdered his cousin for the inheritance, poisoning him most likely, and hiding the body. They said in the servants' hall that the Prince had a friend who was much, much worse, and it was probably him who was behind it all. I paid them no notice to begin with, I thought it was just idle chatter, but once I found your letters I got to thinking. The footman wouldn't have taken them on his own; why would he? So someone must have paid him to do it, and the only person who might do such a thing that I could see was the Prince.'

'So you made an excuse about the handkerchiefs to make sure I would look in the valise,' said Elizabeth.

'Yes, Ma'am. It was the best I could think of at the time. I went back to your room and put them in your valise, but as I closed it I heard footsteps coming along the corridor. I don't mind telling you, it was a nasty moment when they stopped outside the door, and when the door handle turned I took fright and so I slipped through the interconnecting door into Mr Darcy's room. It's a good thing I did. I heard the footman go into the room with the coachman and from what they said I knew they were looking for me. They didn't want me to help you.

'Then one of them walked over to the connecting door and locked it, "So we won't be disturbed," he said. You're too late for that, I thought, I've heard every word.

'I thought it best for me to stay there until Mr Darcy returned, but the coachman was laughing at the footman for locking the door and saying there was no danger from that quarter, the Prince had men waiting for Mr Darcy by the stables.

'I didn't know what to do for the best, but you seemed safe enough for the time being so I thought I ought to warn Mr Darcy. I waited for him some way down the drive from the stables and told him what had happened. He said not to worry, he would take care of you, and then he told me to go to the hunting lodge with his valet, his valet would know the way. He said I should send a message to his valet by one of our grooms. I did as he said, and here we are.'

'And what of the rest of the entourage?' asked Elizabeth. 'Where are they?'

'Gone back to Venice, to the *palazzo*, on orders from the master,' said Annie. 'I never was more glad to see anyone than I was to see you when you rode up to the lodge.'

'And I am here now, safe, thanks to you,' said Elizabeth. 'Without your help...' She shuddered.

'It doesn't bear thinking about,' said Annie.

'No, it doesn't,' said Elizabeth. 'I can never thank you enough.'

'I'm just pleased you're safe, Ma'am.'

Annie took the tray of tea back to the kitchen and Elizabeth sat at last on the sofa, but she was too restless to sit for long. It had all been such a nightmare: the carriage ride, the man in the mask, and then the sight of Darcy with... of Darcy with... with *fangs*.

All the stories she had heard about vampyres, whispered in tones of laughing horror, so strange and odd and unbelievable in Meryton, now took on new shades of dread and terror. She knew now why Darcy had never come to her. She knew the secret that lay between them, the truth he dare not tell.

What a strange fate was hers, to meet a man she took in dislike, then to have to change all her opinions about him and realise she loved him, and then to find out he was a creature of the night. And, perhaps, fate had not done with her yet.

The door clicked and she looked up. Darcy was standing in the doorway.

He was the same and yet different. He was dishevelled from his long ride. He had removed his coat and he was dressed in his breeches with his ruffled white shirt, damp from his exertions, untucked. His hair was wild and his eyes were haunted. He stood before her, completely vulnerable as though he did not know whether he would be welcome or not, and impulsively she held out a hand to him. He struggled with himself for a moment and then restraint broke and he strode across the room towards her, looking deep into her eyes as though he would read the answer to the mysteries of the universe there. Then he put his hand behind her head and kissed her with fierce abandon, dissolving and merging with her... until he bit her lip and unleashed a drop of blood. His whole body jolted as though it had been run through with electricity and there was a change in him, a roaring surge of hunger, an ache of primal need, and he sprang back from her in torment.

'What have I done?' he said in horror. 'Oh, my love, what have I done to you? I've frightened you. You're shaking.' He stepped forward to comfort her, then stopped himself by an effort of will and forced himself back. 'I never meant it to be like this. I thought you need never know, I thought I could keep it from you, I thought we could be happy, and perhaps, if things had been different, if they had been what I thought they were… but I should not have taken the risk, I should never have dragged you into this nightmare. I'm so sorry, Elizabeth. I wanted you so much that I fooled myself into thinking it was possible. But it isn't. It can never be.'

'Darcy—'

'I have wanted to tell you so many times. When you asked me what was wrong I tried to tell you, but I could never find the words, and even if I had found them, I would not have had the right to rob you of your safe and familiar world. How could I plunge you into a world of such nightmares? A deeper, darker world where creatures stalk the night? I never meant to hurt you. I never meant you to know. I never wanted to do this to you, to make you afraid, to see you tremble…'

'I'm not shaking with fear, I'm shaking with relief,' she said with a catch in her throat. 'If you only knew what I have been thinking, the dark thoughts that have plagued my soul. I thought it was something far, far worse. I thought you didn't love me.'

He looked at her in bewilderment. 'You thought I didn't love you?' He stood, astonished. Then he closed the gap between them in one stride and ran his hands through her hair. 'I love you to distraction. I thought I would go mad, being with you every day but never able to touch you. If you only knew how I have longed to do this, to feel your skin, to run my fingers through your hair and over your face, to feel you, touch you, be with you… but I couldn't, I couldn't. It was different when we married. I thought that as long as I didn't bite you that you would never turn, and that I could hide my nature from you; that we could live together at Pemberley and that you need never know. But then I found out on our wedding day that there was a chance, just a chance, that I would turn you if I claimed you, that you might become a vampyre if I truly made you my wife.'

'The look of torment,' said Elizabeth, remembering. 'That was what caused it.'

'Yes.'

'It was one of the messages,' she said, realising it must be so.

'Yes, it was slipped in with the messages of congratulation. I did not know at the time if it was true. It could just have been a cruel hoax, designed to destroy my marriage, but I had to find out for sure. And so that is why I took you to Europe, to consult more widely with people who might know.'

'And did they know?'

'No, my love. No one knows for certain. Whilst there is a chance I will turn you we can never be together. This must be our last kiss. If I have to be with you, day after day, sooner or later my self-control will slip, and you may end up like me, a creature of the night. You have to get away from me.'

'No,' she said resolutely. 'I will never leave you. We are together for ever. Whatever happens, there is only one place I want to be, and that is with you.'

He took her palm and kissed it, sending hot shivers up her arm. Her eyelids drooped and her limbs felt heavy and languorous. She felt rather than saw him lean towards her, and she became very still as she sensed a predatory animal close to her. She instinctively inclined her head, exposing her throat. She knew in some tiny corner of her mind that it was dangerous, but she no longer cared. She felt his breath as his mouth moved towards the graceful arc of her neck and then the soft touch of his lips on her skin and she was held, mesmerised, knowing that if he should bite her, she would be unable to resist.

His hand brushed tiny tendrils of hair away from her neck and his lips found her flesh again and he let out a murmur and her blood responded, coursing through her veins. Then the twigs on the fire shifted and the sound broke the spell and he lifted his mouth from her neck, slowly and unwillingly, pulling himself away from her with every ounce of his strength, his hands lingering on her shoulders until, with a groan he wrenched them away. His eyes were full of pain and his body was contorted with agony, but he forced himself to walk over to the far side of the fireplace where he collapsed into a chair out of temptation's way. Elizabeth, her senses unclouding as he moved away, sank back on her heels.

'That is why you must get away,' he said, his voice low and haunted. 'We vampyres are compelling. If I lose control, you will have no choice but to surrender. If only—but of what use are if onlys now? I let her do this to me; it is done.'

'You said something like it once before,' said Elizabeth, remembering the time he had spoken in such a way, as they had been running from the Count's castle. 'Did someone turn you into a vampyre? Is that what you are speaking of? Do you mean that you were not always this way? That there was a time when you were once human?'

'Yes, there was, long ago.'

'How did it happen?' she asked.

He said nothing.

'I want to know,' she said.

'Very well. You deserve that much. But you are cold,' he said as she shivered. 'You need a hot meal.' He rang the bell and one of the lodge servants answered. Darcy gave him some instructions and the man bowed and departed. 'We will eat first, and then I will tell you everything.'

CHAPTER 14

THE SERVANTS RETURNED AT last to say that the meal was ready. Darcy led Elizabeth through to the dining room, where two places were laid. The silver cutlery sparkled against the dark wood of the table. Oddly assorted chairs were set on either side. There was a wood burning stove on one side of the room. A glow came from the grate and flames flickered fitfully there.

One of the servants held the chairs whilst Elizabeth and Darcy seated themselves and then carried a procession of silver platters into the room. It wasn't until she saw them, and smelt the aromas of roast meat and vegetables, that Elizabeth realised how hungry she was. She had eaten nothing since breakfast that morning, and the time in between had been full of fear and foreboding. She picked up her knife and fork as a plate was set in front of her and Darcy bid her eat.

She needed no urging. Her hands were trembling with the after effects of the day and she felt new strength and energy flooding into her as she put the hot food into her mouth.

He watched her lovingly, tracing the rise and fall of the fork from her plate to her mouth, and each time she parted her lips, his eyes opened a little wider, as if to let more of the sight of her in.

He sat silently whilst she ate, and he did not speak until she had finished her glass of wine.

'It was in the year 1665,' he said, 'the year of the Black Death. The plague was running riot through the streets of Europe, claiming millions of lives. Nowhere was safe. Towns, villages, and cities all felt its dread touch. There was panic on the streets and anyone with the signs of the plague on them was shunned. Doors were marked with crosses to show that they were plague houses, and in many cities the dead out-numbered the living.

'I was in London when it started. My family were landed gentry, connected to the nobility without being noble them-selves, and we had a house in town as well as a country estate. My father was looking for preferment and he decided that we would all move to the London house for a year. There was an outbreak of the plague shortly after we arrived, but it did not seem too alarming. It was in one of the poorer parts of London, and the rest of the city was untouched. But as the summer came, that began to change. It was one of the hottest summers I have ever known. The heat was trapped between the buildings, and in the hot and stifling conditions the plague flourished. It began to spread through the city. The Court moved to the palace at Hampton Court and the nobility began to leave for their country estates. My father stayed for as long as he could, but once his patron decided to retreat to Northumberland, he decided that our own country estate was where we belonged. There was a flurry of activity in the house. I can still remember it: the servants running up and down the stairs and my mother overseeing everything and Georgiana playing in the garden with her doll.

'When everything was packed, we climbed into the coach and set off for the country. Unfortunately, everyone else had had the same idea. It seemed like the whole of London was on the move. The streets were jammed with carriages and we moved at a snail's pace. And then we stopped moving altogether. The Lord Mayor had responded to the panic by closing the gates. The only people allowed out of the city were those who had a certificate to say they were in good health.

'When it became clear that we could not go on, we went back. My father tried to procure a certificate for us to say that we were free of disease. He had friends in high places and after a day of beseeching them to come to his aid—no easy task since few of them were left in the city—he returned home well pleased. He had been promised a certificate and he told my mother that in a few days we would be able to travel.

'But before it was granted, my father fell ill. We knew at once what it was and my mother summoned the physician, and although he prescribed various remedies, none of them had any effect. In the end, we knew we could do nothing but watch and wait. My mother tended my father faithfully until she too caught the plague, and Georgiana and I watched as they sickened and died. I knew that soon it would be my turn, and then there would be no one left to look after Georgiana. This thought spurred me on. I packed a few belongings and some food and I set out with my sister, in the hope that we would be able to slip through the gates and find safety in the countryside.

'London was empty as we made our way through the streets, and when we arrived at the gates, we hid until a noble procession of carriages pulled up before it. As the guards examined the papers, Georgiana and I jumped onto the back of the middle carriage and managed to pass through the gate as part of the noble's entourage. Once safely in the country, we jumped down and ran into a field where we ate some of our food, and then we set off to walk to our estate in the north.

'I knew we would have to travel slowly, but I thought that we would reach the estate before winter set in. I caught fish for us in the rivers and we found fruit and berries growing in the fields and hedgerows. We slept in the open, avoiding towns, for we did not know how far the plague had spread nor did we know if we, ourselves, might already be infected and so be a danger to others. When it rained we sought shelter in barns. On one stormy night, with no barn in sight, we came to the drive of a fine house. My sister was weary and cold, and we had not eaten all day. I decided to take the risk of approaching the house, for we were many miles out of London, and seeing if they would give us something to eat.

'As we turned the corner of the drive I saw that the windows were dark. At first I was downhearted, but then I thought it might be better after all if the house was empty. I found an open window at the back of the house where a catch had broken and we were soon inside. There was a little food in the pantry, some cheese and apples, and I collected eggs from the hen house outside. We ate our fill and then went upstairs, and for the first time in weeks I watched Georgiana sleep in a bed.

'The following morning I wanted to go on, but Georgiana was very young, and she was weary with all her exertions and cried often for our parents. We needed to move on so that we could reach our own estate, but I decided that we would stay in the house for a few days until Georgiana was rested. I caught rabbits, pigeons, and fish, and Georgiana picked fruit and herbs, and together with the remains of the cheese and the plentiful eggs, we survived.

'I tempted Georgiana with thoughts of seeing our own dear nurse. She expressed herself willing to travel and we decided to set out on the morrow.

'But when the morrow came, Georgiana was ill and I saw with alarm that she had the signs of the plague on her body.

'It was a terrible moment. I had thought she had escaped, but there was no mistaking the boils. I looked after her as best I could, but she was sinking fast, and to make matters worse, the owner of the house returned.

'I heard the carriage late one afternoon. It was so long since I had heard the sound of any human endeavour that for a moment I did not know what it was, but as soon as I remembered, I hid. I crouched beneath the window sill and peered over it to see how many people were approaching.

'The carriage stopped in front of the house and a woman climbed out. She was splendidly dressed, evidently a woman of rank and fashion, and she was accompanied by a thin and sickly little girl. She was soon lost to view as she walked under the portico and I knew she was entering the house. I was filled with panic. I darted towards the door, meaning to go upstairs and protect Georgiana, but there were voices in the hall and so I hid behind the sofa, hoping the woman would not come into the room. But I was not quick enough and she saw me.

'"Well, well, what do we have here?" she asked, coming into the room.

'If I had been alone I would have run, but Georgiana was upstairs and so I could not leave. I stood up and told the woman that I didn't mean any harm. I said that I had sheltered in the house for a night and that I was moving on.

'"Are you alone?" she asked me.

'I said that I was, but my eyes betrayed me and she followed their direction upstairs. Catching hold of my wrist she swept through the hall, up the stairs, and along the landing, taking me with her, whilst the pale girl followed close behind. She had no need to ask where my sister was, for Georgiana's moans could by now be heard.

'The woman went into Georgiana's room and, taking one look at her as she tossed and turned on the bed, saw that her end was near. I expected the woman pull back, but instead she stayed where she was, and she made no move to stop her daughter from going over to Georgiana and holding her hand. Georgiana stopped tossing and turning at once and she opened her eyes and gave a weak smile. There was an instant connection between the two girls.

'"Here, you can hold Evelina," the pale girl said to my sister, handing her her doll.

'I expected the woman to snatch the doll back, for people were terrified of contagion in those times, but she made no move to do so, and when I looked at her I saw there were tears in her eyes.

'She blinked them back quickly and her manner became brisk.

'"Do you want me to save your sister?" she asked. "I can save her life if you will it."

'"Are you a doctor?" I asked her.

'"No," she said. "I am a vampyre."

'I thought of all the stories I had heard but I was not afraid. I had seen the way she looked at her daughter. It was the way my mother had looked at Georgiana.

'"If you save her, will she become a vampyre too?" I asked.

'"She will. But you must hurry, her time is short. If you leave it too long, I will not be able to save her. No one will."

'I turned to my sister.

'"Georgie," I said. "This lady can save you, but you will become like her if she does. You will become a vampyre."

'Georgiana had heard the stories as well as I had. She looked at the woman apprehensively, then she looked at the girl.

'"Are you a vampyre?" she asked.

'"Yes," said the girl.

'My sister turned to me and nodded.

'"Very well," I said to the woman. "But only if you will turn me too."

'She looked at me closely.

'"You are not showing any signs of the plague," she said.

'"Where Georgiana goes, I must follow. I promised my mother I would keep her safe, and I can't do that if she lives whilst I grow old and die."

'"Then my Anne will have two playmates instead of one," she said, adding thoughtfully, whilst she looked at me, "and in time, perhaps, who knows?"

'She moved so quickly there was only a blur and then there were puncture marks on my sister's neck. The woman turned to me, her fangs dripping red and then she was next to me and my neck was pierced.'

'So that is the meaning of the scars on your neck,' said Elizabeth in wonder. 'I saw them when we swam in the lake.'

'It is. They have never healed—though they are usually hidden beneath my cravat—and they never will.'

Darcy fell silent. His face was shadowed and Elizabeth sat and watched him, his handsome features brooding in the dim light, his eyes mysterious. She thought of all the things he must have seen in his centuries of living: the rise and fall of nations, and the lives and deaths of kings. She thought of him living at Pemberley down the centuries, and she wondered how it was that no one had noticed his long life.

Seeing her watching him, his hand reached out to her across the table and then drew back.

'I have no right to touch you,' he said.

'You have every right. You are my husband.'

'Still?'

'Yes, still. I love you, Darcy, nothing can ever change that.'

Her hand closed over his own. He took it gratefully and returned her pressure.

'But you are not eating,' he said.

It was true. She had finished her savoury plate of meat and vegetables, and it lay empty before her. He stood up and went over to the wall where he pulled a bell rope then returned to the table.

'You have not finished your meal,' she said, looking at his plate.

He hesitated.

'No,' he said.

'Do you eat? Or do you eat... other things?' she asked with a shudder.

'No, never that,' he said, reading her mind. 'We have a choice of what we eat. There are those who prey on humans but Georgiana and I have never done so; we slake our thirsts in other ways.'

Something Elizabeth had heard in Venice came back to her. She remembered Sophia saying, 'The glory, it has passed, the great days, they have gone. There is no place in the world now for our kind, not unless we will take it, and take it with much blood. There are those who will do so, but me, I find I love my fellow man too much and I cannot end his life, not even to restore what has been lost. But without great ruthlessness, glory fades and strength is gone.'

She had thought that Sophia was talking about the fall of Venice and the plotting of a few to overthrow the French with bloodshed, but now she understood.

'Sophia was a vampyre,' she said, 'wasn't she?'

'Yes,' said Darcy.

'And the other people I met in Venice?'

'Many of them, yes.'

'So that is why they wanted to hold a costume ball; it reminded them of their own pasts—and their own youth?'

'Yes.'

Elizabeth thought of the beautiful clothes. They had not been handed down through the generations as she had supposed; they had been kept by their original owners.

'And that is how you knew the steps to the galliard,' she said. 'You had danced it before. And Sophia, like you, chose not to hunt humans.'

'All my friends, all my vampyre friends, have made the same choice. Only those who choose to turn for evil purposes, or those who are turned by a malignant vampyre against their will, hunt humans,' he said.

'Malignant vampyres,' said Elizabeth with a shudder as she remembered her ordeal. 'Who was the vampyre in the forest?'

'As to who he is, no one knows. He is one of the oldest of us, an Ancient, but how he was made we do not know.'

'Do you think he will find us here?'

'I hope not. We are well hidden, and he does not know I own this lodge. Besides, he has been hurt. He will go underground now to recover and will likely not emerge for many years.'

'So long?'

'To a vampyre, a year is nothing,' he said.

The door opened and the servants returned. Their soft footfalls were almost silent on the thick carpet as they cleared the plates.

'Some fruit and cheese,' said Darcy to them, 'and anything else you have which might tempt my wife.'

They soon returned with a platter of bread and cheese and several bunches of grapes. They set the food close to Elizabeth and with it a clean plate, moving respectfully all the while. She took one of the grapes, pulling it from the bunch and putting it into her mouth.

'And the people at Pemberley? Do they know?' she asked.

'Some of the servants, yes.'

'Mrs Reynolds? She said she had known you since you were four years old.'

'She was our nurse. She was waiting for us when we returned to our estate, where Lady Catherine—for it was she who turned us—took us in her carriage, after she had made us vampyres. The plague had spread there too, and the other servants had fled, but Mrs Reynolds had remained. When she saw us she told us to stay away, thinking she would infect us, but Lady Catherine offered her the same choice she had offered us, and Mrs Reynolds joined us.'

Elizabeth nodded. She took a knife and cut a piece of cheese, eating it with some of the rustic bread and following it with more of the grapes.

'If you were alive in 1665, then you must be 150 years old,' said Elizabeth wonderingly. 'And in all this time you have never married. There has never been a Mrs Darcy?'

'No, never once,' he said.

'Because of the curse,' she said.

'No,' he said simply. 'Because I never met you.'

He stroked his fingers over the back of her hand and stroked his thumb across her palm, then lifting her hand to his lips, he kissed it lovingly.

'Is there nothing we can do?' she asked him. 'No way of changing things? Of undoing what has been done?'

'No,' he said with a look of profound sadness. 'None.'

The servants stirred.

'Have you finished your meal?' he asked Elizabeth.

'Yes,' she said.

'Then let us move into the drawing room and leave the servants to clear.'

'I wish...' said Elizabeth, as they did as he had suggested.

'Yes?'

'I wish we could forget all this, just for a day or two.'

'Then we will, for a few days at least,' he said with a smile. 'Let us be simply Mr and Mrs Darcy as we were meant to be.'

CHAPTER 15

Ensconced in the hunting lodge, away from the world, Elizabeth was happier than she had been since her wedding day. She and Darcy took refuge from the problems facing them and wandered through the gardens in the early morning when the dew was on the grass and the air was fresh and clear. They delighted in the flowers which, although less vigorous than they had been earlier in the season, were still putting forth their blooms. They talked of many things, of their childhoods and their families, and like other newlyweds, they talked of their hopes and dreams. All subjects save one they discussed, and that subject, for the time being, they avoided.

Over the hot noontide hours they retreated indoors and sat on the shady veranda, eating olives and other tasty delicacies. Then, when the heat began to dissipate, they wandered further afield, smelling the sweet scent of herbs, and walked by the side of streams or strolled in the shade of the Lombardy poplars which stood like sentinels on guard in the fields.

'We will take a picnic with us tomorrow. There is a place I want to show you,' said Darcy.

They set off before the heat of the day and wandered down a country lane and onto a track which led to a cliff top overlooking the ocean. There was a small copse of trees, their spreading branches forming an umbrella of shade. Dappled light danced over the ground as the wind stirred the leaves, creating ever-changing patterns on the grassy floor beneath it. Nearby a stream trickled over rocks, the sound of it cooling and refreshing.

Darcy spread out the rug and they sat down, unpacking good, homely fare: bread, cheese, and cold meats, with small cakes, bunches of grapes, and glasses of sweet wine. They ate leisurely, enjoying the view and the novelty of eating in the open. When they had finished, Elizabeth lay back with her head in Darcy's lap and he stroked her hair and kissed her with soft, gentle kisses, and they talked of their plans for Pemberley.

'When we return to England, I would like to have your portrait painted. I have been thinking about it for a long time, ever since the time you walked to Netherfield when Jane was ill. It was Caroline who suggested the idea, although she did so to ridicule me. She was aware that I was interested in you, and she wanted to tease me out of my preference. After telling me to hang a portrait of your aunt and uncle Phillips in the gallery next to my great uncle the judge, she said that I must not attempt to have your portrait painted for what painter could do justice to your eyes? I had offended her by saying that your eyes were very fine,' he explained.

Elizabeth smiled at the compliment and, as her eyes looked lovelier than ever, Darcy was prompted to kiss her again.

'Ever since then I have been thinking how well your portrait would look at Pemberley. I mean to hang it in the hall,' said Darcy.

'No,' said Elizabeth, 'not in the hall. It must go next to your portrait in the gallery, the one I saw when I visited Pemberley with my aunt and uncle for the first time. The artist had caught your likeness very well. There was a smile about your lips, and I remembered I had seen the same smile on your face when you had looked at me. It made me regret all my foolish prejudices, which had made it so difficult for me to like you and to see your worth, and had instead encouraged me to cling to my first impression of you.'

'Which was not very favourable.'

'No. Nor was your first impression favourable of me.'

'How could I not have seen your beauty?' he asked. 'I look at you now and I see you in all your loveliness and I can barely stop myself from…'

He fell silent as he approached dangerous ground.

'We must have a family gathering at Christmas,' he said, changing the subject.

'Yes,' Elizabeth agreed. 'We must invite Mama and Papa and the girls, and Jane and Bingley, and Charlotte and Mr Collins.'

Darcy stopped stroking Lizzy's hair as she mentioned the Collinses.

'Must we have them?' he asked.

'Not if you don't want to, but I would like to have them, or at least, I would like to have Charlotte.'

'She might prefer to go to Lucas Lodge to visit her family,' said Darcy with hope in his voice.

'That is true, but I think I must ask her, all the same. I cannot admire her for marrying Mr Collins; indeed, I am very disappointed in her taste and her judgement, but she was right when she said that we were not alike, and I have no right to judge her for her decision. Although I perhaps cannot feel such perfect friendship for her as I once did, she is still my friend and I would like to see her again.'

'Then invite her,' said Darcy. 'Your Aunt and Uncle Gardiner must come, of course. Without them we might never have met again.'

'If we hadn't come to Pemberley, would you have been content to leave things as they were?' asked Elizabeth, turning to look at him. 'Would you have gone your way and left me to go mine?'

'No,' he confessed. 'I couldn't forget you, no matter how hard I tried, and no matter how great the barriers between us. I think I would have gone to Netherfield again with Bingley whatever had occurred. I knew I had to tell him about Jane, that she had been in London and that I had kept it from him, and once I told him, I knew he would go back to Netherfield. I am sure I would not have been able to resist seeing you again and so I would have gone too.'

'And everything would have been the same.'

'Yes, it would. We were destined to be together, you and I, Lizzy.'

'Yes, I think so too. Although—'

'Yes?'

'I did wonder why it took you so long to propose. You came to Longbourn again with Bingley but then you did not speak to me for weeks. Was it because of your curse?' she asked.

'Yes, it was. I kept telling myself that it was impossible, but in the end, I loved you too much to live without you. I had tried to forget you and failed, and the more I knew of you, the more I knew I had to be with you.'

'Did you not think I would notice that you never grew old?' she asked. 'Or were you going to say that your family was naturally blessed with long life?' she added mischievously.

He laughed.

'I knew you would notice eventually, but I thought I would have perhaps fifteen years with you before you became suspicious. That is more than five thousand days, over a hundred thousand hours, greater than two million minutes, and every one of them precious. But it was selfish of me.'

'Not at all. I am flattered you wanted me so much,' she said happily.

He kissed her softly on the lips.

'Then I cannot regret it,' he said. 'I cannot regret anything, because everything in my life has led to this perfect moment with you.'

They lay there in companionable silence until the sun went behind a cloud, then they gathered up the picnic things and they returned arm in arm to the hunting lodge. Elizabeth played the piano. It was an old instrument and out of tune, but she found the familiar activity pleasurable and Darcy liked to listen to her.

Afterwards they settled down to write letters, Elizabeth to Jane, and Darcy to Georgiana. But as Elizabeth took up her quill she remembered something she had forgotten and turned to him in consternation.

'When I was in the Prince's carriage, I wrote a letter to Jane and threw it out of the window in the hope that one of the local people would see that it was sent. It said that I was being abducted and begged Jane to ask my father to enquire after me.'

'Only you could have thought of such a thing at such a time!' said Darcy with admiration.

'If the letter arrives, my family will worry,' said Elizabeth in some perturbation of spirits.

'I will send the servants to look for it at once. Where was it?'

Elizabeth told him as well as she could.

'If it has already been posted...?' she began.

'We will worry about that later. But for now, we will see if it can be found.'

He walked across the room to the fireplace and pulled the blue bell rope that hung next to it. The familiar jangling noise reached them from far off and soon one of the lodge servants appeared, quiet and respectful.

'Mrs Darcy dropped a letter in the forest,' Darcy said, giving the man directions. 'Find it, if it is to be found. If not, make enquiries in the village. Bring it to me as soon as it has been discovered.'

'Yes, Old One,' he said with a bow, and departed.

'Old One?' said Elizabeth, her eyes widening. She put down her quill in surprise. 'Then they know you for what you are?'

'Yes, they do.'

'But they don't mind,' said Lizzy wonderingly.

'No,' said Darcy. He walked over to the desk and took a seat beside her, sitting down on the battered but comfortable chair. 'I did them a service once, long ago, when I saved the life of the head man of their village. He was travelling between two villages, arranging a marriage, when he was set upon and attacked by bandits. I drove them off and then saw him safely back to his village. He thanked me for my actions and invited me to make a home here, and when I accepted, he set his people to serve me. For many years I lived here and protected the village from attack. The hills and forests hereabouts are mostly safe now, but they were riddled with bandits at the time.'

'There is so much about you I don't know,' said Elizabeth. 'You are not the man I thought you were.'

'I wish I was. I would like nothing better than to take you to Pemberley and for us to live out our lives as you wanted, as you expected... as you had every right to expect.'

The mood had become more sombre. The subject they

had so carefully avoided had risen despite their best efforts to keep it down and now it would not be denied.

'What are we going to do?' asked Elizabeth, looking at him sadly.

'I don't know,' he said. 'I only know that I want us to be together.'

'You no longer want me to go away?'

'No, I could not bear it if you did. But you, what do you want? Do you still want to come home to Pemberley?' His voice was controlled but she could hear the emotion underneath. 'I will release you from our marriage if that is your wish. You did not know what you were marrying in the church all those months ago in Meryton.'

'The church,' said Elizabeth, remembering. 'How were you able to enter it? And how are you able to wear the cross I gave you?'

'It is not my weakness,' he said. 'Every vampyre family has a different weakness. For some, it is garlic, for my uncle the Count, it is that he has no reflection. My family's weakness is that we cannot be out of doors during sunrise or sunset. At those times of day, we become translucent and so we cannot pass amongst humans unnoticed, and if we remain out of doors at those times for too often, then a part of our solidity fades, never to return. And so, as it is not my weakness, I can enter a church and wear a cross, though it chafes me. But you have not answered my question. Do you want to be free of the marriage? A way can be found for a man of my wealth.'

There was something so vulnerable about him as he looked at her that she reached out her hand to him and he took it fervently.

'No,' she said. 'We are meant to be together. I would like

us to return to Pemberley, as we planned. But can we truly live there? Won't your neighbours in Derbyshire notice you never age?'

'I have ways of disguising it. Just before my neighbours begin to notice that something is amiss I leave Pemberley, and a few months later, it is given out that I have met with an accident or succumbed to an illness. Later still, I return to Pemberley as the new heir, sometimes apparently the nephew of my previous self, or the cousin. This time I was the son.'

'Did no one wonder why they had never seen you as a child?'

'One of my Fitzwilliam cousins had a little boy of the right age and so he visited me from time. The servants and neighbours accepted him as Master Darcy, who had been born abroad and whose mother had sadly died in childbirth. His frequent absences were explained by extended visits to relatives, attendance at school, and then at university.'

'Did no one notice you were the same man?' asked Elizabeth.

'The similarity has always been put down to a family resemblance and nothing more, particularly as the prevailing fashions have helped me to disguise my appearance. It has been usual for men to wear wigs until very recently, and a man in a dark wig that tumbles to his waist in a mass of curls will always look different to a man in a short powdered wig. And recently the fashion has been for no wig at all.'

'I suppose a similar ruse is used to hide Georgiana's agelessness?' asked Elizabeth. 'How difficult your life must have been,' she said in sympathy.

'It was not the greatest of my difficulties,' he remarked.

He glanced at her sheet of paper, which was as yet empty. 'Will you tell Jane?' he asked.

'I don't know. I have always confided in her about everything, but this… I cannot decide. Does Bingley know?'

'No.'

'Will you tell him?'

'Perhaps, in time, if you tell Jane.'

'For now, I think I will not mention it. I will tell her that we have been travelling round Europe, but that we mean to be home soon, and leave anything else for another time.'

The blissful interlude could not last. They both knew they would have to face the world again and when the weather changed, with rain falling outside the window, they knew the time had come.

'Annie said that you sent the retinue back to Venice,' said Elizabeth as she looked out at the rain.

'Yes,' said Darcy. 'It seemed the safest place for them at the time.'

'Will we return to Venice on our way back home?'

'No. We will travel home by sea, I think. It will be easier than going across the mountains so late in the year. Are you ready to go back to England?' he asked her.

'Yes, I think I am,' said Elizabeth. 'I would like to be at home for Christmas.'

And once back at Pemberley, she thought, she and Darcy would have to find a way to live, a way to bear the torment of his terrible curse.

'Then I will start making the arrangements. I will have to leave you for a few hours; I must go to the bank in Rome and that is not a task I can give to anyone else, but I will be back as soon as I am able.'

He left the room and Elizabeth heard him giving instructions for his horse to be saddled.

The rain did not last for long, and Elizabeth decided to make the most of her last few days in Italy by walking on the beach. It was very different to the beaches in England. When she had visited the seaside with her family many years before, there had been a cold wind blowing and the other holiday-makers had gritted their teeth, determined to enjoy themselves. They had changed their clothes in bathing machines drawn up on the sand and then dipped themselves in the cold sea. Here there was no cold wind and the sea was warm. There were no bathing machines nor any sign of human endeavour, only the sand, the sea and the cliffs, and above them the sky.

The waves were small and playful, running in and rolling out with a swishing sound that mingled with the cry of the seagulls which wheeled overhead.

On a sudden impulse, she sat down and took off her shoes and stockings, then holding up her skirt she walked down to the water. The sand was hot and she hopped from foot to foot, sinking into the fine grains which enveloped her small white toes as she landed until she reached the firmer sand. It was dark and wet and better able to support her weight, and behind her she left perfect imprints of her well-shaped feet.

Her eyes wandered lazily over the pleasant landscape and followed a carriage that bowled along the wide road on top of the cliff. But when it stopped and turned down the narrow road that led down to the beach she began to feel apprehensive. She ran across the beach to take shelter in the lee of the cliffs and quickly dried her feet on her handkerchief then slipped them into her shoes. The noise of the carriage was growing louder, its wheels rasping and its horses whinnying, with every now and then an oath from the coachman as the way became more difficult for him to negotiate.

Then the noise stopped and she heard the sound of the carriage doors opening. She heard a voice she recognised and was startled to realise that it belonged to Lady Catherine de Bourgh.

'Miss Bennet!'

Any attempt at concealment was useless. Lady Catherine had already seen her and so Elizabeth moved out of the shelter of the cliffs and faced Lady Catherine who, with Anne, was picking her way across the sand.

'Miss Bennet! Where is my nephew? I must speak to him at once. It is a matter of great urgency. I have been to the lodge, but his servants were obstinate and they refused to tell me where he could be found.'

She was dressed, again, in black, as she had been in the Alps. Beside her, Anne was dressed in drab green, her pelisse hanging heavily around her thin form. They looked incongruous in such clothes on the beach.

'He has gone out riding,' said Elizabeth.

'Do not prevaricate with me,' said Lady Catherine. 'Where is he?'

'That I cannot say.'

'You can say at least when you expect him back,' returned Lady Catherine

'Indeed I cannot,' said Elizabeth.

'Headstrong, obstinate girl!' said Lady Catherine in an angry tone. 'You must tell me at once.'

'You have been betrayed,' said Anne, doing with a few quiet words what her mother could not do with her angry tirade, and winning Elizabeth's attention. 'By Wickham.'

'Wickham!' exclaimed Elizabeth in astonishment.

'Yes. George Wickham. We have just come from Paris. Mama had a fancy to stay there for a while after we left you in the Alps and we met George there.'

'He was in his cups,' said Lady Catherine, determined to have her share of the conversation.

'And he was frightened,' said Anne.

'With good reason,' declared her mother.

'If Darcy finds out what he has done—' said Anne.

'Wickham seems born to be a thorn in his side,' said Lady Catherine to Anne. 'First attempting to elope with Georgiana, then running away with Miss Bennet's sister, and now this.'

'This is the worst of all,' said Anne.

Lady Catherine nodded in agreement.

'He has betrayed you to an ancient evil,' she said to Elizabeth, 'a thing old beyond imagining, a monster, a—'

'Vampyre?' asked Elizabeth.

'You know?' said Lady Catherine in surprise.

'Yes, I do. But I did not know that Wickham had anything to do with it,' said Elizabeth with a frown.

'He quickly tired of your sister and left her in England whilst he resumed his debaucheries in Paris,' said Lady Catherine. 'He indulged in drink and women and cards, and in sympathetic company he bemoaned his fate. But one was listening who should not have been there, who should have been dead. He heard Wickham saying that he had married Darcy's sister-in-law and knew then that Darcy must have married. The Ancient believes in the old ways, that every vampyre bride should be his on her wedding night, and he is determined to have you. He has a friend, a prince, who means to invite you to his villa. If you value your sanity, do not go.'

'Your warning comes too late,' said Elizabeth. 'We have already been, and the Ancient has already tried to claim me.'

'Impossible!' said Lady Catherine. 'If he had found you, you would never have escaped.'

'But I did escape, with Darcy's help.'

'Darcy? But then that must mean…' she said, giving Elizabeth a shrewd glance.

'Yes, I know about Darcy,' said Elizabeth boldly.

'And you have not fled in disgust or despair?' asked Lady Catherine in surprise.

'As you see, I am still here.'

'You surprise me. You have more courage than I thought,' she said with grudging admiration. 'But it will do you no good. You will succumb to fear or loathing in the end. When a mortal loves a vampyre, it is always the way.'

'No, Mama,' said Anne. 'Papa never did.'

'Your Papa was the exception,' said Lady Catherine. Her expression softened. 'He was exceptional in every way.'

'I believe that Elizabeth is exceptional, too,' said Anne, turning appraising eyes on Elizabeth.

'She is nothing out of the ordinary,' said Lady Catherine with a dismissive wave of her hand.

'She captured Darcy, and that is something no one else has ever been able to do,' said Anne.

Lady Catherine looked at Anne and said, 'There may be something in what you say. But no matter, it is not important now. What matters is that you claim Darcy saved you from the Ancient. And yet that should not be. Now that the Ancient has reclaimed so much of his former strength, no one can withstand him.'

'It was not easy,' said Elizabeth. 'But when he picked Darcy up by the throat, his hand began to burn. I believe it was because it closed round the cross.'

'A cross could not hurt him,' said Lady Catherine contemptuously. 'A vampyre can only be hurt by something older than itself, and the Ancient was old when Christ was young. Besides, why would Darcy be wearing a cross? He would never wear such a thing.'

'Because I gave it to him,' said Elizabeth.

'Because you…?' asked Lady Catherine, stunned. Then, to Elizabeth's astonishment, she smiled. 'So that is how Darcy managed to defeat the Ancient. I was wrong about you, Miss Bennet—no, I will not call you by that name, I will call you by your true name, Mrs Darcy. You were meant to be together, I see that now, as Sir Lewis was meant to be with me. Instead of giving you my curse, I will give you my blessing.' She lifted her veil and leant forward to kiss Elizabeth on the cheek. 'He was not burnt by the cross, he was burnt by your gift: he was burnt by—'

She was suddenly, without warning, knocked back with great force and Elizabeth, startled, saw that Darcy now stood between her and Lady Catherine. He had returned from his errand and, seeing Lady Catherine's pose, he had moved with supernatural speed to defend Elizabeth.

'Did she hurt you?' he asked, taking Elizabeth's face in his hands and looking at her in concern. 'Did she touch you? Did she bite you?'

'No,' Elizabeth said, reassuring him. 'You don't understand. She was not threatening me. She came to warn me about the Ancient, but when she knew you had defeated him, she wished us well. She sees now we cannot be parted.'

He looked astonished and then smiled.

'I hoped she would see it eventually. She loved a mortal; she knows what it is like to be unable to give up a loved one.'

He turned to help Lady Catherine to her feet, but she was no longer there.

Although he had given her the lightest of taps, the strength of it had hurled her across the beach and into the cliff. But such a blow, whilst it would have been capable of killing a mortal, had done no harm to Lady Catherine. Elizabeth saw her picking herself up and heading for the path that led from the beach, with Anne behind her, leaving an indentation in the cliff. So powerful had the blow been that it had driven her veil into the rock where it remained, blowing in the breeze.

'We came to understand one another a little,' said Elizabeth, watching Lady Catherine go. 'She did not have time to finish her sentence, but I know what she was going to say. The Ancient one was defeated by my gift to you, by something older than himself: by love.'

Darcy's face softened and he leant forward and kissed Lizzy tenderly.

'I cannot bear it any longer,' she said, her hand caressing his face. 'I want to be with you, whatever the cost. Take me, I beg of you, let us be together as man and wife, come what may.'

'You don't know what you are saying,' he said, his voice shaking with the effort of controlling the huge tide of passion she could feel churning within him. 'There are torments to face if you turn. You will never age, but you will have to watch all those around you grow old and die. You will be cut off from life, a part of it and yet not a part of it, forever cast out.'

'I don't care,' she whispered. 'I will bear any fate to be your wife.'

He looked deep into her eyes to make sure that she meant what she said, and then he lifted her from her feet and carried her across the beach and up to the lodge, where he took the steps two at a time and kicked open the door before carrying her over the threshold.

As he crossed the hall to the foot of the stairs a shadow detached itself from the corner and one of the servants stepped forwards.

'There is someone to see you,' he said.

'Not now,' said Darcy, without breaking his stride.

'Yes, now,' came a voice from the shadows.

'It is the head man of our village, Nicolei,' said the servant.

An old, bent man stepped forwards. He was leaning on the arm of a younger man.

'It can wait until morning,' said Darcy, already beginning to mount the stairs.

'No, Old One, it cannot wait,' said Nicolei, looking at Elizabeth and then back to Darcy. 'It must be now, before you do anything you regret. There is a way to relieve you of your burden. There is a way to break the curse.'

CHAPTER 16

THERE WAS SILENCE IN the hall. From outside came the rustle of leaves and the cry of a sea bird, loud in the unnatural stillness. Then Darcy let Elizabeth slip from his arms and onto her feet, and taking her by the hand, he led her into the sitting room, with Nicolei following close behind. Darcy strode over to the fireplace and Elizabeth stood beside him, their arms around each others' waists, whilst Nicolei made his way slowly into the room. The young man helped him into a chair and he sat down with great difficulty.

'You say you know a way to return me to my human self,' said Darcy uncertainly when Nicolei was seated.

'That is right,' said Nicolei.

He spoke in Italian, but Elizabeth was by now so familiar with the language she needed no translation.

'I have never heard of such a thing,' said Darcy.

'And yet it is so,' said Nicolei, looking at him reverently. 'The knowledge has been passed down from head man to head man in our village for many generations.'

'You have never told me about this before,' said Darcy with a frown.

The old man rested his folded hands on the top of his stick.

'I did not know you wanted it, Old One. You are magnificent, a creature of the night, undead, undying. You soar aloft on mighty wings. You are a protector of the weak, a harbinger of both good and ill, a bringer of vengeance, a dealer of swift and sure justice. You scatter your enemies like straw before the wind. Never did I think you would want to give up such greatness. The centuries to you are as the seasons are to your children, for that is what we are in your shadow, nothing but children, weak and blind and pitiful. The land and the sea and the sky are all your home. You travel great distances before we can take a step. Your senses are more keen, more brilliant than ours: you see the ant at his labours, you hear the click of his jaws, you smell the sea when you are on the mountain top, you taste the pollen on the breeze.

'Do we say to the wind, do you wish not to blow? Do we say to the thunder, would you rather be silent? No. We never think of these things.'

'And yet you think of them now,' said Darcy.

'Yes,' he said, nodding slowly, 'that is so. My family, those you have here to serve you, heard you talking when you ate with your so beautiful wife. They knew you had found love and that you were a different man to the one they had known. They saw that your marvellousness was now, to you, a curse, and they were troubled. They take a pride in serving you, it is their way of repaying you for the service you do for them, but that service on both sides has always been willing. Now it is not so. And so they came to me, to ask me what was to be done, and I bid them bring me here so that I might tell you of that which you must know.'

The fire was leaping brightly in the grate. The atmosphere was peaceful. The furniture was faded but wholesome, and the sunlight was beaming benignly through the windows.

How strange it is, thought Elizabeth, that everything should be so peaceful when such dark secrets are being laid bare.

'Can you truly offer me a way to be rid of the vampyric part of me?' asked Darcy, still disbelieving but with a note of hope in his voice.

'I can, if that is what you desire. But think long on this, Old One, I beg of you.'

'I have thought of little else this past year. I have wanted and wished for this thing but I thought it could never be.'

Nicolei nodded.

'If that is so, I will help you. My wish is to serve you, and if this is the service you desire, then I will give it, willingly.'

'How is it to be accomplished?' asked Darcy, looking down at him intently.

'I can do no more than point you on the first part of your journey,' Nicolei said. 'The answers you seek are to be found in a chamber beneath the ground. It is so old that a Roman temple has been built on top of it, and the temple itself is of a venerable age. But before you set your foot on this path, beware, for there is great danger. Once it was tried in my forebear's time many centuries ago. I do not know what happened to the vampyre who tried it, only that he never returned.'

'There is danger in everything,' said Darcy. 'There is danger in living, and an enterprise such as this one does not come lightly; there is always a price to pay. But I am willing to pay it. Where is this temple?'

'That I do not know. I know only that it is set on a cliff in a green hollow, with the sea in front and a greater cliff behind and a tree growing above it. I know of three temples close by but none of them are like this. They have the sea, or the cliffs, or the hollow, but not all three, and I know of no temple with a tree close at hand.'

'And yet it is familiar, what you describe,' said Darcy

thoughtfully. 'I think I have seen this place, some ten miles to the northwest of here.'

Nicolei frowned, as though trying to recall the place of which Darcy spoke. Then his brow smoothed and he nodded, but he said, 'I know the place you speak of, but it is not a Roman temple; it is the ruin of a monastery.'

'But beneath it there is a temple,' said Darcy. 'I found it when playing there once as a boy. I fell through the floor of the monastery when exploring the cellars and found myself in a strange place ringed about with columns and statues. It was very old and I am sure it was a temple. The statues seemed to be of the Roman gods.'

'This, then, might be the place,' said Nicolei cautiously. 'If so, the chamber you seek will be there somewhere underneath.'

'Then I must go there. I saw no way down at the time, but there may be one, hidden,' said Darcy, taking his arm from around Elizabeth's waist.

'I will go with you,' she said.

'No,' said Darcy. 'You heard Nicolei; it will be dangerous.' When she was about to protest, he said, 'You cannot come with me. There is more than just my desire to protect you at work here, there is fate, too. Remember the castle, Lizzy. Remember the axe. Remember when it fell from the wall, and the meaning of the portent, that you would cause my death. You cannot come with me, my love. I must go alone.'

Elizabeth thought back to the days at the Count's castle. How long ago they seemed. She remembered the axe falling and landing closer to Darcy than to herself, and Annie telling her about the talk in the servants' hall, saying that the axe falling meant that she was to cause Darcy's death.

'But that was idle superstition,' she said, though her voice was uncertain. 'You said so yourself.' She saw his expression change and realised, 'You said it to comfort me.'

'Yes, I did,' he admitted.

'Then you believe the portent.'

'I don't know,' he said, 'but I would rather not put it to the test.'

'And yet you do not really know what the portent means,' said Nicolei unexpectedly. 'Portents are wonderful things, but they do not speak to us openly; they speak to us in mysterious ways.'

He looked from Elizabeth to Darcy thoughtfully.

'What do you mean?' asked Elizabeth.

'I mean that a portent, if it is true, will come to pass whatever steps are taken to avoid it. And if it is not true, then it will not affect the future, whatever is done.' He turned to Darcy. 'If your wife is to cause your death, how do you know that she will cause it by going with you? Might she not cause it by staying away?'

Elizabeth and Darcy looked at each other intently and then Elizabeth said, 'I am coming with you,' and this time Darcy did not argue. But still his face was troubled.

'And I too,' said Nicolei, 'with my son, Georgio, to help me, I will come with you. My fate is bound up with yours, Old One. This, I believe, is my destiny.'

Darcy was reluctant but at last he agreed, "Though you will have to travel in the cart which brought you here as I have no carriage at the lodge,' Darcy told him.

'I understand,' he said.

Darcy went over to the bell. When it was answered, he gave instructions for the cart to be readied and the horses to pull it. Elizabeth added her own instructions for some quilts to be put in the cart to soften it and some blankets added for warmth.

Then, turning to Nicolei, Darcy said, 'You have had a long journey to get here. When was the last time you had anything to eat?'

'Many hours ago,' said the old man.

'Then you must have something now, and Georgio must have something too before we go.'

'Thank you,' said Nicolei.

He rose to his feet with the help of his son, and Georgio helped him from the room. He turned at the door and said, 'We will be ready as soon as the horses are harnessed.'

When he had gone, Darcy turned to Elizabeth and said, 'Fetch your cloak, my love. We will be travelling for some time and the wind is cold.'

Elizabeth nodded but then said suddenly, 'Are you sure this is what you really want?' She looked at him searchingly. 'Nicolei was right. I had not thought of it before, but you have great wonders in your life. If you rid yourself of the curse, you will rid yourself of them, too. You will no longer see and hear and feel things so richly or keenly or deeply, and you will lose your immortality. You will no longer be ageless. You will grow old and die.'

He took her face in his hands and said, 'I would gladly swap eternity for one moment with you.'

She gave a long, shuddering sigh, and then he kissed her, a slow lingering kiss, a honeyed meeting of mouths and hearts and spirits, and when he let her go she knew there was no turning back.

She stepped unwillingly out of his arms and went upstairs to fetch her cloak. As she did so, she caught sight of her writing table. She hesitated and then sat down and began writing quickly, in an uneven hand.

My dearest Jane,

I have written you many letters during the course of my honeymoon, expecting them all to be sent, and yet none of them were ever posted. This letter I write hoping it will never leave my writing desk, unless I throw it into the fire at last, but I am going into danger and I mean to give my maid instructions to post this letter if I do not return.

Oh, Jane! If I could only tell you half the things that have happened to me since leaving Longbourn. There have been many difficult and frightening things in my life, but there has been much of great beauty, too: the dread and aweful majesty of the Alps as Darcy and I rode over their snow-capped heights; the peaceful tranquillity of Piedmont; the great river Brenta with its weeping willows trailing their branches in the water; Venice rising like a dream from the lagoon, basking in the morning sunlight, ageless and timeless and serene. And the people: Philippe with his gallantry and Gustav with his irrepressible good humour, and Sophia with her ancient dresses and her love for her city. And her memories: the rise of the merchant princes; the building of the palaces; the creation of the sculptures; the paintings and the poetry; the journeys of the great explorers; the triumphs of Marco Polo with whom she spoke and danced. Yes, Jane, she knew him, and she still sings and dances, though he has long since turned to dust. She is a custodian of all things past, she and others like her, and my dear Darcy is a custodian too—a custodian, a guardian, and a protector: one of the timeless ones. My dearest Darcy is a vampyre. And yet he intends to rid himself of his curse and his blessing for me.

He is going on a dark and dangerous path and I am going with him. How long we will be away I do not know, nor if we will ever return. But I love him with all my heart and

*where he goes, I go. Think of me often if you never see me
again, and call one of your children after me! Not your first-
born; she must be Jane like her mother, but the second, unless
it is a boy and then Elizabeth will not do!*

*Oh, Jane, how good it is to talk to you, even though you
are so far away. Even in a dark and dangerous time, I feel
lighter of spirit just thinking of you.*

*I must go. I hear the horses below. But I could not leave
without letting you know the truth of my life. If I return, I
might never tell you. But if I die in some underground chamber then it will comfort me to think that you will know the
truth, you who have always known everything about me, and
that you will know the truth about my dearest Darcy, too.*

And now, my dearest, most beloved sister,
Adieu.

She called for Annie and gave her the letter, which she
had sealed and on which she had written Jane's direction.

'Annie, I must speak to you about a matter of great importance. Mr Darcy and I are going on a journey and there
may be danger ahead. If we do not return within a week, I
want you to post this letter to my sister. Post it with your
own hand, Annie. Let no one else touch it.'

'I will, Ma'am, I promise you,' said Annie, taking the
letter.

'In the meantime, you must stay here and look after the
lodge whilst we are away. If neither I nor Mr Darcy return,
then you must take passage to England. There is money in
the drawer of my dressing table and you are to have it all.
Mr Darcy's valet will go with you, and he will know how
to make the arrangements. Go to my uncle in Gracechurch

Street, you will find his direction in my writing desk, and he will help you.'

'But what am I to tell him?' asked Annie in concern.

'Tell him...' Elizabeth paused. '...tell him that we went on a journey and that we did not return. Tell him that the area was infested with bandits and that we must have met with an accident or violence in the hills.' The sound of horses' hooves and the wheels of a cart came up from below. 'And now I must go.'

She put on her pelisse and cloak, changed into sturdy boots, and pulled on a pair of gloves, and then she ran downstairs. She went into the sitting room where she found Darcy.

He was dressed in outdoor clothes. His caped greatcoat was thrown over his tailcoat and breeches, and he wore riding boots on his feet. He was looking down at something he held in his hand and there was a look of unexpected pleasure on his face, his handsome features arranged in a smile.

On hearing her enter the room, he held his hand out to her and she saw that it contained a letter. Her heart jumped as she recognised it and she smiled all over her face. It was the letter she had written to Jane whilst she was being driven off in the Prince's carriage.

'The servants found it just where you threw it,' said Darcy.

'Thank goodness! Now Jane will not be burdened with those troubles, at least.'

'No, those troubles are over,' said Darcy.

'It is a good omen!' she said. 'I thought I would never escape that perilous situation and yet I did, and if such a hopeless situation turned out so well, could not another less hopeless situation turn out well also?'

'Indeed it could, it can, and it will!' said Darcy. 'Elizabeth, we were meant to be together. We will rid ourselves of this burden and we will be what we were always meant to be.'

She took his hands and her eyes danced.

'Just think, before long, we may be walking together in the grounds at Pemberley, or visiting Jane and Bingley at Netherfield and walking in the lanes thereabouts, the four of us together, happy and safe, with a blossoming future to look forward to instead of one full of fear and dread.'

'Then let us be on our way,' he said.

They went outside to find that Nicolei was already in the back of the cart, whilst his son, Georgio, was sitting on the box ready to drive it. Darcy's horse stood close by.

'Will you ride with me?' he asked Elizabeth.

Elizabeth gladly mounted in front of him, feeling safe with him at her back despite the horse's restiveness, and they set off for the ruin.

CHAPTER 17

THE WAY TO THE ruin lay along sleepy lanes bordered by olive groves and vineyards. Despite the circumstances, Elizabeth took pleasure in her surroundings and in the steady trot of the horse and in the feel of Darcy's arms around her as he held the reins. He rode well, with an experience born of a lifetime in the saddle, and guided his horse with no more than a gentle pressure of the heel every now and again or a slight movement of the reins. Elizabeth, who was an indifferent horsewoman, thought how different it was to see the world from horseback when she did not have to guide the animal herself.

They passed citrus trees and red-roofed houses and always, on their left hand side, lay the calm blue waters of the sea.

After awhile Darcy turned inland and the cart followed as they traversed a narrow country lane. Some twenty minutes later they left the lane and turned off onto a rough track. It climbed a hill, and once at its summit, Elizabeth could look down to see a ruin far below. It was set in a grassy hollow and it was flanked to the east by the cliff wall and to the west by a further steep drop to the sea. Stretching great branches over it was an old and gnarled tree.

The light was fading as the horse picked its way down the hill and the cart rumbled along behind. As they drew closer she could see that the ruin was large with arched doorways that had fallen in and a collapsed roof. Partial walls still stood, and beneath them lay the stones which had fallen. Long grasses grew between the stones and wildflowers ran riot through them.

Darcy brought his horse to a halt by the side of the ruin and dismounted, then lifted Elizabeth from the saddle, and beside them the cart too rolled to a halt. He tethered the horse to the lower branches of the tree and it began to nibble the grass.

Darcy looked with some apprehension towards the horizon. The sun was beginning to set, spreading bands of red across the sky. He walked briskly towards the ruin, stepping over its tumbled stone walls and striding across its broken floor until he reached a point beyond one of the door arches and stood looking about him, as if trying to recall a distant memory. He walked a few steps further forwards and then knelt down, parting the long grasses that had grown through the tumbled stones in an effort to find the way down.

Elizabeth watched him, and as the sun's colours became more vibrant and more splendid, he started to change. He was no longer entirely solid. His outline was shimmering in the evening light, giving him an ethereal quality, and as she watched in fear and wonderment she saw him becoming transparent. As he faded, she had a sudden urge to reach out and touch him. To her relief, he felt real. She could rest her hand on his shoulder and feel the muscle beneath, but she had the uncanny feeling that if he lost any more form, her hand could slip straight through.

He gave a sudden cry, saying, 'Here!' and she pulled her hand back as he began to tug more vigorously at the grasses, ripping them up in huge handfuls to reveal the dark passage into the earth that lay beneath.

Georgio left the cart, where he had been seeing to the horse, and went to help him, his large brawny muscles making quick work of the debris that was clogging the opening. Once it had been cleared, Elizabeth saw a ramp leading down into the bowels of the earth. It was very dark, and the end of the ramp could not be seen. Georgio went back to the cart and returned with torches. He lit them, first one for Elizabeth and then one for Darcy, and then he went over to his father and helped him out of the cart. Nicolei leaned on his arm and together the four of them proceeded cautiously down the ramp, with Darcy leading the way.

They found themselves in an underground passage with a low roof. Strange shadows flickered on the walls and the *drip, drip* of water could be heard. Down went the ramp. Down and down. Then, just as Elizabeth thought she could stand the confined space no longer, the ramp led into the cellar, where a few bottles of wine were still lying on a wooden rack, coated thickly with dust.

Darcy went forwards slowly, motioning her to stay back. The reason for this soon became clear. In the floor towards the end of the cellar was a gaping black hole where the floor had caved in.

'There must have been a disturbance of the earth some time ago which damaged the foundations and brought the building down,' said Darcy. He looked down into the hole, holding his torch low the better to see. 'This bit will not be easy,' he said to Elizabeth and Nicolei. 'Are you still determined to come?'

'I am,' said Elizabeth.

'I too,' said Nicolei.

Darcy gave a reluctant nod. Then, handing his torch to Georgio, he lowered himself into the hole.

There was silence, with only the steady *drip*, *drip* to mark the passage of time. Then Darcy's voice called up, 'It's all right, you can come down.'

Elizabeth sat on the side of the hole and then gingerly lowered herself down, with Darcy catching hold of her and helping her to finish her descent.

She found herself in an underground cavern which was lit by a weird green light, and she felt a sense of awe as she looked about her, taking in the sublime remnant of antiquity. The temple was large and circular. Roman columns, grooved and topped with elaborate scrollwork, could dimly be seen in the shadows, ringing the temple at the eight points of the compass. Most of them were still standing, but two had fallen and lay broken on the floor. Within that ring, six statues were set, all made of marble, standing on plinths that made them some twelve feet high. She walked round, holding her torch aloft, and upon examining them, she found that they were similar to the statues she had seen in museums when visiting her aunt and uncle in London, portraying as they did the old Roman gods. Behind her, Darcy and Georgio, with great difficulty, managed to lower Nicolei through the hole.

She paused in front of the first statue and recognised him as Neptune, god of the sea. He had a toga half draped across his torso, a long, curling beard, and in his hand he held a trident. Beside him, at his feet, was a monster from the deep. Next to him was Apollo, god of the sun, young and beardless, holding his bow and arrow, with his lyre beside him. Then came Minerva, goddess of wisdom, an owl perched on her outstretched hand. After her was Jupiter, her father, lord of the skies, and then Pluto, god of the underworld. He wore a fearsome aspect and beside him was his three-headed dog Cerberus. After him, completing the circle, opposite the goddess Minerva with her love of learning, came an unsettling image of Bacchus, god of wine, lord of chaos, with an impudent satyr curled around his legs.

Nicolei was at last lowered through the hole and Georgio swiftly followed, until at last they all stood together in the centre of the temple.

'What now?' asked Elizabeth.

'There is a chamber beneath us, if we are in the right place,' said Nicolei, 'and that is the chamber we seek.'

'Then we must look for it,' said Darcy.

Georgio lit two more torches, and with the better light, they could see that there were passages beyond the columns, radiating outwards. Whilst the others examined the passages, Nicolei rested himself on one of the broken columns.

'This leads down,' said Darcy.

'And this,' said Georgio, who had gone to one of the other passages.

'And this,' said Elizabeth, from the mouth of a third.

'Do you know which one we should follow?' Darcy asked Nicolei.

Nicolei, breathing noisily still with the effort of the descent, shook his head.

'No, Old One.'

'Then I will have to try them one by one.'

'We will go together,' said Elizabeth.

'No,' Darcy said. 'We do not know what is lurking in the darkness. You will stay here with Nicolei. I will take Georgio with me. Never fear,' he said, 'once I find the way down, I will return for you.'

He kissed her on her forehead and then he was gone, disappearing down one of the passages with Georgio behind him.

Elizabeth watched him go, but when he had disappeared from view, she went to sit with Nicolei on the fallen column.

'Where do they come from, the vampyres?' she asked. She knew so little about them, but Nicolei seemed to know more. 'Did they have their genesis here, near Rome?'

'I do not know,' he said. 'I only know that they are revered among my people and that they are very old.'

'Darcy said that he first met your people when he saved the life of the head man as he was travelling to another village to arrange a marriage.'

'Yes, that is so. The man he saved was my great-grandfather, and the marriage he was arranging was that of his son, my grandfather. If the Old One had not saved him, then the marriage would not have gone ahead and there would have been war between our villages. It would have been thought that the neighbouring people had refused my great grandfather's proposals and had killed him in pride and anger. But because of the help of the Old One, our villages became united and flourished in peace and prosperity for many years. My whole village is grateful to him for this. And I am grateful to him because, without his help, my grandfather would not have married my grandmother and I, and Georgio, would not be here.'

Elizabeth sat in thought but at last she said, 'Do you know what lies in the chamber we are seeking?'

'No,' Nicolei said.

'But it is older than the temple?'

'Much, much older. It is from a time when nature was greater than man, but also more in harmony with him. The vampyre embodies this, for he is both man and beast.'

'What will you do when Darcy is no longer a vampyre?'

asked Elizabeth, saying *when* and not *if* in an attempt to will it to be so. 'Who will protect your village?'

'Times are not as bad as they were. We are more prosperous now, and more numerous. We have many strong sons, and if need be, we can pay for others to help us. Now too the hills are safer than they were. There are bandits, yes, but they are not so many. We will survive,' said Nicolei. 'But something is passing, something of great majesty, and a power is going out of the world.'

They sat in silence.

At last Elizabeth could bear it no longer, and she relieved her spirits by walking around the chamber. Nicolei watched her, but then, curious as to his surroundings, he begged her for the use of her arm. She gave it gladly. They examined the statues more closely and then the columns, seeing that they had been sculpted by an artist of great talent. Behind the columns the wall appeared to be made of solid rock. Its surface was uneven and water trickled down it in a small, steady stream. Its colour was that of dry sand, shot through with occasional veins of green and rust which gleamed fitfully in the torchlight. Set into them at waist height, one between each two columns, was a basin. To begin with, Elizabeth thought the basins were natural, but they were so regular in their spacing that she gradually realised that they too had been carved.

They had gone some three quarters of the way round when at last she heard footsteps. They were so faint at first that she thought they were in her imagination, but then they became louder and stronger, and she ran to the mouth of the tunnel from which they came. The echoes were deceptive, and it was from another tunnel mouth that Darcy at last emerged.

He was looking dishevelled. His hair was rumpled, his coat

was covered in a fine sandy powder, and his coat was ripped across the shoulder. His cravat was torn and hung from his neck in a tangle of linen. There was a hole in his breeches at the knee, and his boots were caked with mud. Georgio was hard on his heels, his face ashen.

'What happened?' asked Elizabeth, running over to him and lifting her hand to his cheek.

He took it and kissed it, but all he would say is, 'That is not the way. We will have to try another passage.'

Georgio visibly blanched.

'I cannot...' he said in fear and trembling.

Darcy looked at him with sympathy. 'I do not expect it. You have faced a challenge that few would have faced and acquitted yourself with great bravery, but the horrors of the passages are not for your kind. It is for me to face them alone.'

'No!' said Elizabeth.

'My love, it is the only way. I have to do this. For you. For me. For us.'

'And yet,' said Nicolei speaking slowly, 'it may not be necessary for anyone to go there. I think there is another way.'

Darcy looked at him enquiringly and Elizabeth followed his gaze. Nicolei was standing next to the wall at the eastern side of the temple, by one of the basins.

'I have found... I think I have found...' Nicolei said, '...writing.'

He rubbed the surface dirt away with his finger, and Elizabeth could see a fine flowing script underneath.

'What does it say?' she asked.

'It is very old, a dialect. Few speak it now. It says... it says the way will be eased by a... by something close to the... I cannot read this word... something close to the hide... no, the skin... I think this word means father... no, not father, the one who makes. I think it means *sire*.'

'I don't understand,' said Elizabeth.

'It means that if I have something worn by my sire, the vampyre who made me, it will smooth my way,' said Darcy.

'There is more,' Nicolei went on, rubbing again with his finger. 'It says rest in... no, lay in... lay in the hollow. It means, I think, put it in the hollow of the bowl.'

'If only I had something,' said Darcy regretfully, 'but I have nothing. I will have to continue without it.'

'Perhaps not,' said Elizabeth, struggling to recall a slight memory. She turned to Darcy as it came back to her. 'When you came to my rescue on the beach, when you thought Lady Catherine was attacking me and knocked her back, she left an indentation in the cliff, and caught in the indentation was her veil. It must have been embedded in the rock when she pulled herself free. I saw it blowing in the breeze.'

Darcy's face brightened.

'Then I will fetch it,' he said energetically. 'It will not take me long.'

'It took us hours to get here,' Elizabeth pointed out.

Darcy smiled, his eyes bright in the torchlight. 'But I am a vampyre,' he said.

There was a sudden brief stirring of wind and then, quicker than she would have thought possible, he was gone, a black and fluid form disappearing rapidly from view.

She could hardly take in what had happened and she sat down, her legs feeling suddenly weak. It was a day of marvels, fearful and terrible, yet wonderful and strange.

Nicolei resumed his seat next to her on one of the fallen columns, and Georgio sat on the other one, looking down at the floor silently. As Elizabeth recovered her composure, she found herself wanting to ask him what had happened, but she could not bring herself to speak of it. His colour had returned but when one of the torches sputtered and he lit a new torch from the old, his hands were still shaking.

Nicolei too had fallen silent and appeared to be lost in thought.

Elizabeth prepared herself for a long wait, but before she thought there was any hope of Darcy returning, there was a beating of wings and a rushing of air and he stood once more before them. She saw that he was holding, in his left hand, Lady Catherine's black veil.

'You found it!' she said. 'I was afraid it might have blown away.'

'No, it was just where you said it would be,' he said with a warm smile. Then his face became serious. 'And now we must see what it will do.'

He walked past the statue of Apollo and then passed between two of the fluted columns until he stood by the wall. The torches could not illuminate the ceiling—only a small portion of the wall around the basin—and the light flickered constantly. He looked at the flowing script for a moment before placing the veil inside. It lay there, slight and insubstantial, nothing more than a shadow in the hollow bowl.

Elizabeth watched it. But as nothing happened, she began to feel a fall in her spirits. It had done nothing. Nor had she, in her heart of hearts, expected it to.

And then, slowly, with a grating noise, the stone wall in front of them began to move. It swung smoothly open and Elizabeth found herself looking across a balcony of rock and into another, much larger cavern, a vast chamber hewn out of the living stone, set some twenty feet below them.

Darcy took the torch in one hand and Elizabeth in the other, and together they moved forward, going through the massive door and standing on the natural stone balcony, which ran around the circumference of the cavern.

Elizabeth looked down. At first she thought there were columns stretching from the ground far below them to the roof high above, but then she saw that they were not columns; they were trees, and their branches were supporting the roof.

'A petrified forest,' said Darcy.

Elizabeth looked at the petrified trees in awe, wondering how and when they had turned to stone. Some were exactly as they had been when they were growing, with thick branches supporting thinner branches and ending in twigs, the whole of them carrying petrified leaves that glistened with streaks of copper and green. Some had fallen and lay as stone logs across the forest floor. In between them were petrified ferns. The whole thing had an uncanny appearance, lit by an unnatural light, a bluish purple glow.

Hand in hand, Elizabeth and Darcy began to go down the broad flight of shallow steps that led to the forest floor. Nicolei, who, with the aid of his son, was following them very slowly down the steps, said breathlessly, 'It is magnificent.'

'The trees are glowing,' said Elizabeth. She listened intently. 'And humming.'

'You're right,' said Darcy, standing still to listen.

Without the sound of their footsteps the hum could be heard more clearly, like the low buzzing of far-off bees.

Elizabeth and Darcy resumed their descent and came at last to the foot of the steps where they stood for a moment looking about them. Now that they were closer, they could see that some of the trees had been carved into strange creatures, neither man nor beast, startling relics of a long forgotten time.

And yet the carvings were beautiful in their own way. They stood proudly in the centre of small, randomly spaced clearings or peered out from behind groups of trees, some hesitant, some mischievous, and some bizarre yet glorious to behold.

Elizabeth and Darcy began to move forward, picking their way carefully across the forest floor, stepping over fallen logs, and threading their way between stone ferns. By a strange trick of the light, it appeared as though purple and blue sunbeams were falling through the canopy above them and onto the forest floor, though no light entered the cavern from any opening. It seemed to be an effect of the torchlight reflecting from the minerals in the trees and walls.

They found themselves in a clearing in the centre of the forest, without ever having meant to arrive there, as though they had been led there by uncanny paths. In the centre of the clearing stood a broken trunk, and on top of it, illuminated by one of the weird and marvellous beams of purple light, was a stone tablet. They looked down at the tablet and saw that, etched across it, there were strange runes.

'I have seen this kind of writing before, in the Count's library,' said Darcy, holding the torch closer, the better to see it.

'Can you read what it says?' asked Elizabeth.

'Yes, I can, enough to understand the words at least. But I do not understand what they mean. They say something about falling… something will fall…'

As if in answer to his words there was a groaning and then a grating noise behind them. Elizabeth turned, just as a huge slab dropped from the ceiling, guided by mighty channels in the wall, until it completely covered the door. The earth beneath them shifted, disturbed by the impact, and small cracks began to appear in the forest floor. The statues rocked slowly backwards and forwards on their plinths, and Elizabeth held her breath, but gradually the earth began to settle, and after a sigh and a groan, it was still. With a last rattle the statues too came to rest.

Nicolei had not been so lucky. He was still on the steps, but he had been toppled from his feet. Darcy started to move towards him in concern but Nicolei called out to him in a quavery voice, reassuring them that he was not hurt.

'Go on!' he called to Darcy, as Georgio helped him to his feet. 'You must finish what you have started. It is the only way.'

Darcy nodded then turned his attention back to the tablet.

'This word is *break*...' he said.

There was another rumble from below and the earth shifted again, the small cracks widening and new cracks appearing. Something hit Elizabeth on the shoulder, and looking up, she saw that the movement of the earth had caused cracks to appear in the cavern roof too, and that small pieces of rock were falling.

'Hurry,' she said to Darcy.

'All will be bright,' said Darcy, reading, 'if... if... choices...'

The ground rolled and Elizabeth was thrown forward. Darcy caught her and righted her, but there was no one to catch the statues which rocked with greater force, back and forth like giant pendulums, whilst large stones hailed down from above. More alarmingly, a tongue of flame darted up from one of the cracks and was followed by smaller flames from surrounding fissures.

Darcy and Elizabeth glanced at each other and then Darcy read, '...have no fright... no fear... starting to crumble... falling, breaking, destroying...'

The rumbling, which had been low and throaty, now broke forth into a roar as giant spurs of rock thrust their way up through the fissures, toppling the statues and sending them crashing to the ground, where they broke into petrified pieces, sending a cloud of dust whirling upwards into the flame-filled air.

There was a sickening cracking sound, and looking round as one, Elizabeth and Darcy saw that a giant chasm had opened halfway up the flight of stairs, cutting them off from the door. Nicolei, still supported by Georgio, was a small, frail figure on the other side.

'We cannot go back now, even if we wanted to,' said Elizabeth.

Darcy held the torch higher and moved a few steps to the side, the better to see the inscription.

'Hold on…' he read, as the roaring grew louder, drowning out the forest's hum, '…hold on to the truth… no, hold on to that which is true.'

There was a great splintering sound and a deep fissure opened between Darcy and Elizabeth, widening with frightening speed until they were separated by a sea of molten lava, and another appeared, and then another, separating him from the tablet.

'The inscription!' cried Elizabeth.

'It's finished,' shouted Darcy, above the noise of the flame. 'That is all it said.'

'Then do as it says,' called Nicolei. 'Hold on to that which is true. It is the tablet, Old One. The tablet is true.'

Darcy looked at the tablet. But as he was about to spring across the vast lava-filled chasm, he experienced a moment of calm, and whilst the tempest raged all around, a voice spoke in the quiet of his soul.

'No,' he said, 'It's Elizabeth. Elizabeth is true.'

He leapt to the opposite chasm and held on to her as the ground heaved and the mighty trees collapsed and roof began to fall. Huge pieces of stone rained down on them, and he cradled Elizabeth protectively to his chest, sheltering her head with his hands.

The ground was seething all around, a boiling mass of garish red, and a fierce wind sprang up with a wild roar, buffeting them and battering them, threatening to whip them from their island and cast them into the lava. Elizabeth clung to Darcy and he to her.

And then the waters appeared. Up from the newly made crevices they spurted, drawn from the deepest reaches of the earth, as an icy river started to rise.

Elizabeth watched in horrified fascination, torn between despair and hope as fire and water waged battle before her. The fire boiled the water into steam, but still the water rose, consuming the fires in a great hissing rasp.

'It's going to be all right,' she said with wild hope as she saw the flames flicker and die.

But her hope was short-lived. As the fires died all around them, the waters kept on rising, creeping over the island of rock on which they stood with arms entwined and bodies pressed close together. It was over their feet, then over their knees, a blood-warm sea, rising quickly until she and Darcy were thigh deep in water.

'It was the tablet,' cried Nicolei sorrowfully, his voice barely audible above the tumult of cracking earth and sizzling fire and roaring wind. 'You should have held on to the tablet, Old One. The tablet was true.'

Elizabeth looked up into Darcy's eyes.

'I shouldn't have let you come,' he said, turning all his

attention to her and taking her face in his hands. 'I should never have allowed it.'

'It was not your fault; it was mine,' she said. 'I should have stayed behind. You tried to make me listen. I should not have gone against the portent.'

'We could not have escaped it whatever we did, I see that now,' said Darcy. 'I only wish that you could have been spared and that you did not have to die with me.'

'You are immortal,' she said. 'You will not die.'

'I cannot die of old age, but even I can drown,' he said. 'But you should not have had to share my fate. You should be at home now, in Meryton, safe.'

'I don't regret anything,' she said as the waters swirled around her waist and rose with frightening speed to her shoulders. 'I don't mind dying if I can die with you. Only kiss me and I will die happy.'

He turned up her face to his and kissed her fiercely, and she returned his kiss with passion as the waters swirled over their shoulders, and there amidst the noise and turmoil, they kissed and kissed again as they waited for the end.

But the end did not come. The waters started receding, going down slowly at first, retreating to their shoulders and then to their waist, then moving more rapidly, sinking to their knees, and then to their ankles before disappearing beneath the rocky floor as quickly as it had appeared. There was one final convulsion of the earth and a shower of rocks rained down from above, and then everything was silent. They stood amidst the dread and terrible wreckage, and yet miraculously the two of them were untouched.

Elizabeth lowered her hand from Darcy's neck and as she did so she was filled with a sense of awe.

'Your puncture marks. The bites,' she said, running her

fingers over the smooth skin of his neck. 'They've gone. The water has washed them away.'

He lifted his hand to his neck and ran his fingers over the spot where they had been, then his eyes filled with profound wonderment.

'What does it mean?' she asked.

'I don't know. I hope—'

He was interrupted by Georgio's hail and looking round, they saw that Nicolei and Georgio were unharmed. The two men had climbed back up to the top of the steps and were standing by the door. Nicolei was leaning heavily on Georgio's arm.

'Go on,' called Darcy across the chasm that separated them. 'Don't wait for us. I will find a way out for Elizabeth and myself. Go back to the lodge, we will meet you again there.'

Georgio waved in acknowledgement and he and Nicolei disappeared through the door.

'And now, we must find a way out,' said Darcy. They were surrounded by cracks and crevices and the way would not be easy. 'I think, if we go this way,' he said, indicating a path that could be negotiated by small jumps over narrow cracks, 'we can approach the door more nearly.'

Elizabeth, having come to the same conclusion, agreed.

They began to jump across the cracks, but they had crossed only two of them when the earth rocked again and Elizabeth was nearly thrown from her feet. She righted herself quickly, then put her hands to her ears as there was a terrible rumble, and to her astonishment, the side of the cavern started to slide away.

She stared at it in amazement. Faster and faster it went, slipping downwards to reveal glimpses of blue skies and daylight.

Before another minute had passed, she found herself in a newly-opened cave overlooking the bright blue waters of the Mediterranean. Darcy, beside her, let out an astounded exclamation, and the two of them looked out in wonderment.

'It is the most beautiful thing I have ever seen,' said Elizabeth.

The sun was rising on the horizon, spreading its golden light over the world. She hardly dared turn towards Darcy for fear of what she might see, but she did so at last and felt herself awash with relief.

'You are not transparent!' she said.

He looked down at himself.

'So that is what the portent meant,' he said. 'The curse has been broken, the shadow lifted. You have caused my death after all, Lizzy, or at least a part of me. It was the death of the vampyre you caused.'

He turned his face to the sun then he stretched out his arms and threw back his head as he basked in the glow of the sunrise.

'It is many, many years since I have done this,' he said. 'To see the dawn of a new day, without fear, is something wonderful indeed.'

She watched him with an overpowering love.

And then he turned towards her.

For the first time since she had known him there was no tension in him, no aloofness, no painful restraint. There was only a man without burdens or curses. Free.

His eyes darkened and they began to smoulder, and she felt her legs grow weak. He ran the back of his hand across her cheek and she began to tremble. And there by the sea, in the new light of morning, they came together as one.

EPILOGUE

My dearest Jane,

I am sure you must have written to me, but none of your letters have reached me and I know that none of my letters have reached you. The post is very unreliable in these parts! No, not the Lake District, my dearest Jane, but the Continent. My dear Darcy took me through Europe and we have had many adventures along the way. I have learnt a great deal about him, much of it unsuspected, but all of it, in its own way, wonderful; by which I mean, my dearest Jane, that it was full of wonder. I know now why he was so reserved and why he would never let other people near. I know everything about him. And I have learnt this, Jane: that to know another human being absolutely, and to love them, is the greatest adventure of our lives.

I must go now; the carriage awaits. But it will not be long before I am back in England. I am longing to see you again. How much we will have to say to each other!

And how much I will have to conceal, she thought, as she read her letter through, adding to herself, *though perhaps I will tell Jane everything, one day.*

The door opened and a respectful servant stood there.

'The carriage is at the door,' he said.

'One minute,' said Elizabeth. She signed her letter, then

folded it and wrote the direction. The servant stepped forward to take it. 'Thank you, but I will post it myself,' she said.

'Very good.'

Darcy came into the drawing room, looking happy and carefree.

'Are you ready?' he asked. 'The carriage is waiting. It is not as comfortable as our own coach, but I was lucky to be able to hire anything at such short notice, so far away from a city. We will not be travelling with it for long. We will soon be on board ship and heading for England.'

'England and Pemberley,' she said. She let her gaze wander for one last time around the hunting lodge and then she took his arm. 'Then let us be off. It's time to go home.'

ABOUT THE AUTHOR

AMANDA GRANGE IS A bestselling author specializing in creative interpretations of classic novels and historic events, including Jane Austen's novels and the Titanic shipwreck. Her Jane Austen sequel *Mr. Darcy's Diary* is a bestseller in the US and the UK. She lives in England.

Mr. Darcy's Diary
Amanda Grange

"A gift to a new generation of Darcy fans
and a treat for existing fans as well." —AUSTENBLOG

The only place Darcy could share his innermost feelings...

...was in the private pages of his diary. Torn between his sense of duty to
his family name and his growing passion for Elizabeth Bennet, all he can
do is struggle not to fall in love. A skillful and graceful imagining of the
hero's point of view in one of the most beloved and enduring love stories
of all time.

What readers are saying:

"A delicious treat for all Austen addicts."

"Amanda Grange knows her subject...I ended up reading the entire book in one sitting."

"Brilliant, you could almost hear Darcy's voice...I was so sad when it came to an end. I loved the visions she gave us of their married life."

"Amanda Grange has perfectly captured all of Jane Austen's clever wit and social observations to make *Mr. Darcy's Diary* a must read for any fan."

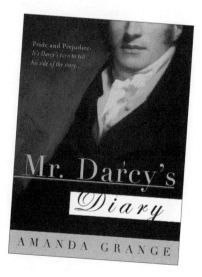

978-1-4022-0876-8 • $14.95 US/ $19.95 CAN/ £7.99 UK

Mr. and Mrs. Fitzwilliam Darcy: Two Shall Become One
SHARON LATHAN

"Highly entertaining... I felt fully immersed in the time
period.
Well done!" —*Romance Reader at Heart*

A fascinating portrait of a timeless, consuming love

It's Darcy and Elizabeth's wedding day, and the journey is just beginning
as Jane Austen's beloved *Pride and Prejudice* characters embark on the
greatest adventure of all: marriage and a life together filled with surprising
passion, tender self-discovery, and the simple joys of every day.

As their love story unfolds in this most romantic of Jane Austen sequels,
Darcy and Elizabeth each reveal to the other how their relationship
blossomed from misunderstanding to
perfect understanding and harmony, and
a marriage filled with romance, sensuality
and the beauty of a deep, abiding love.

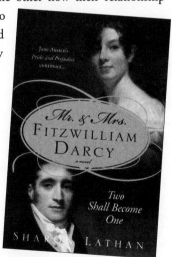

What readers are saying:

"This journey is truly amazing."

"What a wonderful beginning to this
truly beautiful marriage."

"Could not stop reading."

"So beautifully written...making me
feel as though I was in the room with Lizzy and
Darcy...and sharing in all of the touching moments between."

978-1-4022-1523-0 • $14.99 US/ $15.99 CAN/ £7.99 UK

Loving Mr. Darcy: Journeys Beyond Pemberley
SHARON LATHAN

"A romance that transcends time." —*The Romance Studio*

Darcy and Elizabeth embark on the journey of a lifetime

Six months into his marriage to Elizabeth Bennet, Darcy is still head over heels in love, and each day offers more opportunities to surprise and delight his beloved bride. Elizabeth has adapted to being the Mistress of Pemberley, charming everyone she meets and handling her duties with grace and poise. Just when it seems life can't get any better, Elizabeth gets the most wonderful news. The lovers leave the serenity of Pemberley, traveling through the sumptuous landscape of Regency England, experiencing the lavish sights, sounds, and tastes around them. With each day come new discoveries as they become further entwined, body and soul.

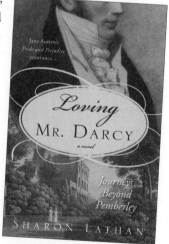

What readers are saying:

"Darcy's passion for love and life with Lizzy is brought to the forefront and captured beautifully."

"Sharon Lathan is a wonderful writer… I believe that Jane Austen herself would love this story as much as I did."

"The historical backdrop of the book is unbelievable—I actually felt like I could see all the places where the Darcys traveled."

"Truly captures the heart of Darcy & Elizabeth! Very well written and totally hot!"

978-1-4022-1741-8 • $14.99 US/ $18.99 CAN/ £7.99 UK

Mr. Darcy Takes a Wife

LINDA BERDOLL

The #1 best-selling Pride and Prejudice sequel

"Wild, bawdy, and utterly enjoyable." —*Booklist*

Hold on to your bonnets!

Every woman wants to be Elizabeth Bennet Darcy—beautiful, gracious, universally admired, strong, daring and outspoken—a thoroughly modern woman in crinolines. And every woman will fall madly in love with Mr. Darcy—tall, dark and handsome, a nobleman and a heartthrob whose virility is matched only by his utter devotion to his wife. Their passion is consuming and idyllic—essentially, they can't keep their hands off each other—through a sweeping tale of adventure and misadventure, human folly and numerous mysteries of parentage. This sexy, epic, hilarious, poignant and romantic sequel to *Pride and Prejudice* goes far beyond Jane Austen.

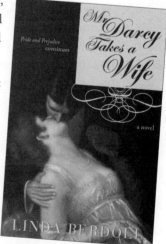

What readers are saying:

"I couldn't put it down."

"I didn't want it to end!"

"Berdoll does Jane Austen proud! ...A thoroughly delightful and engaging book."

"Delicious fun...I thoroughly enjoyed this book."

"My favorite *Pride and Prejudice* sequel so far."

978-1-4022-0273-5 • $16.95 US/ $19.99 CAN/ £9.99 UK

My Cousin Rachel

DAPHNE DU MAURIER

> "From the first page…the reader is back
> in the moody, brooding atmosphere of *Rebecca*."
> —*New York Times*

A classic story of mystery and love from the bestselling author of Rebecca

One of the world's great storytellers, Daphne du Maurier spins a dark gothic tale of passion and unswerving love that turns to suspicion and fear. Rachel, a woman of exquisite beauty, descends on the great Cornwall estate of Philip Ashley. Despite his aroused suspicions, she soon enchants him. In this tale of good and evil, Philip must decide whether the glorious Rachel, the recent mysterious widow of his beloved cousin, is out to destroy him or is the innocent victim of devious men. His fate and his future lie in the answer to this deadly question.

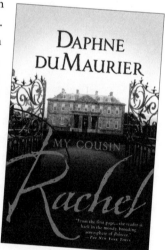

978-1-4022-1709-8 • $14.99 US/ $15.99 CAN